A Critical Edition of Caroline Norton's
Love in "the World"

A Critical Edition of Caroline Norton's *Love in "the World"*

Edited by
Ross Nelson and Marie Mulvey-Roberts

ANTHEM PRESS

Anthem Press
An imprint of Wimbledon Publishing Company
www.anthempress.com

This edition first published in UK and USA 2023
by ANTHEM PRESS
75–76 Blackfriars Road, London SE1 8HA, UK
or PO Box 9779, London SW19 7ZG, UK
and
244 Madison Ave #116, New York, NY 10016, USA

© 2023 Ross Nelson and Marie Mulvey-Roberts editorial matter and selection;
individual chapters © individual contributors

The moral right of the authors has been asserted.

All rights reserved. Without limiting the rights under copyright reserved above, no part of this publication may be reproduced, stored or introduced into a retrieval system, or transmitted, in any form or by any means (electronic, mechanical, photocopying, recording or otherwise), without the prior written permission of both the copyright owner and the above publisher of this book.

British Library Cataloguing-in-Publication Data
A catalogue record for this book is available from the British Library.

Library of Congress Cataloging-in-Publication Data: 2023937879
A catalog record for this book has been requested.

ISBN-13: 978-1-83998-728-1 (Hbk)
ISBN-10: 1-83998-728-6 (Hbk)

Cover Credit: *Caroline Norton* by Henry Pickersgill (1830), Beaverbrook Art Gallery

This title is also available as an e-book.

This book is dedicated to Lady Antonia Fraser, one of Caroline Norton's greatest champions.

CONTENTS

Manuscript Cover Page and Frontispiece	ix
Caroline Norton: England's First Feminist Law-Maker By Diane Atkinson	xi
Introduction By Ross Nelson and Marie Mulvey-Roberts	xv
Editorial Note	xxix
Chronology	xxxi
Foreword By Ross Nelson and Marie Mulvey-Roberts	xxxv
Volume I	1
Volume II	95
Notes	147
Publications, Websites and Archives Cited	157

MANUSCRIPT COVER PAGE

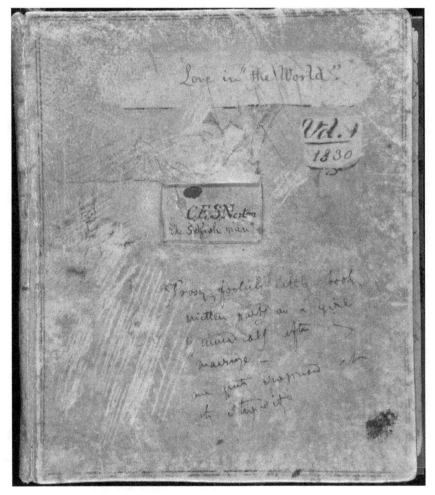

Title page to Vol. 1 of the MS of *Love in "the World"* (Beinecke Library). The position of authorial initials suggests that they were originally "C.E.S." [standing for either Caroline Elizabeth Sarah or Sheridan]. This was extended to "C.E.S.N." after her marriage in 1827 to reflect Caroline's married surname. Underneath her initials, she has written the curious descriptions "The Selfish M'am" [i.e. Madam] and: "Prosy, foolish little book, written partly as a girl and immediately after marriage – am quite surprised by its stupidity."

MANUSCRIPT FRONTISPIECE

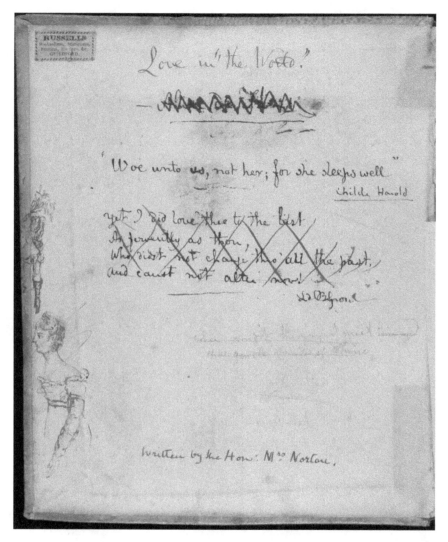

Frontispiece to Vol. 1 of the MS of *Love in "the World"*. The alternative title, "Alixe de Fleury," has been deleted. The Byronic quotations are adapted from "Woe unto us, not her; for she sleeps well:" (*Childe Harold*, Canto 4 (1818), Stanza CLXXI, l. 1); and "Yet did I love thee to the last/As fervently as thou,/Who didst not change through all the past,/And canst not alter now." (from "And Thou art Dead, as Young and Fair," ll. 19–22). "When midst the gay I meet that gentle smile of thine" is a quotation from Thomas Moore's "When 'Midst the Gay I meet'" (Thomas Moore, *Poetical Works* (London: Longman, 1840-41): V. 183–84).

CAROLINE NORTON: ENGLAND'S FIRST FEMINIST LAW-MAKER

By Diane Atkinson

On 17 August 1839, the Infant Custody Act, the first piece of feminist legislation to be passed in the United Kingdom, became law. The four-hundred-word act gave mothers of "unblemished reputation," who were separated from their husbands, the right to have access to their own children. The silent architect of this groundbreaking law was the poet, songwriter, novelist and scandalous woman Caroline Norton, known in the press as "Norty" Mrs Norton.

Born Caroline Elizabeth Sarah Sheridan in 1808, she married George Norton in 1827 and had three sons: Fletcher, in 1829; Brinsley, in 1831; and William, in 1833. From the beginning it was a deeply troubled marriage: for almost a decade she was the victim of her husband's drunken violence which started on their honeymoon in Scotland. In 1831 she was asked by her husband to secure him a well-paid job from an old friend of the Sheridan family, William Lamb, Lord Melbourne, the Home Secretary in the Whig government. Mrs Norton succeeded in getting her barrister husband a job as a magistrate for east London. Several other favours for the siblings of George were demanded by him and given by Melbourne. Caroline Norton and Lord Melbourne, who was to become Prime Minister in April 1835, started an affair in 1831, that was encouraged by her husband. Norton's elder brother Lord Grantley, an Ultra Tory, wanted to topple the Whig government and instructed George Norton to cite Prime Minister Melbourne in a "criminal conversation" case, which was heard on 22 June 1836, a sultry summer's day, in the Court of Common Pleas.

"Criminal conversation" was the antique legal term for adultery: "conversation" was a euphemism for sex, "criminal" described having sex with another man's wife as criminal, alluding to the fact that a husband's property – his wife's body – had been trespassed upon. George Norton accused the Whig Prime Minister of "crim con" and sued Melbourne for the modern equivalent of about a million pounds in damages for his hurt feelings, and being denied "domestic harmony," a euphemism for sex. The trial only lasted a day: Lord Melbourne and hence Caroline Norton were found not guilty and George Norton was humiliated and then hell-bent on revenge.

George locked Caroline out of her home in the spring of 1836 with only the clothes she was wearing. Her possessions, her manuscripts and most importantly her three sons, now aged seven, five and three, were lost to her. In law, a mother was not considered to be a parent of her children and therefore had no rights to see them when the marriage failed. Caroline Norton had no hope of seeing her sons again unless George agreed – which he adamantly refused to do – or until the patriarchy was challenged and defeated.

Caroline Norton, reeling from the scandal, said at the time to be the sex scandal of the century and which destroyed her reputation, wrote to Mary Shelley, the daughter of Mary Wollstonecraft and author of *Frankenstein*, "A woman is made a helpless wretch by these laws of men."[1]

Thanks to her persistent and discreet lobbying, the Infant Custody Act (1839) said that if a wife was legally separated, or divorced, from her husband, and had not been found guilty of adultery, such a mother was entitled to have custody of her children up to the age of seven and periodic access after that.

This legal landmark was the direct result of Caroline Norton's struggle with her drunken and abusive husband and the patriarchal values of English law that presumed that a father was the only parent of a child and mothers had no parental rights at all. Once a woman married, the rights she had were subsumed into those of her husband.

The Infant Custody Act opened a much wider debate on wives' and mothers' invisibility before the law. Her ongoing struggles with her abusive husband prompted Caroline Norton to deploy her outstanding rhetorical skills to become a pamphleteer on issues around the inability of women to escape violent and controlling husbands and the loss of their earnings and inheritances to their husbands on marriage.

Caroline Norton's pamphleteering influenced four key clauses of the 1857 Matrimonial Causes (Divorce) Act which became law on the 1st of January 1858. Before then a divorce could only be obtained by an Act of Parliament, which was expensive, complicated and public. No matter how powerful the case for a woman's right to divorce her husband she could only be granted a divorce if the House of Commons *and* the House of Lords agreed, which only happened four times in two hundred years. This Act took divorce away from the Church and Parliament and established a new civil, secular court which made divorce more affordable for women who were stuck in bad marriages. When the Matrimonial Causes Act became law, hundreds of women petitioned for divorces, often after decades of misery.

The groundbreaking Married Women's Property Act of 1870, which was informed by 30 years of Norton's lobbying and pamphleteering, allowed married women to keep their own earnings and to inherit property after they were married (if it was not part of a trust) and to inherit two hundred pounds. The Act also made wives liable, like their husbands, to pay for the maintenance of their children out of their own earnings and assets. The law was not retroactive and many women did not benefit, as any property a wife owned prior to marriage had become that of her husband. It took another 12 years, by which time Caroline Norton had died, for the law to recognize that a wife was entitled to her own legal status, equal to that of her husband, and to address the issue of property law, which was further considered in 1882, and beyond, by successive Parliamentary legislation.

This previously unpublished novel which you are about to read was written between 1828 and 1830, during which time Caroline Norton marked the first anniversary of her disastrous marriage to George Norton and gave birth to her first child Fletcher Norton.

Caroline Norton is a heroine to every woman who has made a mistake in judging a man. Her wretched marriage drew her out of her own life and into the world of the law. Caroline Norton was an accidental feminist who changed women's lives for the better.

Today Caroline Norton's name is not widely known, but every time a mother is granted custody of her child and is successful in her application for financial support, her struggle with her dreadful husband and success in informing our laws should be saluted.

INTRODUCTION

By Ross Nelson and Marie Mulvey-Roberts

Caroline Norton's forgotten novel, which has remained unpublished until now, tells of the perils of courtship facing a naïve young girl Alixe, who has been launched onto the London social season. Her encounters with both a worthy and an undesirable suitor open an intriguing window onto the fashionable society of the 1820s in which *Love in "the World"* takes place.[1] Caroline was able to draw upon her own experiences of the bon ton and those of her elder sister, Helen.[2] The time in which the novel was set coincides with her first ball in the late summer of 1825. It was then that her sister Helen asked their mother to relate "every little incident [...] and whether she is admired or no."[3] In anticipation of her younger sister's entrée to society in March 1826, Helen wrote to her: "I wish you joy with all my heart of all the pleasing anxious cares of coming out and all attending circumstances."[4] That Spring Caroline burst upon the scene with all her beauty and brilliance, later recalling "the night upon which she made her début, coming down dressed to the room where her mother and aunt were awaiting her." She added, "I came out [...] to find all London at my feet."[5]

Caroline believed that London, "where the cry of the drowning suicide is lost in the hum of gathered multitudes restlessly pursuing the pleasures or the business of life,"[6] could be as callous as the metropolitan social scene might prove treacherous, and in alerting the reader to the dangers of fashionable society, she could make ample use of her own observations as a debutante at her first London season. In a highly readable and coherent narrative with an indeterminate ending, which throws a spotlight onto her life and times, the plot of *Love in "the World"* initially follows a pattern broadly representative of her own experience and anticipates that of her young heroine Beatrice Brooke in her later novel, *Lost and Saved* (1863). All three women had to respond to the advances of an apparently virtuous, but in reality immoral, suitor. For Alixe, this is Everard Price, for Beatrice, the Jekyll and Hyde persona of Montagu Treherne, while Caroline had to grapple with the advances of George Norton, who had first proposed to her when she was about sixteen. Like Alixe's friend Emily Price, Caroline had early in life lost someone to whom she had been passionately devoted and wished to marry. The death from a fever in April 1827 of Leveson Smith, a lawyer and poet, and a nephew of the celebrated wit Sydney Smith, had fatally propelled her towards George Norton. As the artist Robert Haydon concluded after speaking with Caroline on the subject, she "married an Ass to get rid of her pang."[7]

Her unhappy marital experience may help explain the novel's pessimistic commentary on the pitfalls of sudden marriage and the superficiality of society flirtations. Early in her first season, Alixe is warned by Lady Townley of the dangers in marrying for either love or convenience. Lady Louisa Whittaker, "a beauty" who "did what all beauties are sure to do, married a poor man, a mere nobody, shocked her friends and struggles on in poverty with three children whom she is obliged to educate herself,"[8] is contrasted with "pretty Lady Harriet Dure, only married a year and a half and flirting already as if she had no husband at all."[9] Meanwhile, the unmarried characters become involved in a series of concurrent attractions and rejections. The coquettish Annette Aimwell, having been passed over by Everard Price, who then set his sights on Alixe, goes on to flirt with both his friend Darlies, who has been rejected by Emily Price, and Colonel Manners. Alixe is as much shocked by Annette's decision to marry Darlies hastily before the imminent death of his father, with his inheritance in mind, as by his sudden change of affections: "What a strange thing that Darlies, who hardly a month before has been so evidently in love with Emily, should have not only changed, but engaged to marry a girl the most completely opposite in every respect to Miss Price."[10]

Norton makes clear that Emily Price is a more grounded and sensible character than her wayward brother Everard, despite their close relationship. Her scepticism towards the type of marriages of convenience practised in the novel reflects Norton's own experience of marriage. A conflict between the marriage of convenience and the ideal of companionate marriage emerges through the heroine Alixe. Even though the wife was expected to submit to the will of her husband, the companionate marriage was based on comradeship and valorized such qualities as mutual loyalty, protection and duty.[11] It was a prospect which was perfectly feasible for Alixe as the future wife of Charles St Clair, but one that was denied Caroline Norton on her marriage to George. After her wedding in 1827 to the Hon. George Chapple Norton, the younger brother of Lord Grantley, a briefless barrister and MP for Guildford, she and her family subsequently felt that they had been misled over the extent of the fortune and prospects of this good-looking young man. Regarded as rather slow and lazy, he earned the sobriquet, "the late George Norton,"[12] living up to that appellation when he turned up late for his own nuptials at

Westminster owing to his horse having run away with him in his cabriolet, a lightweight two-wheeled chaise.

The control that Emily exercises over her life as an unmarried woman correlates to Norton's independent spirit. Emily's "dark beautiful eyes," "hair literally jet black" and "very fair clear skin without the slightest colour but in her lips, which were the brightest crimson,"[13] closely match Henry Pickerskill's 1830 portrait of the author (on the cover of this edition). Antonia Fraser points out that Susan Dalrymple, a protagonist in Norton's next novel, *The Wife* (1835), "was surely a self-portrait of Caroline: 'The most Grecian of heads [Grecian was a description often applied to her] [...] dark eyes, black silken hair', with her 'most lovely feature', her mouth."[14] Emily shares a "rich, deep and powerful"[15] singing voice with Norton, with whom another comparison may be made, this time with Alixe, who sets lyrics to music. This was an occupation from which Norton gained a substantial income, the most famous of her songs being "Juanita" (1853).[16] She also co-wrote numerous lyrics with her sister, Helen. Along with their youngest sibling, Georgiana, the three sisters, whose maiden name was Sheridan, became known as "The Three Graces" in recognition of their beauty and elegance. In *Love in "the World"*, this equates to how Alixe, Annette's sister Pamela, and Emily Price go to a ball as The Three Graces. The following passage captures the sense of fashion and style that the Sheridan sisters brought to society:

> There was to be a grand fancy ball at the Opera House in a week, that fancy ball to which Everard predicted the engaging appearance of the gentlemen of Guards and of one in particular. Great were the discussions as to the important topic – dress. Mr Price proposed a Caucasian costume, Captain Aimwell thought they might appear as the three graces. Lady Townley thought Sultana dress would be particularly becoming, and she had quantities of trinkets and beads to lend. Alixe wished to go as a French peasant. Pamela thought Flora might do for her. Both these were objected to on account of their being common. At length, after much debate, Emily Price's opinion was universally agreed to. She proposed that the three friends should go as the spirits of air, water, and earth.[17]

Norton mentions in the novel that the description of the women's dresses at the fancy-dress ball in Chapter 11 was written "for the benefit of young ladies & in humble imitation of some pages in '*Pelham*' devoted to the costume of the other sex."[18] She was an ardent admirer of Edward Bulwer Lytton's fiction, most notably his best-selling *Pelham*, an early example of the Silver Fork novel. This genre, which flourished between the 1820s and 1840s, was intended to impart an insider's view of high society for the delectation and even aspirations of members of the middle classes. The term was adapted from William Hazlitt's article "The Dandy School" (1827), where it was used in a derisory manner to explain how authors with social ambitions upwards would impart such facts about the lives of the higher echelons of society to their lower-class readers such as "the quality eat with silver forks."[19] The first generation of Silver Fork novels were primarily male writers who satirized dandies and aristocrats, notwithstanding their own identification with the object of ridicule, as in the case of Bulwer Lytton himself, who had been dandified as a young man. On first meeting him, his wife Rosina described him as wearing his hair in long golden ringlets and clad in a highly embroidered and laced cambric shirt front on which "a perfect galaxy glittered along the milky way down the centre of this fairy-like *lingerie*."[20]

Norton's early social satire, *The Dandies Rout*, a poem written in 1820 with her sister Helen,[21] when she was aged 11, about preparations for a ball, anticipated the vogue for the Silver Fork genre, which was established by 1826,[22] the year in which she came out in society. The poem was inspired by a children's nursery rhyme book entitled *The Dandies Ball: or, High Life in the City* (1819), presented to her by a family friend, Lady Westmoreland. The same publisher, John Marshall, after seeing the version created by the Sheridan sisters, decided to publish it and gave them 50 copies.[23] They derived their title and incentive for this sequel from the closing lines of the anonymously written poem, "Though I very much doubt,/But at the next rout/We shall see all these dandies again."[24] Here various foppish male characters are caricatured and illustrated by the artist Robert Cruikshank (1789–1856) in 16 coloured engravings. Caroline and her sister Helen may have responded by producing 14 for their own poem: Caroline's fondness for drawing is evident from the frontispiece to the manuscript of *Love in "the World"* (see frontispiece to this edition). Her comedic mockery of fops and dandies was directed towards their preoccupation with fashionable clothing and takes its cue from the source text, which describes a Mr Pink fainting with exhaustion in his grandmother's arms from the over-exertion of dressing himself. He is one of the corseted men in the poem who are so tightly laced that they are unable to enjoy their dinner. They inspired the creation of Norton's Sir Peter Tightstays in *The Dandies Rout*. These characters anticipate Thomas Carlyle's famous depiction of the dandy in *Sartor Resartus* (1831), as one who does not dress to live rather than "he lives to dress."[25] Norton demonstrates how pretentiousness can be bolstered up by artificiality in her depiction of her own version of Mr Pink wearing false whiskers and padding out his calves. His friend is a Jew, another character borrowed from *The Dandies Ball*, in which he is described as skilled in "boots, calves and whiskers."[26]

In *Love in "the World"*, a parallel may be found in the vacuity and vanity of the moustache twirling and ironically named Colonel Manners, which prompts the following authorial digression:

> And during the pause which ensued, I may be allowed to remark that a moustache answers precisely to a male conscience, being a something which he cannot forget without great exertion of thought, and even in that case it returns more strongly to his remembrance after the lapse of attention to it of which he has been guilty. Even allowing (which happens but seldom), that they be neither curled plaited or dyed, they occupy much more of the wearer's attention than the most beautiful head of hair belonging to a lady. They assimilate themselves in a manner with the feelings of their possessor. Unfortunate civilians who possess not the graceful privilege of wearing a tuft above, a tuft below your mouths! (as the bourgeois of former times might not wear a sword) to express your sentiments you are forced to speak, to smile, to frown. But with a *militaire* no such labour is necessary. Be he pleased, he strokes his moustache down with his finger and thumb, at once throwing form and contempt into his countenance. Be he at a loss for conversation, he twists the end of it into a curl or holds it in the corner of his mouth.
>
> And this was in truth the most efficient way Colonel Manners had of making his sentiments known, his countenance being destitute of what the fastidious in beauty are apt to call expression.[27]

These hints of the dandy, as an appropriation of the feminine, can be applied elsewhere in the novel as in Lord Darlies' "great talent for sighing."[28] Silver Fork novels, which sometimes took the form of the roman à clef, in exposing the affectations, excesses and extravagances in high society, were popular with bourgeois readers, who relished reading about the vices of the upper classes. In *Love in "the World"*, we discover that the villainous Dunston is addicted to gambling, the "turf, gaming-table and dice-box."[29] In Chapter 20, he poisons a racehorse, Beauty, the favourite for a race taking place that day, in order to rig the outcome for his own financial gain. Earlier in the novel, Dunstan is exposed for having won his election as an MP through bribery with the result that he loses his privilege of immunity from arrest for the debts he had incurred.

A publisher who cashed in on the success of these novels of fashion and frivolity was Henry Colburn, who later published Norton's poem, *The Dream and Other Poems* (1840). Colburn encouraged Caroline "to devote her talents to the fashionable vices of the day"[30] but this did not lure her into making a career from writing lucrative Silver Fork novels.[31] Nevertheless, *Love in "the*

World" contains elements of this fashionable fiction. Indeed, Randall Craig regards Norton's later novels, *Woman's Reward* (1835) and *The Wife* (1835), as having similar preoccupations.[32]

Compared to the light-hearted tone of many Silver Fork novels, *The Wife* has a more serious trajectory. In the conclusion, Susan Dalrymple makes a marital sacrifice for her disabled sister Catherine, "described (by herself and others) as 'born crooked' to indicate that her spine was twisted."[33] Susan provided Catherine with security and a home by marrying the wealthy Lord Glenalton, rather than the suitor she is in love with. The "years rolled away"[34] and at the end of a fast-moving final chapter, the author herself, in the guise of an anonymous male guest,[35] makes an appearance at the wedding of Lady Glenalton's daughter, where he notices Lady Glenalton's wayward former lover, by now "an old dandy [...], making the agreeable to a fair giggling girl, who was pulling a magnolia to pieces."[36] In the final chapter of *Woman's Reward*, the death of the domineering Lionel Dupré releases his sister Mary to live abroad. Here again, the "years rolled on,"[37] brightened by occasional news of the public and married life of Lord Clavering, whose marriage proposal Mary had earlier been persuaded to reject out of a misguided sense of loyalty to her brother. After 13 years, Clavering's wife died. Two years later he wrote to Mary with a second proposal, which on this occasion she accepted and thereafter "preside[d] over his house and daughters."[38] For those who felt that Mary's "trials were too bitter and cup too full," the author had the following cautionary advice:

> I can only remind the reader that I am but a poor historian of past events; that I do not recollect any instance of poetical justice in real life, and that I conceive the suffering and sorrow of the humble and pure hearted were specially intended to show how little it is the Creator's will, that either man or woman should look to this world's portion of happiness, as their REWARD [*sic*].[39]

This melancholy conclusion was no doubt informed by Caroline Norton's appalling eight-year experience of marriage to a wife-beating drunk, a depressing situation that deteriorated even further with a six-year separation from her three sons, the youngest of whom died before she was able to obtain shared custody. By returning to George Norton in 1835 after previously leaving him, she found herself unable to obtain a divorce. In turn, he had failed in his attempt to prove her culpable of "criminal conversation," the first step to obtaining a divorce, with the result that their disastrous marriage carried on through the 1840s, as they battled over issues of financial support and how to raise their sons. The literary outcome for Caroline was her most autobiographical novel, the melancholy *Stuart of Dunleath* (1851), in which the protagonist also finds herself trapped in a loveless marriage where she undergoes several of the author's own tragedies and humiliations. The fortuitous avoidance of such a marriage by Alixe St Clair and Emily Price is therefore followed in Norton's fiction over two decades by increasingly sombre narratives exploring the consequences of failed marital relationships, one of "the consequences of her life's trauma" which she has "referred to as a species of insanity."[40] *Love in "the World"* could be said, therefore, to support Lovesey's conclusion that "Norton in her first novels may have effectively inaugurated a new sub-genre of the early Victorian novel, a type of anti-romance: the divorce novel."[41]

In the 1850s, her personal situation had begun to improve: her sons became more independent and she became a grandmother. Moreover, she very publicly exposed her husband's earlier mistreatment of her: at Westminster County Court, in *The Times* and in two pamphlets: *English Laws for Women in the Nineteenth Century* (1854) and *A Letter to the Queen on Lord Chancellor Cranford's Marriage and Divorce Bill* (1855). These developments may explain the more upbeat character of her "sensation" novel, *Lost and Saved*, which initially adapts several elements from *Love in "the World"*. Captain Brooke, while abroad, marries an Italian widow with a young daughter, Marianna, and brings both to England. Alixe St Claire is the daughter of a British Captain and a French woman and is subsequently brought to England by her aunt, who had adopted her. Although the back story to the novel is unclear due to the excised opening chapters, it is possible that Alixe's mother was originally widowed. By the time Marianna reaches adulthood, a neighbour, Maurice Lewellyn, falls in love with her but, as Charles St Clair discovers in the opening chapters of *Love in "the World"*, his feelings are unreciprocated: "She felt for Maurice nothing of that love – nothing but the regard of a friend – a deep and true regard – nothing more. She did not think she ever would feel a different sort of love; she did not expect ever to marry."[42] Like Alixe St Claire, Marianna's half-sister Beatrice arrives in London "blooming with health, bright with joy, in an ecstasy of eagerness and curiosity,"[43] to become infatuated with a fashionable politician, Montagu Treherne. Like Everard Price, Treherne is unable to break off a previous arrangement with a married woman, Lady Milly Nesdale, who represents a charismatic decoy in "his London life of business and temptation"[44] and to whom he also feels tied by his political ambitions and a sense that she is "in 'the world.'" At the opera, Milly is "very prettily dressed, with a strange and pretty wreath."[45] By contrast, Treherne notes of Beatrice that "her dresses were neither the right width or length nor even of the right material" and "was positively annoyed, one day, at the thickness of her neat little boots."[46] As he sees it, she is essentially, to cite the earlier novel's sub-title, "out of 'the world'" of fashionable society, presenting a conundrum he cannot comfortably resolve:

> It is not so easy to get rid of your old love, in a society where the same people meet every day, belong to "the same set", and when your promotion

in your profession and your parliamentary success may be damaged by weakening such ties. [...] although Treherne was "in love" with Beatrice – though he passionately admired her beauty, was amused with her conversation and the echo of her rich voice, when she sang, seemed to thrill his whole being, – yet he experienced in a degree, on her arrival in town, that strange *désillusionnement* peculiar to worldly persons, when the habits and tastes of those who are not "accustomed to the world" jar with theirs.[47]

In *Love in "the World"*, Emily Price explains her brother's inveiglement by his mistress in very similar terms:

But Madame de Valcone, whatever she may have been, is *now* a woman "of the world": that comprehensive expression which signifies that all your best and most maternal feelings are swallowed up, all your holiest ties and duties hidden by the false glare and excitement of an all-engrossing vanity. Happy are they whose hearts have been saddened early into reflection, whose love and friendship are not of "the world."[48]

Indeed, the Beatrice-Montague-Lady Nesdale triangle is to such an extent an echo of the Alixe-Everard-Madame de Valcone relationship in *Love in "the World"*, that the development of the plot after Beatrice agrees to marry Montague in *Lost and Saved* could be said to offer one direction the earlier novel might have taken, if in the conclusion Alixe had *not* released Everard from his "voluntary engagement" to her.

For *Love in "the World"*, Norton was doubtless indebted to several illustrious female predecessors, most notably Frances Burney, whose protagonist in *Evelina: Or the History of a Young Lady's Entrance into the World* (1778) may well have inspired her naïve heroine. Like Burney's ingenue Evelina, Alixe's entry into society is made potentially perilous by the presence of an unsuitable beau. Even though both heroines are unworldly, they are shrewd observers of fashionable society around them. Alixe witnesses with amusement those mothers who are intent upon securing desirable matches for their unmarried daughters, and scrutinize, "as the spider watches its prey, self-entangled in the mesh spun for its destruction; some young unconscious heir, who saw nothing round or beside him but the blue eyes and long curls of the would-be wife."[49] Conversely, Norton notes ironically that, "Without accusing young men of being mercenary, I may observe that their admiration for a young lady certainly is not lessened by knowing them to be heiresses."[50] Alixe is in receipt of two thousand a year, which in today's money is around £80,000 a year, though her value is lessened by those who realize that she is not, in fact Lady St Clair's daughter, but only her niece.

Her romantic way of looking at the world echoes Jane Austen's Catherine Moreland in *Northanger Abbey* (1817) who, like Alixe, is caught between a worthy and less suitable beau, and Eaton Stannard Barrett's Cherubina in *The Heroine* (1813), who has to ward off a dissolute young suitor. Norton's narrator informs us that "Alixe had too much romance in her disposition. She was too fond of making a *dreamy* world of her own to live in."[51] But her natural and unaffected disposition does suggest that she is regarded more favourably by the author than those who are dubbed "women of the world." Besides the previously mentioned Baroness de Valcone, with whom Everard is infatuated, there is the coquette Annette Aimwell, described as a "painted automaton."[52]

Norton created a series of coquettish figures in her early fiction, including Milly Nesdale in *Lost and Saved*. During her loveless marriage in *The Wife*, Susan Glenalton maintains relations with a former admirer, arousing her husband's jealousy and at one social event alienating the admirer in a passage reminiscent of the conclusion to *Love in "the World"*:

> "Glenalton, have you thought of calling the carriage?" said she; and with another bow to Lord Frederick, as he returned the broken rose, she was gone. Frederick Osborne followed two of three steps mechanically; offered his arm to Mrs Clinton, and attended them to the carriage. He fancied till the last moment, that a look, a sigh, a gesture, would tell him that at least she had heard him without resentment – but no; Lady Glenalton looked not again towards her young love, she was now "a woman of the world."[53]

Lady Clarice Lyle is a superficial woman in *Woman's Reward*, who flirts with and discards both Mary Dupré's brother and the foppish Altamont Percy. The "spirit of coquetry" of the protagonist in the tale, *The Coquette* (1833), prompts her "to encourage every one around [...] – to traffic for compliments – to barter looks for words, and words for feelings."[54]

In certain respects, *Love in "the World"* functions as a quasi-conduct book imparting the codes of etiquette and good manners, as well as of moral behaviour. When Alixe learns that Everard is going away, her collapsed posture is upbraided by the author in no uncertain terms: "she laid her arms crossed on the table and bent her head down on them, a very bad attitude for any young lady."[55] As part of her female education, Caroline Norton would have been acquainted with conduct literature which almost certainly would have included *The Memoirs of Miss Sidney Biddulph* (1761) a novel, written by her great-grandmother, Frances Sheridan. This conduct book fiction exposes the suffering of a virtuous woman at the hands of a cruel husband, while trying to live up to the standards of female conduct imposed upon her by society. Her eponymous heroine, like Alixe, has to choose between a virtuous and a morally dubious suitor. The man who Sidney eventually marries later bans her from their house and, in an uncanny foreshadowing of Norton's own predicament many years later, prevents her on a whim from seeing her children.

Conduct literature, by reinforcing a submissive female role, was instrumental in condoning the legal powerlessness of women, which extended to their exclusion from politics. In Silver Fork novels written by male writers, such as Bulwer Lytton's *Pelham* and Benjamin Disraeli's *Vivian Grey* (1826), the heroes are in pursuit of parliamentary careers. In stark contrast, there is a reminder in *Love in "the World"* of how even the physical presence of women as spectators was denied in the chamber of the House of Commons. This is revealed in Chapter 17, when Alixe goes to St Stephen's Chapel in the old Palace of Westminster to hear Everard's maiden speech. At that time, the only way in which ladies could follow the proceedings was to listen through a stuffy and dirty ventilator lantern, designed to funnel the heat and smoke arising from candles on a chandelier below, suspended above the Commons' chamber. This wooden structure had a platform with chairs around the side and contained a limited number of apertures, through which the female spectators would have to poke their heads and crane their necks to catch sight of the Members below. This highly compromised access was available for no more than fourteen women. It is sobering to realize that Norton was basing her account of this cramped and uncomfortable viewing arena on historical fact.

Sketch of the ventilator by Lady Georgina Chatterton © Shakespeare Birthplace Trust/Baddesley Clinton

There is a description of the ventilator by another prominent novelist Maria Edgeworth, who describes the effort involved in having to peep hard in order to catch sight of any figures below:

> In the middle of the garret is what seemed like a sentry-box of deal boards and old chairs placed round it: on these we got and stood and peeped over the top of the boards. Saw a large chandelier with lights blazing, immediately below: a grating of iron across veiled the light so we could look down beyond it: we saw half the table with the mace lying on it and papers, and by peeping hard two figures of clerks at the further end, but no eye could see the Speaker or his chair, – only his feet; his voice and terrible "ORDER" was soon heard.[56]

This restriction on female observers had been imposed after an incident in February 1778, when some women refused to obey the Speaker's injunction to clear the visitor's gallery. It had taken three hours to eject the recalcitrant Mrs Sophie Musters, the wife of the High Sheriff of Nottingham, a society beauty whose portrait as Hebe, handmaid of the gods, was painted by Sir Joshua Reynold in 1785. She also appears on horseback alongside her husband in a painting by George Stubbs in front of their home, Colwick Hall in Nottinghamshire.[57] Her wayward nature extended to her marriage since her cuckolded husband had her painted out of the portrait almost certainly because of her liaisons with her admirer, the Prince of Wales (later George IV).[58] A parallel can be seen with Caroline Norton, when accused by her husband of having an affair with the Prime Minister, Lord Melbourne, which triggered the notorious Criminal Conversation trial.[59] As a direct result of the intransigence of Mrs Musters, women were barred from the visitor's gallery. Consequently, the only access available to them for over 50 years was via the ventilator in the loft space above the House of Commons. It was not until the fire of 1834, when the Houses of Parliament were rebuilt, that a Ladies Gallery was provided in the new Palace of Westminster.

In the novel, Alixe leans into the opening in the side of the ventilation shaft in order to listen to Everard's speech, which from the height of the ceiling would have been barely audible in the echoing chamber.[60] As Norton reported, it was to this "cold and dreary" place that "the wives and sisters of young members may creep unseen, unheard, in breathless anxiety to the eight-inch square hole."[61] This description aptly sums up the marginalization and invisibility of women who were deprived of a political voice. A few years hence, Norton proved herself to be instrumental in defying limitations imposed upon women as political advocates through her campaigning, which led directly to the passing of the Custody of Infants Act (1839) and the

Matrimonial Causes Act (1857) in the Houses of Parliament. At the time she wrote *Love in "the World"*, she could never have dreamt that one day she would be celebrated as the figure of Justice in a fresco hung in the House of Lords or even that it would still be on display there hundreds of years later.[62]

As her biographer Diane Atkinson explains in the Preface to this edition, Caroline Norton is now recognized as an important English social reformer who campaigned successfully to improve the legal rights of women. In her own time, however, she was known chiefly for the violent vicissitudes of her life and as a prolific author of poems, lyrics, novels and short stories. So it is ironic that *The Wife* was recently republished as an edition with other fictional works by "Victorian Social Activists." The editor of this series suggests that *The Wife* was Norton's first published work of fiction[63] and the novella certainly has strong similarities in tone, language and subject matter to *Love in "the World"*.

Norton has created some confusion as to when exactly the manuscript was actually produced. On Volume I, she has written that it was "written partly as a girl & immediately after my marriage," which took place in July 1827, and on Volume II that it was composed "when I was yet 'in my teens'" (i.e. before 22 March 1828, her twentieth birthday). She appears to have adroitly extended her unmarried initials from C.E.S. (for Caroline Elizabeth Sheridan) to her married name: C.E.S. Norton, the "S" here presumably standing for Sarah. So it does seem that the novel was started before her marriage, although a part, or all, of the material from this period may consist of the initial 76 folio pages excised from Volume I. However, it does appear to have been completed later than she has indicated. In February 1829, Norton's sister Helen Blackwood wrote to their brother Brinsley Sheridan that she and Caroline were "each writing a novel,"[64] "1830" is inscribed on the title page of the Volume I manuscript and in late January 1830 the siblings' younger sister, Georgiana, wrote to Brinsley:

> Caroline [...] has written two volumes of a novel called "Love in the World" and "Love out of the World", which I want her to finish as prose sells better and easier than poetry. She means to ask five hundred for it, and thinks six weeks more hard writing will finish.[65]

Out of commercial considerations, publishers then preferred works of three volumes, while for library members a subscription to borrow a maximum of one volume was much cheaper than for multiple volumes and also tended to result in a wider availability of titles, as three people could then read a three-volume work at the same time.[66] Norton's two subsequent works of fiction, the novella *The Wife* and the two-volume *Women's Reward*, were published in 1835 as a three-volume work, as were two novels written by her mother, Caroline Sheridan, *Aims and Ends: and Oonagh Lynch* (1833). Although *Love in "the World"* succeeds as a two-volume work, it is therefore unlikely to have been submitted for publication in that form and whether or not a third volume was ever completed has yet to be established: the phrasing of Georgiana's "I want her to finish" and Caroline's reference to "hard writing" could suggest that the novel had become problematic and that further production was delayed.

Norton's creation of an ambiguous chronology for the writing of the novel may have been inscribed on the manuscript covers at any time from 1830 onwards, as could her dismissal of the work as a "prosy, foolish little book," the shortcomings of which embarrassed her: "am quite surprised at its stupidity." Possibly this happened many years after the novel had been laid aside and partially forgotten, as her critique is puzzling: the novel compares well with any of her finest narrative writing, such as *The Wife* and *Lost and Saved*, hitherto her only fiction to be republished in a new edition since 1877,[67] and the autobiographical sections of her pamphlets. It is hoped that *Love in "the World"*, finally in print after almost two centuries, might achieve comparable recognition and inspire a wider reappraisal of Caroline Norton's novels and stories.

We would like to thank Lord Richard Grantley for granting a publishing licence for this edition, the Beinecke Library at Yale University for generously providing scans of the manuscript, the Beaverbrook Museum for permitting publication of the portrait of Caroline Norton and the Shakespeare Birthplace Trust for permission to reproduce the Ventilator sketch. Thanks are also due to Diane Atkinson for writing the Preface to this edition, Margaret C. Jones, for proof-reading and correcting the novel transcript, the review panel for the edition, in particular Professor Mariaconcetta Constatini of D'Annunzio University of Chieti-Pescara, our editors at Anthem Press, Jebaslin Hephzibah and Megan Greiving, and Gomathy Ilammathe at Deanta Global. Diane's biography of Caroline Norton, together with Lady Antonia Fraser's biography and Randall Craig's critical account of Caroline Norton as a writer and a public figure, have all informed this publication and greatly enhanced recent Norton studies in general. This edition arose from a documentary conversation about *Love in "the World"* between the editors that took place at Markenfield Hall a year ago. We would like to thank Caroline Norton's descendent, Lady Deidre Curteis, for allowing us to use her home and Sarah Robson for her hospitality and making arrangements for the event.

EDITORIAL NOTE

Caroline Norton's manuscript for *Love in "the World"*[1] has few paragraphs, the use of speech marks is irregular and speech is very rarely indented. Hyphens are used to indicate a wide range of punctuation, such as full stops, commas, semi-colons, colons and question marks. It is clear that manuscript for Volume I of the novel, which is available online, features two contrasting styles of handwriting. As other contemporary samples of their handwriting demonstrate, the initial three-quarters of Volume I was transcribed from an earlier draft by Caroline Norton's sister, Helen Blackwood, while the remainder of Volume I and all of Volume II are in Caroline's hand. Both Helen Blackwood and Caroline Norton annotate the script, Helen using pencil and Caroline ink. Helen's annotations are referenced in the endnotes, Caroline's corrections acted on.

For the sake of readability and authenticity, the editorial practices in Caroline Norton's novella and novel, published under the collective title of *The Wife and Woman's Reward* (1835), have been adopted to transform the manuscript into a text that might have been prepared for publication by Norton and her editors. Where necessary, pages have been reordered, standard paragraphing and speech mark styles of the period have been introduced, hyphens and dashes have largely been replaced by a range of punctuation features and emphasis of underlined words had been reproduced through italicization. The most plausible substitute for a missing or indecipherable word is given within square brackets. The chapter numbering is conventional, from 1 to 22, replacing the original chapter structure, which begins midway through Chapter 3, as the first 76 folios of the MS have been torn out. There are also 18 missing folios (as we can establish since the pages have been numbered), which incorporate part of Chapters 14 and 15 and the transition from the neat copies produced by Helen Blackwood and Caroline Norton. A summary of likely aspects of the two missing sections, as can be deduced from the extant text, has been included. In all other respects, every effort has been made to faithfully reproduce the author's manuscript.

CHRONOLOGY

Date	Events (in chronological order) including publication of works (italicized)
22 March 1808	Caroline Norton born at 33 Charlotte Street in London.
1814–1818	Lives at Ardkinglas Castle in Argyll and Rossie Priory in Perthshire, while her parents are in Cape Town, where father dies in 1818.
1818	Reunited with her mother, sister and two brothers on their return from South Africa.
1820	*The Dandies Rout.*
	Sheridan family takes up residence in Grace and Favour Apartment 44 at Hampton Court.
1823	Sent to Miss Taylor's Academy at Shalford, Surrey.
1824	George Norton's first marriage proposal.
1827	Marries George Norton.
1828	Moves with husband to 2 Storey's Gate, Westminster.
	The Sorrows of Rosalie and Other Poems.
1829	Oldest child Fletcher Pennington born.
1830	*The Undying One and Other Poems* published.
1831	George Norton appointed Police magistrate for Lambeth by Lord Melbourne.
	Her operetta *The Gypsey Father* first performed at Covent Garden Theatre.
	Appointed editor of *La Belle Assemblée*.
	Second child Thomas Brinsley (known as Brinsley) born.
1833	Third child William Chapple born.
1834	Visits Rhineland and Paris with husband and Sheridan family.
1835	*The Wife and Woman's Reward.*
1835	Leaves husband after a violent incident and stays in Grosvenor Square with her brother while he negotiated terms on her return to Norton, which the latter does not uphold. CN has a miscarriage.
1835	Meets Edward Trelawny.
1836	Her husband prevents her return to their house at 2 Storey's Gate.
	George Norton brings an action for criminal conspiracy against Prime Minister Lord Melbourne.
	Norton vs Melbourne: Prime Minister cleared.
	Moves to 16 Green Street.
	A Voice from the Factories.

(*Continued*)

(Continued)

Date	Events (in chronological order) including publication of works (italicized)
1837	*Separation of Mother and Child by the Law of Custody of Infants Considered.* Infant Custody Bill, modelled on her pamphlet, *Separation of Mother and Child by the Law of Custody of Infants Considered*, introduced to the Commons by Thomas Talfourd. Later withdrawn for revision. Tours South Wales with her uncle, Charles Sheridan. Moves with her uncle to 22 Bolton Street, Mayfair. Talfourd re-introduces Infant Custody Bill to the Commons.
1838	Infant Custody Bill rejected by Lords. Tours the Isle of Wight with Lady Harriet d'Orsay.
1839	*Plain Letter to the Lord Chancellor.* Infant Custody Bill, allowing separated and divorced mothers custody of their children under seven and access to their older children, passes 3rd Reading in the Lords. Tour of Italy with her uncle Charles Brinsley Sheridan.
1840	Presented at Court by her sister Georgia Seymour. *The Dream and Other Poems.* Edward Piers tried after spying on CN on her husband's orders.
1842	Wins out-of-court appeal for custody and begins to see her sons on a regular basis. Youngest son William dies.
1843	Proposes herself as the next Post Laureate. Uncle Charles Brinsley Sheridan dies.
1844	Becomes friends with the Dorset poet William Barnes. Becomes seriously ill while completing *The Child of the Islands*.
1845	Moves to 3 Chesterfield Street. *The Child of the Islands.* Reputed to have leaked inaccurate story in *The Times* on cabinet unity over Corn Law abolition.
1846	Breaks off her relationship with Sidney Herbert due to scandal. Starts to edit *Fisher's Drawing Room Scrapbook*.
1847	*Aunt Carry's Ballads for Children.* Brother Charles Kinnaird Sheridan dies. Son Fletcher joins the British Legation in Lisbon.
1848	*Letters to the Mob* published in *Morning Chronicle*. Sits as subject of Daniel Maclise's *Spirit of Justice* fresco in the House of Lords. Leaves Portsmouth for Portugal, where her son Fletcher is ill.
1849	Stays with sons in Lisbon and Cintra.
1850	Stays in Brussels with son Fletcher, an attaché at British Legation in Brussels. Son Brinsley starts at Oxford.

(Continued)

(Continued)

Date	Events (in chronological order) including publication of works (italicized)
1851	*Stuart of Dunleath.*
	Death of mother, Caroline Sheridan.
	Visits Naples, where son Fletcher is an attaché with the British Legation.
	In Naples when George Norton suspends monthly allowance.
1852	Tours Scotland with son Brinsley.
	Visits Fletcher at Naples with Brinsley.
1853	*Thrupps vs Norton* trial: carriage firm sues George Norton for the costs of repairs to a carriage Caroline had purchased. He uses the trial to restate many of the accusations of the 1836 case.
	In Ireland, staying with sister Helen Dufferin at Clandeboye.
1854	*English Laws for Women in the Nineteenth Century.*
	Returns to Naples, then moves to Florence with Brinsley and his wife Mariuccia.
	At Vienna, Milan and Paris.
1855	*A Letter to the Queen on Lord Cranworth's Marriage and Divorce Bill.*
1856	In Naples and Capri to see son Brinsley and grandchildren.
	Staying at Keir with Sir William Stirling-Maxwell.
1857	Parliament passes Divorce and Matrimonial Causes Bill: four clauses in the Act protecting the income and property of married women were originally proposed in Caroline's pamphlets.
1858	Visits Scotland.
1859	*The Moral Responsibilities of Lawyers.*
	Son Fletcher dies in Paris.
	At Dinan in Normandy with son Brinsley and his family
1861	*The Lady of La Garaye.*
1863	*Lost and Saved.*
	Visits son and family in Italy.
1864	Tours north Germany.
1865	Tours Scotland.
1866	*Old Sir Douglas* serialised in *Macmillan's Magazine.*
1867	*Old Sir Douglas* published as book.
1868	On holiday at the Isle of Wight with grandchildren.
1869	At Cowes on the Isle of Wight.
1870	Tour of Scotland.
1871	Appears at Marlborough Street court for the non-payment of parochial rates.
	Stays at Keir.
1874	Death of George Norton.
	Lady Stirling-Maxwell's dress catches fire and she dies from serious burns.
1875	Visits Italy.
1877	Marries Sir William Stirling-Maxwell.
15 June 1877	Caroline Norton dies in London at Sir William Stirling-Maxwell's house.

FOREWORD

By Ross Nelson and Marie Mulvey-Roberts

Although taking place two decades after *Mansfield Park* (1814), the plot of *Love in "the World"* has similarities to Jane Austen's novel. However, the background circumstances of *Love in "the World"*, which seem likely to form part of the excised quarter of the Volume I manuscript, have to be concluded from the extant text. Like *Mansfield Park*, the key extended family in *Love in "the World"* involves a trio of siblings. As with Austen's Ward sisters, the marital fortunes of Sir William, George and Gertrude Marwood are very different. Sir William inherits his family's estate in England, where he settles down into married life. One plausible back-story for George Marwood is that after joining the Royal Navy he is promoted to the rank of Captain and meets the widowed Madame (or Mrs) de Fleury, who has a daughter, Alixe. The de Fleurys are known to have been among French emigrants to Canada in the seventeenth and eighteenth centuries. So it is at least plausible that Alixe's grandparents were also included with the thousands of French Canadians deported by the British from New France to Louisiana in the later eighteenth century. Many of these people were merchants engaged in the lucrative fur trade and other enterprises. The story's chronology suggests that Alixe was born in 1807–1808, which raises the possibility that her biological father, de Fleury, died or was separated from her mother during the War of 1812, and that her widowed mother soon afterwards decamped and possibly married Captain Marwood. Such a hypothetical back-story could explain why Alixe is an heiress and why she retained her mother's de Fleury family name. She does not mention any biological father but may have been too young at the time to remember him. In *Lost and Saved*, Captain Brooke is also married abroad to a widow with a young daughter. And Norton is known to have had an interest in American history, having as a child written a long poem "whose scene is laid in America, an early instance of that constant interest and liking for persons and things beyond the Atlantic which we find in her to the end of her life."[1] Meanwhile, Gertrude has married St Clair, a titled gentleman holding a position in the Caribbean, where the couple live and have a son, Charles. After several years they adopt Alixe, whose parents had recently died when their ship, the *Calliope*, was wrecked off New Orleans, a disaster Alixe witnessed and later painfully recalls when the subject is raised at a London dinner party. Only Lady St Clair and another guest are aware of her connection with the tragedy:

> At the bottom of the table near General Koss sat a gentleman describing in an animated and interested manner a shipwreck from which he had escaped. Twice General Koss tried to turn the conversation. He asked the gentleman to take wine, but he was too much engaged in conversation to reply, otherwise than by a hurried "No, I thank you."
>
> Alixe, who had at first answered, grew paler and paler, as the description of the storm of winds and waves and the agony of those on board to escape with life only recalled the first painful scenes in which she had known her adopted mother and lost her parents. She struggled with herself. No one observed her, for by this time all were listeners. She raised her eyes to her mother, but Lady St Clair's were fixed on the table and Alixe only saw from a slight compressing of her lips that she heard and felt. Alixe determined to show no symptom of agitation. She tried to fix her eye on the speaker, but she could not. She was on the shore at Port St Louis with the storm above ground and before her. She dimly remembered the form of her stronger father plunging in the waves and thought no more of those present, when the name of that father struck her ear with an electric shock.
>
> She heard the sentence distinctly. "Poor George Marwood was lost at that very time. He was a great friend of mine and I saw him drowned, poor fellow, almost within four yards of me. That was a day indeed."
>
> And she heard too General Koss in a low voice say, – "For God's sake stop him," to his next neighbour.

As children of around the same age, Alixe and Charles form a close bond. After her husband's death, Lady Clair returns with Alixe to England, Charles having by this time gone to sea with the Royal Navy. Alixe stays temporarily with Sir William and his wife, whom to her annoyance call her "Miss de Fleury." Wishing to be seen as Lady St Clair's biological, as well as her adopted, daughter, Alixe changes her surname to St Clair when she resumes living with her aunt in the latter's villa outside London. Lady St Clair then moves to the capital with Alixe, later revealed as an heiress due to inherit

£2000 a year, for the season. They stay with Lady St Clair's widowed aunt, Lady Townley. Chapters 3–11 describe the events of Alixe's first season, but the novel begins shortly before the start of her second season, the story of her first season forming a prolonged anamnesis within the entire narrative. By the start of the novel, Charles St Clair has returned to his family and, as soon becomes clear, has developed feelings for Alixe of an intensity that she does not share.

Volume I

Chapter 1

"Oh!" in a half-satisfied tone was the only answer Charles made and the evening passed off as usual. Alixe took her guittar [*sic*] and sang her prettiest airs, Charles occasionally singing second to those he knew, or occupied in watching the beautiful laughing mouth and dark blue eyes of the fair songstress, while Lady St Clair, whose health was by no means good, reclined on the sofa.

In this happy manner some days and weeks past [*sic*] till the time drew near for the annual visit to town. Alixe prepared for this with great alacrity and Charles more than once caught her at the glass, balancing between two colours or hesitating whether a chaplet of pink or white roses became her best. This was a great matter of amusement and "Oh Alixe! fie how vain you grow" and "Yes, but dear Charles which *shall* I take?" were repeated I will not say how many times.

A few days before the departure Alixe, rising with her guittar in her hand, dropped some trinket which was suspended to a gold chain around her neck. Charles stepped hastily forward to prevent its fall, but it had reached the ground and his foot was on it before he was aware where it had fallen. Alixe clasped her hands as he drew his foot away. "Oh my harp, my poor little harp," said she. And stooping, she picked it up, gazed on it a moment and to Charles's astonishment actually burst into tears.

He stood petrified, and at length, gently taking it out of her hand, said, – "I dare say it can be mended. Do not cry, pray do not dearest. Any jeweller can do it. I could do it myself. I am very sorry indeed, it was great awkwardness."

"Oh no, dear," said Alixe who had recovered and was apparently rather ashamed of having wept for a trinket. "You could not help it. It cannot be mended, it need not be mended. Indeed, I do not care about it."

She extended her hand eagerly for the trinket, but Charles smiled and put it in his pocket. "No, no, as I did the mischief, I will endeavour to remedy it. And as you do not care for it, why the attempt, if it fail, can do no harm." Alixe made no answer and they soon after separated for the night. When Charles retired to his own room, he could not help recurring to the little scene he had just witnessed. Was it possible that Alixe, the perfect, the lovely, the good-tempered, should have been foolish enough to weep for the loss of a paltry ornament, when she knew what pain those tears would give the author of the damage done? And then to declare she did not value it, what could such a contradiction mean? The question could not be answered, and Charles fingered the trinket with no very satisfied feeling. It was a minute and exquisitely finished harp, apparently of gold and of foreign manufacture, with strings of dark hair wound with the greatest nicety round the fairy pegs of the instrument. Charles thought it very pretty. He was near thinking it beautiful, but he could not make his mind up to it. The strings were most of them broken, but otherwise it had received but little damage. A sudden thought struck Charles. It was satisfactory, for he finished his contemplations, said his prayers and got into bed. For a long, long time he did not sleep. And when he did, confused visions of Alixe and Mr Everard Price, weddings in which he had no share and above all an enormous harp, the chords of which struck of themselves to prevent his approaching it, flitted before his eyes. And restless and disturbed he lay till morning, when he started from a vision of Alixe, in a white dress with a great quantity of pearls on it, refusing to speak or shake hands with him. And jumping out of bed, proceeded to dress himself in haste.

Chapter 2

He[1] descended into the breakfast room, where Alixe and his mother were waiting. "How lazy you are this morning Charles," said Alixe laughingly, holding out her hand. Charles kissed her, sat down and watched intently the important operation of tea-making.

"Will you have some toast Charles?" said his fairy. "Charles will you have some toast? Charles will you have –?"

But the voice of the fairy and even the silver sound of her laugh were unheard and after a pause of some moments the abstracted youth gravely said, without raising his eyes from the bread he was buttering, "I have been examining your poor little harp,[2] Alixe and I think it could be easily mended. Only," added he, looking up, "the strings must be of gold wire I think, as they are almost all broken. So I will take it, if you like, to Mr Humphrey's, shall I?" Alixe had dropped her knife (a thing that had never happened in her life before) and she had stooped for it. But Charles's sentence was so long that the precautions were wasted. For with a countenance flushed (by the heat of the tea) and [in] a voice almost inarticulate, she answered.

"I told you Charles, I did not want it mended and, – and, – and, –"

Said Lady St Clair, – "if you want it mended, perhaps it had better be done in town?"

This was no doubt intended as a relief, but from some cause not understood Alixe's confusion augmented visibly, and at length she rose, saying, – "I think I had better finish packing up, dear Mamma." Lady St Clair nodded and smiled and the fairy glided out of the apartment. There was a long pause, during which Charles seemed struggling with some painful feeling. At last, just as Lady St Clair rose, he caught her arm:

"Mother, dear mother, is Alixe in love with him?"

"In love with who?"

"Oh you know, dearest. That man, that Everard Price."

"My love, I cannot pretend to say. Alixe is very pretty and she has been out a great deal and been very much admired by many people." Charles groaned, and his mother continued:

"And if you had any suspicion of Alixe being attached to any one, it was not very manly or very kind of you to teaze her so. And I cannot tell why it should offend you, even were she in love with Everard Price."

"Oh, I am not offended. I do not care. Mr Price is the same to me as anyone else. Only I should think you would not wish her to marry a merchant's son."

"Indeed, I should not think that any objection, if Alixe did not."

"Then you will really let her marry this man? 'Mrs Price'! How well it sounds!" added he, hardly knowing how to vent the bitterness of his heart on the offending object.

"My dear son, you have certainly taken a great prejudice against poor Everard. There are twenty men who admire your adopted sister as much as he does or more. I can only say that I will never constrain Alixe's inclinations on the point most essential to her future happiness. I suppose you would wish to see her well married?"

"Never!" said Charles vehemently

"You wish her *never* to be married?"

"Oh no, no. It does not matter. Thank you mother, for listening so long to my … I am grown very foolish."

"God forbid, my dear boy," added she, as she rose to leave the room. "Do not let this mystery of Mr Price make you unhappy." Lady St Clair smiled, but it was a mournful smile and she sighed as she closed the door. And poor Charles echoed the sigh from the bottom of his heart and swallowed his cold tea hastily in hope to prevent the tears that were rising.

He was roused by the silver voice of Alixe. "Charles, Charles what are you thinking of? Come here and help me to choose my flowers."

"Thinking of you always," thought Charles as he rose slowly. "And now," he half answered, "I must go and help to choose flowers that others may look and admire."

Everyone knows that lovers have the worst tempers in the world. Our disconsolate walked up stairs where his fairy[3] stood pondering with white lilies in one hand and white roses in the other.

"Now dear, which shall I take? The lilies are the most uncommon but then they have green and yellow in them and the roses –"

"I think I should like you best with nothing but your hair. I hate those artificial ornaments. I never saw any girl who looked as well with them as without."

"Oh Charles, it was but the other day that I came dancing down in a wreath of the convolvulus and you said I looked beautiful."

"*You* look beautiful in anything," said Charles sadly.

"Well, don't say it so sorrowfully," said his companion laughing. "But exert your judgement and choose for me, for I cannot take them all."

Charles did as he was commanded. And the remembrance of Everard Price was half absorbed in the attempt to decide between crimson, blue, pink and white. After dinner the younger part of Lady St Clair's family went out to enjoy the sweet spring feel of the air.

"Oh I have forgotten my guittar [*sic*]," said Alixe. "I must have my guittar." And she turned back to fetch it.

"*I* have forgotten it you mean," said Charles, "for I always bring it: I cannot think what makes me so stupid to-night." No more could Alixe, and she continued ruminating on the subject till he again joined her.

"What a fine minister you would have made," said the fairy, "in the days of old when gentleman went about playing and singing as the beggars do not!"

"Yes, I dare say I should. Only you know the minstrels of old did not carry a guittar but a harp." This required no reply. Alixe asserted silently to its truth and they walked on till they reached a trellis seat at the end of a lawn, which commanded a view of the house and the rest of the garden, in which violets and primroses were blowing in proportion and every variety of crocus laying their faded or fading heads by the green nests of leaves, where snowdrops had budded and bloomed for a little while and then disappeared entirely. Alixe sat like a nightingale singing in the little bower, the honeysuckle of which had been trained by her own hands and which was now twisting in little pale green buds, as if to thank her care. Song after song had been gone through, interrupted only by an occasional observation. At last, the topic seemed nearly exhausted. She paused and turned to Charles,

"Do you remember any more?"

"Ah," said he, "I was thinking, do you remember our first visit to the garden when you were a little joyous thing and I, –"

"Oh yes, that puts me in mind, how could I forget it, – 'Ma patrie.'"[4] As she spoke, she played a light prelude and then sang in a voice, whose tones might have bribed the departing souls of the blest to pause on their way to Heaven, a little French chansonette as simple as might be, the burden of which at every stage was "Ma patrie." As she finished, she bent her head to slip the guittar off her neck and the bright evening soon fell on the still brighter locks through the trellis work above. Charles kissed her cheek as she stooped, and she turned her rosy innocent lips to him, unconscious of the painful reflections which were passing in his mind.

"Ah, Alixe, dearest Alixe," said the young man mournfully, "I wish we had never left that country. Not for its sunny and beautiful skies, nor its rich flowers, nor its high mountains, but there are at least, *there*, you would have loved me, for there would have been none *like* us, or *with* us."

"Dear Charles what do you mean? I *do* love you, sincerely *would* have loved you!"

"Yes, you love me, but not as I love you. You are my world and if we had lived till now in our own island, I should not have seen you make your world away from me."

"Charles! dear Charles," said Alixe, whose surprise almost bordered on tears.

"Have I not a right to love you!" continued he passionately.

"*Love* me?"

"Yes, a right to love you! Am I to live with you for years; to see you, to hear you, every day. And then because I have spent my life with you, because I *know* you to be more perfect than others can even imagine you, am I to be denied the privilege of strangers? The privilege which the merest coxcomb, who sees you for a quarter of an hour, may claim to admire, to love? And I am expected to sit tamely by and see it all? No, by heaven!"

"Oh Charles," said the almost weeping girl, "for the sake of the power you invoke so passionately, be more calm! I do love you. Indeed I do! Perhaps not so wildly, so –"

"Wildly?" repeated Charles vehemently. "You can love others at least as, – as I love you. You love that paltry fool Everard Price or I should not be so miserable. You would rather be his wife than mine. Him, whom you have, can only have known a few months. And I have spent a life in loving, in worshipping you."

Alixe sobbed bitterly and Charles, moved even in his own agony by the sight of his tears, paused. Alixe wiped her eyes, struggled for composure and attempted to speak. She took his burning hand in both her own and looked earnestly at his agitated countenance.

"Charles," said she, "you have been gentle and kind to me from childhood. Do not be unjust and cruel now. If you had seen some girl abroad, whom you had loved –."

"It is impossible," said Charles passionately, "absolutely impossible. In the calm and the storm, in the hours of death and danger and those of mirth and joy, sleeping or waking, I thought of you, I blest you. When I saw other girls, I thought, so tall Alixe must be now! And at the foreign bridals, at which others stood looking on in mere curiosity, I turned from the dark swarthy bride with the wild songs and wilder ceremony, to reckon the years that would pass before I should be able to claim you. I thought of the blue eyes and golden locks I had left behind and of my return –." And overcome by his own remembrances, Charles sobbed aloud.

Confounded, agonized, Alixe sat painfully silent, till starting up, her young lover cried, – "and you say nothing, you do not contradict me. You do not care for me or you could not do it."

"Charles, hear me," said Alixe firmly. "You reproach me as if I had wronged you. Had I made a promise, however slight, however thoughtlessly given, and you had claimed it, no power should have prevented my being there. [As] to my word, I have none to fulfil. I consider myself as free as I considered you when we parted last. If I have loved another, it is not a fault of mine. You say you love me. Were I to bid you change, you would think it strange, impossible. Why should not the rule apply to both?"

"Then it is true," said Charles, "it *is* true. I am come back from my voyages to find a stranger usurping my place. Would to God I had been [over]whelmed in the ocean before I had lived to see it! But no, I will not see it. If Everard Price aspire to be your husband, he shall cut his way through me before he reach the church."

"There is no need of so wild a threat, Charles. If it were to make you miserable to see me the wife of another, if you were to tell me so coolly and dispassionately, I would make the sacrifice."

"But would you love *me*? Oh say that Alixe, and I will worship you, forgive you all the agony you have given me."

"Charles, dear Charles, you will make me miserable. I would not marry against your wishes, though unreasonable. But I would not marry at all if the sacrifice was once made. Oh Charles, drive this wild thought from your heart," added she, her tears again rushing to her eyes as she spoke, "and be my brother again, the kind, gentle, generous."

But the appeal was lost.

In a quivering tone subdued to apparent calmness, Charles said, – "Where did you first meet this man? At a ball? How long have you known him?"

"About five months. You may read my journal. It is only a narrative of my season. But I would rather you should read it, than have to explain [it] to you."

"Read your journal? No, keep your narrative, your love, to yourself. I will go and sail again on the waste of waters, on waves less changeful, and winds less varying than you. Unkind, ungrateful Alixe, my life has been spent with one end in view: the effort to please you. That has sunk and my life may finish. When you first came to our house, I little thought how hard-hearted –"

Charles could say no more. He darted out of the summer house. And Alixe, after weeping bitterly till she lost the power of reflection, rose to return to her mother. At the entrance of the bower, she met Charles. He had been crying, she knew, by the sound of his voice. He silently put her little broken harp into her hand and then said in a low voice, "can you, will you, forgive me Alixe?"

And they entered the house once more as brother and sister. The next day Charles bent over Alixe as she was preparing her drawing and timidly requested the loan of her journal. Alixe gave it without speaking and Charles, after having perused it, silently returned it, only vowing (in the most brotherly way) that there was nothing he could not or would not do which he thought would conduce to her happiness. As it would be unfair not to allow my readers the privilege of knowing the contents of the journal, I lay before them the narrative (collected from many sources) of Mlle de Fleury's season.

Chapter 3

On the fourteenth of April A__ D__ Lady St Clair and her interesting protégé reached London for the express purpose of producing Alixe, according to the absurd practice of the world. Mlle de Fleury was just eighteen, very beautiful on a very small scale, with a slight and almost childish figure and a face whose sparkling and varied expression struck all who saw her with admiration. Lady St Clair had proposed taking a house while in town. But she was induced to relinquish the plan by the pressing invitation of an old aunt, who had lost sight of her since her marriage and who having no children of her own, and being very fond of young people, thought it would be an agreeable society to have her niece and grandniece staying with her during a London Season. Lady Townley, widow of Sir Joshua Townley, Rear Admiral of the Red,[1] was sitting in a magnificent drawing room in a superb house in Park Lane, when the expected visitors were announced. The dignified hostess took off a pair of gold spectacles and laid them down on the book she was reading, rose slowly and stately and walked forward (with a large green fan closed in one hand and a worked handkerchief in the other), with a step like a queen receiving her ambassadors, to her niece.

"Welcome my dear Lady St Clair, welcome to my house and home with your daughter. And double would your welcome be if Sir Joshua, poor man, was alive. He was a good friend to your father and a good husband and a good man, but we'll not think of that just now. Won't you be seated?"

The invitation was complied with and Alixe, to whom the old Lady's attention was by no means directed, sat motionless, gazing at her with surprise. Accustomed to the simple appearance and subdued manner of her adopted mother and having always looked on her as a model of female excellence, the present object of her thoughts appeared to some disadvantage. Highly rouged and dressed, according to poor Alixe's taste, somewhat too *young* with false curls of the lightest flaxen, she sate [sic] upright, majestic and pompous, talking *oratorically* to her niece, who fatigued and exhausted, sate patiently waiting till some pause should allow her to request permission to retire and take off her hat and cloak. At length, a pause did actually take place and Lady

Townley rose and escorted her niece to the room she had set apart for her, observing as she left the room that no doubt Miss St Clair would find great amusement in watching the carriages in Hyde Park till their return. Alixe was easily amused and though this was not precisely the entertainment she would have chosen, yet its being a novelty had temptation in it and she moved her chair to the window, which shaded by light muslin blinds with green drapery above, concealed her while it allowed her full view of the groups below. As she gazed, she felt more and more interested and her heart beat high at the thought that soon she too would be one in the gay crowd. Lady Townley returned in about a quarter of an hour and sate down by her. To Alixe de Fleury's surprise she told the name of every carriage as they past with anecdotes of their possessors.

"There Miss St Clair, my dear, do you see the yellow liveries belong[ing] to Mrs Archdale? She is an acquaintance of mine, a very disagreeable woman indeed, so proud, so overbearing. And the next is Lady Louisa Whittaker; was a beauty poor thing and did what all beauties are sure to do, married a poor man, a mere nobody,[2] shocked her friends and struggles on in poverty with three children whom she is obliged to educate herself. Ah, there is the Duchess, dear Duchess, such a sweet woman, only rather insincere, but that is a confidence. And there is old Mrs Price's carriage. She is a good soul, but so prosy and dry I never can hear her talk without feeling enuyée.[3] And there is pretty Lady Harriet Dure, only married a year and a half and flirting already, as if she had no husband at all."

Alixe repeated "flirt" to herself, and subsequently "as if she had no husband," without being able to comprehend the least what her new friend meant thereby, losing the history of Sir Samuel Repringer and his four ugly daughters and only coming in for half the account of the Misses Annette and Pamela Aimwell, girls of great fashion, great accomplishments, great beauty and fresh from Paris, who were to be the models of visitation by whom Alixe was to square her conduct. A loud double rap at the door summoned visitors.

"You had better go and take off your bonnet, child, and then return and we shall have people to dinner tonight, which it is always fair to warn young ladies of, because of their dress."

So saying, the majestic Lady Townley rose to meet her friends and Alixe retired to the opposite door, glad to escape to her mother. She stood for a moment irresolute, for her friend had entirely forgotten to give the least direction respecting her way upstairs. She looked to the end of the passage or gallery. It led into a library. She stood helpless for a minute, considering what she should do, when a side door opened and she heard the well-known voice of Lady St Clair speaking to the maid. She bounded forward and laughingly stepped into the room.

"Oh Mamma, I have been this half-hour considering where you could be. Lady Townley sent me away at last and she says I must dress, for there are people to dinner."

"Very well, my love, choose your gown and make haste, for it is getting late and we must be downstairs soon. For my Aunt makes small allowance for travelling," added she, smiling. "The next room is to be yours. And when you are dressed send the maid to me. And I will lie down till then."

Alixe accordingly returned to her own room with the maid. But it was some time before she would fix on what she should wear. "At dinner in London!" What a dreadful sound! Too much dressed! Too little dressed! What rock to split upon.

At length the toilette was finished. Lady St Clair smiled and was satisfied and they went downstairs. Long before the drawing-room door was opened, Alixe heard strangers' voices and laughter. The door flew open, the voices hushed, and Alixe, with a beating heart, stepped forward holding her mother's arm. Lady Townley rose, took her niece by the hand and made her sit down by her, having first introduced her to Lady Aimwell and said to the daughter of the latter in a half whisper, –

"My dear Miss Pamela, I hope you and your sister will afford a little of your countenance and support to Miss St Clair, as she knows nobody in town."

The young ladies gracefully curtsied. Miss Pamela asked, accordingly, how long Alixe had been in town and Miss Annette whether she liked the thought of "coming out"? To which, having received satisfactory answers, they seemed to consider their duties over and took no more notice of the young lady so forcibly recommended to their countenance and support, than by once turning with a quiet stare and "do you think so?" when someone remarked that Alixe was very pretty, adding as she turned round again: "She wants *airs*."

Poor little Alixe, thus forsaken, sate by her mother, contemplating the party. On the sofa sat, or rather *lay*, Pamela Aimwell, leaning back, while a man with his elbow on the arm of the sofa sat quietly gazing on the rest of the strangers and occasionally half turning to her. This was Captain Aimwell of the Guards, as Alixe presently discovered. At the other end sat Annette, the liveliest and most talkative of half-French young ladies, but not near so pretty as her sister, of which the latter was certainly as much aware as Annette seemed ignorant or averse to believing it. No less than three beaux did she entertain at once, much to her own delight. There was one other young lady on whom Alixe's eyes riveted themselves, as the most beautiful object she had ever seen. Her profile was turned, for she was talking to Captain Aimwell. But that profile was a most lovely one. With hair literally jet black, she had a very fair clear skin without the slightest colour but in her lips, which were the brightest crimson. She turned in a minute, fixed her dark beautiful eyes on Alixe and after a moment's pause, she rose and came forward, saying with a kind smile, "I thought you looked very solitary, so I am come to sit by you a little while till some of your beaux come." Alixe smiled.

"I have no beaux, for I know nobody yet. This is my first spring."

"Indeed then, you have many pleasures to come. Are you fond of dancing?"

"Oh, very."

"And you can play and sing, I dare say?"

"Yes, I have learnt."

"And you are very pretty. Here we have all the chief requisites for 'coming out'. I wish my brother had been here tonight. I could have introduced him and he would have made a nice beau for you."

"Thank you," said Alixe gratefully. And feeling it her duty to continue the conversation without knowing exactly how, she said, "Is he like you?"

Her companion laughed. "You shall judge when you see him. He comes very often, but he had an invitation somewhere else tonight."

"Are you speaking of your brother, Miss Price?" said Lady Townley.

"Yes Ma'am, he begged me to make every excuse for him. But your note only reached him this morning, as he was here in the country for a few days. I dare say he will call tomorrow and speak for himself."

"I am very sorry indeed," said the urbane hostess, turning to praise him to Lady St Clair, with the usual modifications, which in the present instance were confined to "rather too wild." In the meantime, the room gradually filled with a proportionate number of men, making in all sixteen. Lady Townley was content. Captain Aimwell offered his arm to Miss Price, much to Alixe's surprise and mortification, who did not wish to be separated from her new friend. She stepped back to her mother.

"Oh, my dear Miss St Clair!" said the hostess. Then, turning to a gentleman who had for the last five minutes stood twirling his mustachios and looking at his own feet, or the black silk stockings which covered them, [added], "Colonel Manners, perhaps you will take care of Miss St Clair?" The mustachios stepped forward, offered his arm in the most graceful way imaginable and they proceeded forward.

"How wide these stairs are." (Colonel Manners was famous for knowing how to *begin* a conversation). "They are nearly as wide as those at Forbes's house don't you think?"

"I never was there."

"Oh –" brought them into the dining parlour. Alixe found herself miraculously seated, by the care of her companion, without the slightest trouble and proceeded to glance round the table, having never dined out before, with surprise and something like awe. She was endeavouring to judge between the dresses of Miss Price, the Misses Aimwell and their mother, who chose to appear quite as gainly as her daughters, and was a very pretty little widow about seven and thirty, and as nobody had told her she was *passée* she overlooked the difference of years with great complacency. Miss Price [wore] plain pink silk with one rose in her hair, Miss Pamela Aimwell blue, very much trimmed. And Miss Annette? To observe her, it was necessary to glance across a gentleman who had cruelly raised his eyeglass at that moment.

The scrutiny was but momentary. The instant Alixe's eye passed him, his glass was put down and turning to Annette he said –

"Who is that simply dressed girl? La belle Marguerite?"[4]

La belle Marguerite blushed excessively. Surely he need not have said it so loud? She did not hear the answer. She was thinking only of her ciasse[5] dress and headdress of white daisies.

"Will you take some wine Miss St Clair," said the attentive Colonel. But Alixe did not hear. She had turned her head and gave the brightest look of joy to a somebody who sat at the further end of the table.

"Do you see any of your friends," said Colonel Manners, with a most intelligent smile.

"Yes," said Alixe simply. "It is a General Koss. Do you know him?"

"No, I do not," said her companion, rather disappointed, and he gave his moustache a twirl upwards.

And during the pause which ensued, I may be allowed to remark that a moustache answers precisely to a male conscience, being a something which he cannot forget without great exertion of thought, and even in that case it returns more strongly to his remembrance after the lapse of attention to it of which he has been guilty. Even allowing (which happens but seldom), that they be neither curled, plaited or dyed, they occupy much more of the wearer's attention than the most beautiful head of hair belonging to a lady. They assimilate themselves in a manner with the feelings of their possessor. Unfortunate civilians who possess not the graceful privilege of wearing a tuft above, a tuft below your mouths (as the bourgeois of former times might not wear a sword) – to express your sentiments you are forced to speak, to smile, to frown. But with a *militaire*[6] no such labour is necessary. Be he pleased, he strokes his moustache down with his finger and thumb, at once throwing form and contempt into his countenance. Be he at a loss for conversation, he twists the end of it into a curl or holds it in the corner of his mouth.[7]

And this was in truth the most efficient way Colonel Manners had of making his sentiments known, his countenance being destitute of what the fastidious in beauty are apt to call expression. After some few more attempts at conversation with Alixe, having discovered that she had never been to Almack's, nor indeed any place in London, that the opera was a novelty and a fancy ball a sort of paradise, looked forward [to] with delight, his moustache gradually took the upper turn and he ceased to speak; as Alixe thought, from having nothing more to say; as Colonel Manners himself thought, from her not being worthy to hear.

After this, the dinner which Alixe de Fleury already thought particularly tedious grew more and more dull. They all talked and laughed, but they talked of things she had never seen and laughed at jests she did not comprehend. Her mother was seated at some distance, Miss Price nearly opposite and an encouraging smile from the latter alone relieved the form and monotony of the scene, till nearly at the end of the dessert, when the conversation became more interesting, from eating being but a secondary object, her attention was suddenly awakened in a very painful manner. She listened eagerly, though she would have given worlds that she had not been present. At the bottom of the table near General Koss sat a gentleman describing in an animated and interested manner a shipwreck from which he had escaped. Twice General Koss tried to turn the conversation. He asked the gentleman to take wine, but he was too much engaged in conversation to reply, otherwise than by a hurried "No, I thank you."

Alixe, who had at first answered, grew paler and paler, as the description of the storm of winds and waves and the agony of those on board to escape with life only recalled the first painful scenes in which she had known her adopted mother and lost her parents. She struggled with herself. No one observed her, for by this time all were listeners. She raised her eyes to her mother, but Lady St Clair's were fixed on the table and Alixe only saw from a slight compressing of her lips that she heard and felt. Alixe determined to show no symptom of agitation. She tried to fix her eye on the speaker, but she could not. She was on the shore at Port St Louis[8] with the storm above ground and before her. She dimly remembered the form of her stronger father plunging in the waves and thought no more of those present, when the name of that father struck her ear with an electric shock.

She heard the sentence distinctly. "Poor George Marwood was lost at that very time. He was a great friend of mine and I saw him drowned, poor fellow, almost within four yards of me. That was a day indeed."

And she heard too General Koss in a low voice say, "For God's sake stop him," to his next neighbour. Had she been at home, she could have wept, but there was something strange and oppressive in her present feelings. She had started so visibly at the mention of Marwood's name that the Misses Aimwell turned with a satirical smile. And Colonel Manners (who was worn out with endeavouring to appear attentive to the wreck) anxiously asked if she was ill. Perhaps nothing ever rouses and revives one more completely from deeply interesting feelings, and certainly nothing ever so effectually prevents a *genuine* flood of tears, than the forced and affected sympathy of persons who are utter strangers, incapable of feeling with you or for you, and unable to comprehend what is passing in your mind. Happy was it for Alixe that Colonel Manners *was* a stranger. Happy that she was near none who could sympathize with her. She neither wept, nor did she adopt the still more interesting expedient of fainting. She answered with tolerable calmness that she was not ill. And Lady Townley, who had perceived something was the matter, conjectured Lady St Clair's evident dislike to the account of the wreck of the *Calliope* to proceed from her having a son at sea. As soon as she had made this discovery (that is, when the tale was ended), she rose and retired, followed by her female train to the drawing room. As they past upstairs, they stopped for a moment at a window which opened into a sort of greenhouse. They followed Lady Townley into it, as she begged, to look at her beautiful plants. Mrs Aimwell declared her nerves were so shaken by that terrible story, that she must lie down on the sofa till the gentlemen came up. Miss Price, who had watched poor Alixe with deep interest and felt for her from the bottom of her heart, spoke kindly to her. It was some indifferent question, "whether she knew or cared much about flowers." The greenhouse was only partially lighted and she could hardly see the countenance of her companion. She continued the obvious subject by offering to let her have some seeds – of what will never be known, for Alixe, whose feelings had been frozen for some time, so unnaturally overcome by the tone which meant so much more than the words, uttered a low distinct sob. A deep pause followed.[9]

"You had better fetch a shawl, my love," said Lady St Clair. "It is cold here." Alixe, according[ly] glad of the relief, went upstairs, where her mother soon joined her, leaving the rest of the party adjoining to the drawing room.

Chapter 4

The Miss Aimwells loudly accused Miss St Clair, when she had left the drawing room, of affectation and *missiness*.

"So actress-like, so disgusting, as if we did not all feel as much."

"I am sure" (said their interesting mother), "I felt far, *far* more. I shall not be well for a week." Miss Price had a brother, loved perhaps better than he deserved, and she instantly considered her own feelings with those of Alixe's and undertook her defence.

"I have heard Miss St Clair had a brother at sea. Perhaps she has lost him, and in that case…"

"Well, we will ask Lady Townley," said Miss Aimwell. And skipping or tripping across the room, she said to Lady Townley, who was cutting the stalk of a geranium and at the same time viewing herself in the mirror opposite:

"Dear Lady Townley, I am afraid that story has affected Miss St Clair."

"Yes, poor little thing. I saw something was the matter at dinner-time."

"She has a brother at sea, has she not?"

"Yes."

"I thought perhaps he had been drowned."

"Drowned? Oh no, he is quite well, or was, when they last heard from him. Is not this a beautiful specimen of the Duchess of York geranium?"

"Yes, indeed. They seem to me to grow better than ever in your greenhouse. You are not a witch are you, dear Lady Townley?"

"No," said the Lady smiling. "I leave all arts of witching to you young ladies, you and your sister in particular."

"Yes, Lady Townley, you will quite spoil us, and what will Mamma say?"

And after this serious enquiry about Miss St Clair, Annette Aimwell returned to her seat.

"Well?" said her sister enquiringly, "what of her brother?"

"Oh, he was quite, quite well in their last letter, so you see it must be affectation after all," said the amiable young lady, turning to Miss Price.

"No, I cannot say I am convinced. Even if he is not drowned, he was at risk every hour of losing his life. If war was to come on, you would feel very unhappy about your brother, and Mr St Clair's is quite as uncertain a profession as Captain Aimwell's."

"Yes, but if war was to come on" said the persevering Annette, "I would not go out at all rather than expose myself to strangers."

Perhaps in her heart Emily Price rather wished her fashionable friend put to the test, but she merely said, "Probably Miss St Clair did not foresee the conversation which was to take place after dinner."

This was a self-evident fact and Miss Aimwell changed her mode of attack. "Ah no, I see Miss Price you are determined to defend your new friend at all hazards; this is one of your prepossessions."

"Yes," said Pamela, who sate with her beautiful eyes half closed, as weary of the debate. "And remember how ill the last person you took a fancy to turned out."

"Ah yes," said Annette, "poor Lady Louisa Brandon, who ran away with Mr Whittaker."

"Oh no, Miss Aimwell. She did not run away. She told her uncle she meant to marry Mr Whittaker and he refused his consent. But she was of age and she certainly did right in following her inclinations, even if it was an imprudent match."

"Ah, I see you will defend her even now against all the world."

"I do not wish to place my opinion in opposition to all the world," said Emily with a half-smile. "But certainly, I see nothing in Lady Louisa Whittaker to alter my affection for her. She is an excellent wife, an excellent mother, and anyone who knows Mr Whittaker will excuse the capital crime."

"Yes, but nobody *does* know him, that is the worst of it."

At this moment the door opened and Alixe and her mother returned.

"Are you better now?" said Miss Price, kindly making room for her on the sofa.

"Yes, thank you," said Alixe, blushing and sitting down, ashamed of the look which Miss Aimwell gave as she past. No explanation was given, no misplaced enquiries made. Miss Price was as kind as before, but it was without a hesitation or appearing to think that Miss St Clair required consolation and amusement. The ten minutes above stairs had been employed by Lady St Clair in gently reasoning and endeavouring to convince her adopted child that there was nothing extraordinary in the accidental turn the conversation had taken. And preparing her to hear with fortitude and composure allusions to that or similar subjects.

Soon after their return to the drawing room, the gentlemen came up. Colonel Manners hoped Alixe was better. Alixe wished herself at the bottom of the Red Sea, which is the one generally chosen by people who suffer under great embarrassment to hide in. The graceful Colonel walked on to the sofa, where Miss Aimwell was reposing in a languishing mode and who greeted him with much affection. He was soon engaged in conversation with her. They suited so much better than with any other people. She was all *minauderie*,[1] he was all affectation. And what they wanted in words they made up in grimace[s]. The balance, however, was in favour of Colonel Manners. He was affected from mere folly to add to the charms of a good figure and face what he fancied were agreeable qualities. She was affected from vanity and emptiness of heart. Singing was proposed, in order to give people "something to do," by the mistress of the house. The Miss Aimwells were great musicians. Pamela sang. Her sister did not. Lady Townley advanced to them.

"My dear Miss Aimwell, I know you sing beautifully, no denials are allowed. I shall make you all sing in turn, so pray begin with a good grace."

"Pray do now, Miss Aimwell," resounded through the room. Gentlemen heaped books upon books and turned over leaves which nobody thought of playing from. And Annette slowly rose, saying "my fingers are quite out of practice," and walked towards the piano. But Pamela Aimwell acted better than she sang, and she protested she must hear someone sing first to give her courage. She was sure Miss St Clair sang; she knew it by the shape of her mouth. Alixe protested her willingness to do anything that was required of her. She would sing, but she did not think she could play the pianoforte accompaniment. She had not been used to it. Anything so contemptuous as the mouth of Annette Aimwell could not be well imagined.

"Not play the accompaniments! Do you sing without accompaniment then?"

"Oh no, but I generally sing with my guittar and it is not unpacked yet."

"Well then Pamela, you had better come and sing," said her sister, on whose countenance there was a displeasure for which Alixe could not account. And Pamela sang. Alixe de Fleury did not like her singing much. It was a *taught* voice, and though she could hardly tell why, she felt disappointment at this little display of Lady Townley's models. A confused buzz of praise sounded through the room, however.

And Pamela, drawing on her gloves with a little bend of the head to one side (which in these degenerate days stands proxy for a blush), turned and said, "Now Miss Price, it is your turn."

But Captain Aimwell, who had no reason to be jealous of Alixe, said, –

"Oh are we to lose the pleasure of hearing Miss St Clair sing? Annette, I am sure you could play anything. Suppose you try the accompaniment to some song?"

But this was the last step Miss Aimwell chose to take. She replied with the sweetest smile, that "she only played the song her sister was in the habit of singing and she was afraid that perhaps –"

But Miss Price relieved her fear by stepping forward. "Miss St Clair has mentioned several songs I know, and I shall be delighted to play them for her."

Alixe sang in a sweet clear simple style. She was not thinking of herself and she was not timid in consequence. There was a deep silence and many who dared not openly declare they preferred Alixe St Clair's singing to that of many girls of Miss Aimwell's set, gave a more sincere murmur of approbation that they were accustomed to do. Captain Aimwell was loud in his applause. She was requested to sing it again. Alixe was quite willing, but she felt as if she was engrossing more of the time and attention of those around her than she ought.

"Oh, you know, Miss Price, it is your turn. You were to have sung before."

"Well, I am not going to deprive you of the pleasure of hearing me, but you see the gentlemen have quite forgotten me, and they wish to encore you, so begin."

"What shall I play?" But the song Alixe mentioned Miss Price did not know. The next was a duett [*sic*].

"Oh, that will do, if you will sing Charles's part?" said Miss St Clair. "Can you?"

"Oh certainly, but I am afraid my voice will be but a poor substitute for that of a gentleman."

Alixe was about to explain that Charles was *only* a boy when she last sang with him, but the symphony was already run through and the duett began. If Alixe had been disappointed in the Miss Aimwells' singing, she certainly was not now. Miss Price's voice was rich, deep and powerful beyond what Alixe had ever heard. She almost forgot her own singing in listening to her companion's. And when they finished, she said with the most genuine admiration, "Oh, how beautiful, how very beautifully you sing. I am glad I sang first, or I should have been almost ashamed."

Miss Price laughed and the rest of the company heaped praises on the young performers. It was followed by a trio of Colonel Manners, Pamela – and her mother! – who seemed rather offended at having been left out of the list of young ladies. At length, the party broke up and Alixe was once more alone with her mother. Weary and half asleep, she stood with her candle in her hand, looking at her mother.

"Well my love," said the latter. "Are you not going to bed?"

"Yes, Mamma," said Alixe, standing motionless.

"How do you like your evening?"

"I hardly know. I have not been very happy tonight, but I dare say it will be better soon. Perhaps this was dull."

"I advise you to moderate your expectations if this party has not pleased you, for Lady Townley took great pains to choose her people to be companions for you. She told me so when I remarked on her fondness for young people, in having so many girls to dinner, which does not often happen. So, go to bed and try to be more moderate," said she, patting her [niece's] cheek.

Alixe sighed and wished herself home again, or at least that Charles was with her. A night's sleep, however, put her in better spirits. The next day she went with her mother and Lady Townley to call on the friends of the latter. Visit after visit was paid. Some admitted them. At others, the welcome answer of "not at home" was returned. At length, the list seemed over and Lady Townley held the check string[2] in her hand, asking Alixe whether she would like to dine in the Park, when she suddenly interrupted herself –.

"Oh, by the bye, there's old Mrs Price, yet I don't think I need go there. Gertrude my dear, do you wish to make acquaintance with Mrs Price?"

"Certainly, my dear Aunt, if she is a friend of yours."

"She is an acquaintance of mine, but I am not particularly partial to her. However, as she gives little parties and has balls sometimes, we may as well go for Alixe's sake."

Alixe gave grateful thanks for this attention to her future interests and to Mrs Price accordingly they drove. They stopped at a large house in Grosvenor Place and were ushered into a large and handsome drawing room. At one end sat Miss Price, occupied busily with a most beautiful little girl about four years old. She rose as they entered and walked to the other end of the apartment, where sat her mother making a purse for Everard, her son. Mrs Price was the beau ideal of Alixe's imagination for an old woman. She was dressed in an old-fashioned black velvet gown with a black crape scarf or veil over her white mob,[3] under which her grey hair was seen divided in two straight bands on each side. Her eyebrows had been black and in spite of the silver which had ever mingled with them, they were still so dark as to give almost an unearthly expression to her calm kind eyes and pale placid countenance. Alixe gazed on her with feelings it were hard to describe. She wished to know her, to love her, and had set down the *maison* Price to be models of perfection in their different ways, when she was roused by the ceremony of introduction.

"I have heard a great deal of you this morning, Miss St Clair, from my daughter and was coming purposely to see you today though I do not often go out. You see what a length an old woman's curiosity will carry her?" She kindly shook Alixe's hand as she spoke and looked at her for a moment with deep interest.

Alixe then sat down and was beginning a conversation with Emily Price, when the little girl, creeping round and looking up at her, said, –

"You are not going to talk, are you? Oh, do come and play. I have sat still so long, I am quite tired, *quite* tired," asked she in a wistful tone, laying her little arms on Alixe's knee. "I see you are coming by your face, and you shall see my picture, if you will."

"I will come and see your picture, where is it?" said Alixe, looking round as if expecting it to hang on the walls.

"Oh no, not there Miss Price," said the child, watching the direction of her eyes. "My Emily is doing it, come!"

And putting her hand in that of Alixe and shaking her little head with a rebellious smile at the offered rebuke of Emily Price, they stepped forward to the scene of her labours. It was a miniature picture, half-finished, but what was done was beautiful and the image of the child before her.

"Oh, how beautiful," said Alixe. "How clever you must be!"

"Yes," said the little chatterer. "It's very pretty and just like me, everybody says. And Mamma wanted my picture and she said she could not buy a picture of me, because it cost, oh, many, many guineas, and so –"

"Look dear," said Emily laughing, "here is nurse come to take you away to your dinner." This was an interruption, but it availed but little. All the time her maid was buttoning on her pelisse, the indefatigable narrator continued.

"And I had to sit, oh hours! With a little fat puppy in my arms. And they gave me the little puppy to make me sit still. And I did sit quite still, only I wanted so to look into my Puppy's ears, and Miss Price wouldn't let me look into my puppy's ears (Oh nurse, you pinch my arm!) because it made my eyes go down instead of up. And somehow I did not think the puppy was quite mine when I might not do what I please to her. And *she* did not sit *very* quiet, because I stroked her hair the wrong way and I kissed her nose and made her sneeze."

"Well now, you must say goodbye, love," said the maid. "Kiss your hand[4] and come."

"Yes, but I must just show my puppy. She wants to see my puppy, I know. Do let me fetch it." And she ran out and returned with her favourite. "It is to go away from here when my picture is done. And then it will be *quite* mine. Just kiss it and put your finger in its ear and feel how soft it is."

Just as she held it up for Alixe to kiss, it jumped out of her arms and ran away.

"There now, you *must* go," said the maid. And with much trouble the little rebel was taken downstairs, talking all the way.

"I cannot think," said Alixe, laughing, "how you can make her sit still for one quarter of an hour? Whose child is she?"

"Lady Louisa Whittaker. She is a dear little thing, but very troublesome. And they send her to me often, as a companion. And as Lady Louisa wished her picture to be done, I thought I might as well do it."

Alixe understood the delivery of her motive and admired it. And while Emily Price continued to praise her friend without the affectation of enthusiasm, describing her little comfortable home, her occupations, the way in which she educated her children and made their clothes and finally described the man for whom she had relinquished the hope of a grand parti,[5] Alixe de Fleury sighed to think how differently people spoke and thought about the same thing. But the most interesting conversations have an end and Alixe was summoned to depart. Emily shook hands affectionately and Mrs Price added a little invitation to a tea party.

"Or rather," said she, "it is no party, but I have a few people, and if you have nothing else to do?" Lady St Clair assured her that she would come and they departed, all satisfied with their visit, except Lady Townley, who with a gentle yawn declared her intention of not accepting any invitation to so insufferably dull a house; at any rate not till the young man returned. *He* was pleasant and amusing.[6]

Chapter 5

Days past and Hyde Park, Kensington Gardens, Almack's and the Opera became objects of increasing interest to Alixe. Always gay, always unaffected, she was a universal favourite. Among all the different people she saw, none interested her so much as Emily Price. None of the girls she knew were so completely natural, so devoid of envy, so willing to allow all their due share of praise. The little parties at her friend's house became her favourite amusement. Even Almack's, with all its attractions of dancing and beaux, held but the second plan in her esteem.

One evening when Lady Townley had accompanied them to Mrs Price's, Emily said with great joy, "Ah, my brother will be here tonight, and we are all so happy. He has been staying there six weeks with a young man, a great friend of his, who broke his arm by a fall when he was hunting." And Emily slightly coloured as she spoke. Alixe watched with great curiosity.

At last, the door opened and a party of young men entered, some of whom she knew. One of them was remarkably handsome and had his arm in a sling. He advanced immediately to Miss Price, who again blushed and looked so lovely at the moment, that her young friend almost regretted she had not an habitual colour. The last who entered Alixe instantly guessed to be Everard, from his likeness to his sister. But she was not satisfied with the resemblance. He was not the sort of being she had pictured Emily's brother, nor did she think him so handsome for a man as Miss Price for a woman. He had the same paleness of complexion, the same dark hair and high forehead, but his expression was stern almost to harshness and even his smile seemed to imply a conscious superiority that approached to contempt. Altogether, Alixe felt disappointed. She turned to speak to Emily, but she was busily engaged talking to the young man with the broken arm. In a moment, however, she turned and said, "I must introduce Everard to you, Alixe."

This was accordingly done and the young man seated himself by Alixe; and after conversing for some minutes, he leant back behind her on their ottoman and said to his sister Emily, "Where are the Aimwells? It is very late for young ladies to arrive."

"Oh, they are not coming. They do not always honour us and I could not put in a postscript that you would be here."

"Oh, how unfeeling of you, not to prevail on them. I shall certainly become inconstant. I have not seen them for two months. I do not think I could recollect what they are like in the least."

Emily laughed and her brother, turning with mock earnestness to Alixe, said, "Now Miss St Clair, seriously do you not think two months a long time to be constant, when the lady does not even write to the gentleman?"

"I do not know the rules," said she, smiling. "But I think two months a very short time indeed to cease to love a person. I think you must have loved them very little at first."

"Not at all, Miss St Clair. Suppose the person to be tenderly beloved, and the absence to consist of two long months. The first five weeks are spent in lonely dejection weeping for the lost one, the next fortnight in entirely forgetting her, and the last week in seeking for a few objects."

"Then be your own argument," said Alixe. "The balance is in the lady's favour; if you are *five* weeks before you cease to grieve for your separation, I do not think you could dry your tears and change in *three*."

"Oh, I beg your pardon, your ideas of proportion are quite wrong. She is a long time forgetting a sorrow, but the moment it *is* forgotten, any pleasure is welcome immediately. Darlies has had his arm useless these six weeks, but you do not expect him when it is well to sit for six weeks without using it, merely from the recollection of the preceding period, when necessity obliged him, do you?"

Alixe laughed and Emily said archly, "In short Everard, all this incomprehensible arguing is to remind us that this is the last week of your two months and to prepare us for the catastrophe of your inconstancy. Oh, sad to think all young men are alike!"

"Not *all* young men," said the interesting Darlies. And he laid the hand that was not in a sling on his heart, or rather on his left waistcoat pocket, in which he always kept (blest memorials of past triumphs!) some few little notes, a locket or two, a seal ring, the motto "*fino alla morte*"[1] and locks of hair of various shades. Alixe thought the tones and the action rather moving. Not so Everard –

"You wish thus to insinuate that though I may be inconstant, *you* are not. Oh Darlies, conscience, conscience! Emily, I beseech you, beware he is grown so doubly formidable now, that he wears his arm in a sling, that he will be the conquering hero wherever he goes." But Alixe did not think he was likely to be the conquering hero on the present occasion, for Emily's smile for a moment slightly resembled her brother's and Miss St Clair sagaciously concluded that the handsome Darlies had not only the misfortune of failing to inspire Miss Price with love, but that he had further, though perhaps unconsciously, excited her contempt. To save trouble and avoid long explanations, I assure my readers that she was right on the present occasion. Darlies was heir to a large property and a title. He rode inimitably and waltzed inimitably and had not an idea beyond hunting, dancing and flirting. But few ventured to call Darlies a stupid man, though many pronounced him decidedly "not clever." But he was a good fellow and here for a moment I must observe that nothing can stand more against a man than being demonstrated by his friend a "good fellow," it being always a proof that nothing further can be said in his praise. Does a man gamble, swear, fight duels and break hearts, his indulgent companions pronounce that he is rather wild, but after all he's a good fellow. And when a man says this of an absent friend with energy and warmth, I take it for granted the gentleman spoken of had every fashionable vice under heaven. Just as a nurse always says of the most troublesome and unruly child under her care that he has a "good heart at bottom."

Singing was as usual proposed in the course of the evening. Everard, his sister and Alixe sang in parts. The voice of the former was superb and while he was singing a part alone, Alixe stood lost in admiration.

"Are you endeavouring to find out whether he is like me?" said Emily half laughing. Alixe blushed and answered "no." Certain it is that when she returned home and reflected on her evening, she discovered that Everard Price was much handsomer than she had at first expected herself to think. His countenance was certainly harsh sometimes and to some people. But it could alter beyond any countenance she had ever seen. The dark melancholy eyes could flash with eloquent brightness and his smile soften with playfulness. And his voice, that at least was *never* harsh. The tone of it still sounded in her ears as she shook her head and tried to compose her thoughts to prayer. And she got into bed with the satisfaction that he was not unworthy.

The maison Price, before a fortnight, was over, alas! Alixe thought him the most perfect being in it. Her heart beat when his name was announced. Kensington Gardens became dull when he did not walk in them, and balls were not balls unless he was there. What greater proof could he give of strong attachment in London? And Everard Price? Everard was a man of the world and it is a long time before such men love, if they ever contrive it. But he was amused by the extreme artlessness of Alixe's disposition, thought her style of beauty perfect and his vanity was gratified by the discovery of the sort of worship she paid him. Emily Price wished heartily, not only that Alixe could become her sister, but that she was Everard's wife for his own sake. All she could do, she did. And [was] Alixe [so] unaccustomed to the language of "young men about town," that she fancied Everard loved her as well? No, no, not quite, but almost as well as, she loved him.

Everard had paid a good deal of attention to several young ladies, nay it had been whispered that he had been seriously in love more than once. This was totally incomprehensible and incredible to Alixe. First, she could not admit the possibility of any woman preferring any man to Everard. And if he fixed his heart on any one person, she did not understand how it could end except in marriage! Awful word, simple Alixe! Certain it is, that previous to his acquaintance with Mlle de Fleury, he had devoted himself to the lively Annette Aimwell in such a manner as to lead many wise heads to prognosticate a match. But no match resulted, and he now appeared totally to forget that she even had any claim to his attentions, which were bestowed almost exclusively on Alixe. She had heard this said, but she was incredulous, nay Miss Annette Aimwell seemed not to be the least chagrined at his desertion, if desertion it was. She was in the midst of a violent flirtation with the handsome Darlies, who it was privately understood and publicly contradicted had made an offer to Emily Price and – disgraceful report! – been refused.

Chapter 6

One night there was a large party at Lady Townley's. Alixe, Everard and Emily were on a sofa together. Captain Aimwell was talking to Miss Price. Annette was sitting nearly opposite on a low ottoman with Darlies, Colonel Manners, her mother and Pamela, who with her gloves off to display the whitest and roundest arm possible, was raising her beautiful sleepy eyes with a vain endeavour to catch the sense of what some gentleman was saying to her about the castle of Drachenfels on the Rhine.[1] Suddenly, Annette rose and shot across the room, followed by the eyes of the Ottoman party and attracting the attention of all those immediately opposite. Everard stopped short in an animated discussion he was beginning with Captain Aimwell.

"See what a sensation I have produced," said Annette, laughing. "What do you all expect me to do or to say, that you now honour me with so much notice!"

"Something very extraordinary we always expect when Miss Aimwell moves or speaks," said Everard with a half-smile.

"Your comprehension has grown clearer or your ideas of female excellence have changed depuis peu[2] Mr Price," said Annette. "I remember the time when you would not have thought it wonderful had I moved from the ottoman to the sofa, even had you been sitting on that sofa. But that was when 'Zuleika and her lute were *new*.'"[3]

And with a glance of meaning at the unconscious Alixe and a mock sigh, the young lady paused. Everard paused too, and having gravely measured the distance with his eye, he said:

"Now seriously, Miss Aimwell, I have been contemplating, and I find you have come five times the distance. Any moderately courageous young lady would have come without the help either of chaperon or pastor, from whence I infer that you are superior by five degrees to the rest of your sex, or if the compliment be better, that you are worth five ordinary women."

"You are unworthy [of] my wrath," said Annette, "and I shall not please to understand you when you are satirical. I shall take your compliment in the most matter of fact way and am willing to consider myself equal or superior to ten ordinary women, if any one will swear it."

The party laughed and Annette continued, "now pray all of you attend to your own conversation, while I speak to Miss St Clair." Alixe almost started.

"Are you frightened," said Miss Aimwell.

"Oh no, only I was surprised, because – because –"

"Because I so seldom talk to you, you wish to say? Well, but tonight it is a very serious affair. You know, I suppose, that you have taken him from me?"

"*Him*!" said Alixe, looking *half* at Darlies.

"No – no – no – no – don't pretend, you know who I mean. Stay, I will mention his name. Mr Everard – Charles – Augustus – Price. See how that little blush betrays you."

"Indeed Miss Aimwell –"

"*Indeed*, what? I accused you of nothing except of blushing and the crime of having seduced the cœur volage[4] of my beau from its allegiance."

"If the cœur volage *is* mine," said Alixe laughing, "I certainly have not seduced it willingly."

"Oh yes! you have, you have taken the little heart and sung to it, and played the guittar to it, and danced to it, and smiled at it, and talked to it – and – oh!" and she looked up piteously in her face.

Alixe could not help laughing. "I am sure I would give you the little heart if I could."

"Would you? I will tell him so."

"Oh pray, Miss Aimwell!" said the startled girl. But the entreaty was in vain.

"Mr Price, Mr Everard Price, Miss St Clair does not think your heart worth keeping, and she had returned it to me."

"Indeed?" said Everard. "I did not know Miss St Clair had my heart in her custody, but she knows best. Pray however, don't part with it without consulting me because I should [have] wished to take it back before it is quite worn out."

He turned to Captain Aimwell again and Annette said with a triumphant laugh, "There! He has begun to quarrel with you already. His smile was a very bitter one, but perhaps *you* were pleased with it?" And so saying, she returned to the ottoman, leaving Alixe very little disposed to be pleased at anything.

"How unkind," (thought she), "Miss Aimwell does not care for him and yet she tried to make him dislike me. How forward she is, how forward he must have thought me by her speech. His heart! Heaven knows if I had it."

But the *if* prevented the conclusion even of the thought. And to her shame, be it spoken, a real undeniable tear fell on her white glove. She dared not stir even to wipe it away, till she felt her fan gently drawn out of her hand. She coloured and looked up. Yes, it *was* Everard.

"Was my speech too satirical, my gentle bird of paradise?" said he.

Alixe smiled. "No, it was not, at least it did not seem so now."

"She is a naughty girl, Miss Aimwell? Is not she? Do not you dislike her very much?"

"Oh, no, I do not dislike her."

"Don't you really? How very good-natured," and Everard paused and sat with his teeth over his underlip, contemplating, as he always called it. At length, he spoke.

"You are a sweet creature, if you really are what you seem."

Alixe smiled. "Do you suspect me of being affected then?"

"No, God knows I don't. But I was thinking whether – Do you think you really have my heart, Miss St Clair?"

Alixe coloured deeply. She tried to laugh it off, but the attempt was a bad one. However, she answered: "Oh, I thought you knew Miss Aimwell's manners better than to think she said it seriously."

"You allow for great intimacy then, for I think no woman so difficult to understand as Miss Annette and I think a woman the most incomprehensible and wonderful of God's creatures. Now as for you, I think I understand you. There is so much ingenuousness in what you say, so much expression in your little eyes, that I think I could draw your character easily, but Annette Aimwell is the oddest compound of heavenly and diabolical that I ever saw. Sometimes, she even puzzles me. I can hardly decide whether she is ill-natured or no, nor whether I ought to think her clever, or *only* half mad."

"I do not think she is really ill-natured, but people who say anything must sometimes do mischief," said Alixe gently. "It is a pity she is not more quiet."

"You think so do you, my little moralist," said Everard half-laughing. "Well, so do I. First, she is a coquette, which is a thing I abhor. Secondly, her frankness has more of impudence than truth in it and an impudent woman is a devil in my eyes, whatever perfections she may have. Thirdly, so much want of gentleness *without*, argues a total absence of it within. And depend upon it, violence of temper must accompany extreme vehemence of manners. Thus, she is vain. That alone would spoil her. The consciousness of her attractions prevents her from being the least attractive. And the restless spirit of showing off, the wish to please all, and be admired by all, prevents her pleasing half the number she might. And to conclude my long oration, I should be ashamed of her if she was my daughter, I should grieve if she were my sister and I should go mad if I thought it possible she could be my wife."

Everard gave a half sigh as he concluded and Alixe could not help suspecting that he had had a more narrow escape from the last mentioned danger than he was willing to allow; particularly when he added in rather a melancholy tone, –

"And yet I remember thinking her so charming, so perfect, so éblouisante[5] how she loves on being known and how little she is aware of it." I remember hearing Colonel Manners say of her that she was like a fruit shop, where the best of everything is seen exposed for sale and when you are tempted to go in, you find nothing equal to what you expected from the view outside. "Changeons de sujet,[6] what do you think of the colonel?"

"Oh, I think he is rather silly."

"Wrong, he is not silly. He is only very affected and somewhat wrongheaded and shows very bad taste in choosing to pay attention to that little painted automaton, Miss Aimwell. What do you think of Captain Aimwell?"

"I really never thought about him, he is so totally uninteresting."

"Well, do not let him hear that or his poor heart will be broken, for he *has* looked at you and does not think you totally uninteresting. His only fault is that he can neither take a joke or make one. And his greatest merit, that he has contrived out [of] the most heartless and conceited family to be the only one with good feelings and 'du [conduit] naturel'.[7] And now what do you think of me? Thank you for blushing. It is a most flattering reply in my favour. Shall I tell you what I think? What I *feel* about you? As I won't, I will reserve it till I come back."

"Are you going away?" said Alixe surprised.

"Yes, the day after tomorrow. I shall see you once again, shall not I? You must see your picture finished."

"Oh yes, I had almost forgotten, how naughty Emily must think me? I shall come and sit tomorrow."

"Is that for your picture, you little deserter?" said Emily, whose beau had now left her. "I have waited with extraordinary patience and made extraordinary allowance for you're not sitting these four days past. You must come tomorrow and see it. It is nearly finished. I have made a little fair shoulder and dressed it in a blue gauze scarf. Will that content you? I was obliged to *drapery* it out of my own head, you have been so negligent."

"Oh, thank you a thousand times," said Alixe, who however had only heard half [of] what was said. "When do you come back, Mr Price?"

"Belle Alixe, je reviendrai lorsque vous me rappellez."[8]

"No, no," said she, half mournfully. And she was going to repeat her question, but there was something in his smile that made her pause and she thought it would seem too eager. She was silent.

"Do you not wish to know when I come back, Miss St Clair?"

"Yes," said Alixe, laughing.

"Well, I shall come back in a month for one week and then you will never see me again."

"Oh fie, Everard," said his sister. "You really are trying to make yourself interesting like Darlies."

"Not like Darlies, or at least with better success, I hope," said he, with a look and emphasis which brought the colour into Emily's cheeks. "After that week, I shall depart till next year for I am going abroad. But of course, you will be here next spring will not you?"

"Yes, I believe we shall, I hope so." And Alixe sighed. To Everard Price, next spring seemed like saying "tomorrow." To Alixe, it was a *long* year.

This memorable party at length broke up and they all went to the separate homes. In the morning, as Alixe had just finished trying on a new white hat with a trimming of violets and primroses that she might go and *see* her own picture, which Miss Price had been taking, a note was brought her from Annette Aimwell. The contents were as follows:

Dear Rival

Had you received me last night with more composure and not been so terribly alarmed at every word which came from my unfortunate and offending lips, you would have heard all I had to say, instead of the part you were satisfied with. What I wished to have finished with is this: Darlies has made me an offer and I have accepted him. His father is very ill and Mamma wishes me to be married soon, in case he should die, and "delays are dangerous," particularly in these matters. If you are not married yourself before tomorrow fortnight, perhaps you would be my bridesmaid. Otherwise, you will see my erring form no more till I am sobered into a wife.

Yrs sincerely
Annette Aimwell

Alixe stood transfixed with surprise. What a way of mentioning the most solemn of all engagements! What a strange thing that Darlies, who hardly a month before has been so evidently in love with Emily, should have not only changed, but engaged to marry a girl the most completely opposite in every respect to Miss Price. Alixe did not know that grand merit of all young ladies who are looking out for a matrimonial engagement, viz. that nothing is easier than to catch a man who has just been disappointed, provided he has no sense and no heart, or too much of either. She went to her mother, showed the note and asked her opinion and advice. Lady [St Clair] folded the note and returned it saying, –

"Well, I did not expect Miss Aimwell would have been married, at least so soon. I hope she will be happy. Do you wish to be her bridesmaid?"

"I do not wish exactly to be her bridesmaid," said Alixe, laughing. "But I should like to go to the wedding. I have never seen one."

"And you cannot wait till your own. Well, I have no objection, and if I go you shall certainly fill the distinguished office Miss Aimwell has so kindly left vacant for you." A note was accordingly dispatched signifying her consent to Annette and Alixe got into the carriage and drove to Grosvenor Place.

Chapter 7

On her entrance, she found no one in the drawing room. Her picture was lying on the table, quite finished as it appeared to her. She took off her hat, looked in the glass, which young ladies do almost mechanically, then at a picture of Emily's mother, which hung on one side of the mantelpiece, and lastly at one unfortunately more interesting to her eyes: that of Everard himself. She looked at it for a long time and sighed. Young ladies always do sigh when they see interesting portraits. She wiped away a little dust with her cambric handkerchief and sat down. She thought Emily a long time coming. She thought it a great pity poor Emily's brother was going away and with these two thoughts in her little brain, she laid her arms crossed on the table and bent her head down on them, a very bad attitude for any young lady.

She was roused from this reverie by the entrance of Emily who, tapping her on the shoulder, said, "Why my dearest, after what has happened, what have you been saying to one another?"

"One another," repeated Alixe in astonishment, as she started up and saw Everard sitting opposite.

He answered calmly, "Oh, I assure I have said nothing. I was in the back drawing room and Miss St Clare's step is so light that I dare say I did not discover her for some time. And since my entrance she has not vouchsafed me a word."

"I did not know you were there," said Alixe, laughing, though she felt extremely uncomfortable. "Why did you not speak?"

"I did not like to disturb your meditations, particularly since I discovered the subject of them." Alixe grew crimson. "Are you not aware, Miss St Clair, that you have uttered a soliloquy since you began your reveil?"[1]

"Oh no!" said she, half terrified, half incredulous. But Everard was gravity itself.

"It is but too true, Miss St Clair. I am sorry for you, very sorry."

"Now pray Everard, don't be so foolish," interrupted Emily. "Alixe, if you will come to the light, I will finish your picture in a quarter of an hour."

"Dear me, it seemed quite finished. But I will come." She seated herself accordingly, and Everard stood to watch the proceedings.

"Now put a little light on that curl. No, that one near her forehead. What a pretty little thing it is (the picture I mean). And now a shade of pink on that cheek. Oh, Miss Alixe you must not blush, you will spoil the picture entirely. And now, let me see what is there to do."

"Nothing love," said his sister. "And you had better go and get the frame I ordered. The shop is close by and Alixe perhaps would like to take it home as a surprise to Lady St Clair."

"Very well," said he slowly, contemplating the portrait. "Oh, wait a moment, you must put a ring on her little finger, the one that is touching the string of her guittar."

"No, I shall not indeed, Everard, it only makes a delay. Now pray, do not be foolish."

"Well, obstinate Emily, I will do it myself." And he sat down, painted a ring and [a] rose. "There now, I think that is the master stroke of the portrait. Do you not think so, Miss St Clair?"

Yes, Alixe thought so.

"Now, I shall go and have it framed. But first —" He was interrupted by the entrance of Mr Whittaker and Lady Louisa.

"Now Alixe, you will see them both," said Emily, her eyes sparkling with enthusiasm. And Alixe looked and admired, though her head was full of other things. Mr Whittaker was not quite so handsome as she had expected. His face was not remarkable, he was not very dark, nor indeed *very* anything, except graceful, and that he was in no common degree. His smile, too, was beautiful. But he was not Alixe's beau ideal for the excellent reason that he was totally unlike Everard Price. Lady Louisa, tall, gentle and dignified, suited the idea Alixe had formed of her very well and the quick brilliancy of her eye when she spoke contrasted with the habitual seriousness of her countenance [and] gave a striking relief to her style of beauty. The little girl was with them, endeavouring to be sober and well-behaved, a resolution which the sight of Alixe totally overthrew. After the ceremony of introduction was over, the picture became the object of notice. It was thought beautiful.

"The attitude is so natural," said Lady Louisa. "I can almost fancy that I shall hear a chord struck presently from that pretty guittar. And the convolvulus in her hair and the light blue scarfe suit Miss St Clair's complexion so well. But why have you put on her a wedding ring, my dear Emily? What an odd fancy." And she looked up, laughing, at Miss Price. Her husband had been gazing intently on the original, who coloured deeply even to the tips of her little ears and bent down to see – what? She knew there was a ring in the picture.

"*I* drew the ring," said Everard, seeming not to notice Alixe's confusion. "Miss St Clair particularly wished it and Emily refused harshly, so I thought I would be more indulgent." A momentary glance of Alixe's dark blue eyes altered the careless look and tone. He paused.

"Well I have loitered too long. I must get the picture framed. I shall find you on my return, I hope, Lady Louisa."

She smiled in reply and he left the room.

"Naughty Everard," said Emily, laughing yet vexed. "He has been an interruption all the morning."

"Oh, I dare say," said Mr Whittaker. "His society has not been very disagreeable, nothing he does can be ill done."

Emily laughed. Alixe blushed and took up her hat.

"You are not going dear, till the frame comes?"

"Oh no, I will wait. Only, as I am not sitting for my picture, now I may as well put my hat on." A hat has a veil and a veil is a convenient thing when the conversation grows *particular*.

"What did they give you to make you sit still?" said the little girl.

Alixe laughed. "I am to have the next puppy that is given to Miss Price."

"Oh well – I am glad my picture was taken first because else you would have had my puppy, and I should have been so sorry."

The conversation had become general and all seemed mutually pleased with one another; each talked of what they thought the other would like, not what they themselves felt most interested in. In about twenty minutes Everard returned. He carried the picture to the other end of the large drawing room.

"Now Miss St Clair, this is the proper light. Come Lou, won't you look at this pretty painting?"

"Oh yes!" said the child joyfully. And Alixe rose and followed her. Everard took down his own picture and gave it to the child to look at. He then looked at it, hanging up Alixe's in its place, sighed, wiped the frame with his handkerchief and sat down in the attitude which Alixe had previously chosen. She felt excessively confused. Everard rose and continued, smiling.

"Had it been Annette Aimwell instead of you, I should have thought she was acting a part. And you will excuse me, belle Alixe, but you must have been extremely preoccupé[2] not to have observed me."

Alixe was silent. Indeed, she felt a strong inclination to cry but she repressed it. "Well," said her companion, "you certainly might have had your revenge had you seen me in my lonely hours, for I have done nothing but sigh over your picture, look at it and talk to it, since yesterday evening."

"Oh, Mr Price!"

"'Oh, Mr Price?' Cannot you say, 'Oh Everard!' I had not known Annette three nights before she called me 'her Everard' and 'dear Everard' and '*her idol*' and I don't know how many more names. And as for you, I can never hear anything but 'Mr Price.' I will not answer to it anymore."

"Well, but give me my picture Mr Price and let me –"

"Ask properly! Say 'My dear Everard can you part with my picture?'"

Alixe laughed, in spite of the tears in her eyes. "My –"

"Well go on."

"Oh, pray do not. It will look so odd," said she, glancing at the party.

"'Look so odd?' Why, you are not obliged to kneel while you say it! And they are going. Look!"

Yes, they went. And Emily attended them to the door and then she began putting by her drawing materials.

"Now Alixe, it is my last day at home, my last hour with you. Cannot you say 'dear Everard' *once*?"

"Dear Everard, will you –" But she could get no further.

"No, my beloved Alixe, I will not return the picture. I meant it for myself."

"For yourself!"

"Yes, I shall then perhaps be able to live without you for a few months. And I can say what I please to it, without its answering 'Oh, Mr Price!' and I can fancy it saying 'dear Everard,' as often as I please. All I can do is to leave you my own in exchange. Will you have it?"

"Oh no, no –," said Alixe. And she looked up with a mixture of feelings hard to be described. There was a deep pause. It was broken by Everard.

"Alixe, I am going for some time, or I would not say what I am going to say. I do not easily fall in love, nay I will confess that I am, or have been, un *peu volage*,[3] but I do love you with my whole soul. I am sure, quite sure, I shall never change, but it would not be fair to expect from you who are but just come out and perfect as you are, that you should fix in so short a time, you might repent it afterwards: 'l'absence et le temps detruisent l'amour.'[4] That is some sort of love – you will have time to change."

Alixe interrupted him by a half sob and "Oh no!" – said with all the sorrowful energy of truth:

"You will love me then till I come back," said he, as he took her hand. "Oh, I hope you will. And when you come here after I am gone, while all the idle flutterers are around you and admiring you, you will think of me when you see my picture, at least for a moment."

And he hung the picture up in its place, while Alixe walked forward to Emily. The latter turned round.

"Are you going already? Oh, I wish you would stay and dine with us. It is the last day we shall be all together. Could you not ask Lady St Clair?"

No, Alixe knew it would be of no use, for they were to drive in the country with a cousin of Lady Townley's.

"Well, it can't be helped then. So, goodbye. But where is the picture?"

"He will not let me have it," said Alixe.

"He? What, Everard? Oh, surely Everard, you are joking?"

"No indeed, I never will relinquish the artificial Alixe, though I am obliged to lose the real one for a time."

"How lucky you are only to be away *one* month," said Alixe, rallying her spirits. "Otherwise, you might quite forget what I was like."

"Oh, you wicked little girl," said he, looking at her with some surprise. "I see at least *your* heart will not break in the interval. Take care, don't let me find you Mrs Aimwell of the Guards, when I come back. There is to be a fancy ball soon and the uniform is very becoming."

"Good bye, Emily."

"I hope we shall see you as often, though the portrait *is* finished?"

"Oh yes."

"And though I *am* going away," added Everard. And Alixe went. Weary and agitated, she walked into the drawing room in Park Lane. It was full, quite full of people. How provoking, when she wished to speak to Lady St Clair! She spoke to the persons she knew and sat down with patient resignation. But the affectionate eye of her adopted mother glanced towards her in a moment.

"My love, you [look] very pale and tired. You had better go and take off your things, that you may have time to rest before we set out." Alixe obeyed. She hoped Lady St Clair would soon follow, but there seemed an endless train of visitors. And when at last she did come, there was but just time to dress. The evening passed away. The formal dinner, the strange company, the half-heard conversation passed before Alixe like a dream. But at last, oh happiness! she found herself alone with her mother. She began the story of the picture which had been meant as a pleasant surprise to Lady St Clair. She grew more and more confused as she proceeded, and at last she paused: "Mamma, dear Mamma, indeed I wish to tell you everything as it happened, but –"

Lady St Clair smiled. "My love, I will excuse you. For tonight, go to bed. I have a great deal to say on the subject, but it is too late now and you may comfort yourself with the assurance that I do not think you to blame for the loss of that precious miniature which was to have been presented to me."

What Lady St Clair had to say was doubtless said in due time and the substance of her discourse was, first – she suggested (horrible suggestion) that Everard Price appeared not only inconstant, but that he was more likely to wish to marry a woman of some rank and family than a girl like Alixe, as he has a good future of his own and, according to Lady St Clair's view of the case, not likely to marry *at all* at present. Secondly, she pronounced the wonderful opinion that "even were Everard to come the next day and lay his heart at Alixe's feet, she would wish her to weigh well before she accepted him, as by all accounts he was wild, thoughtless, extravagant and, to say the least, dissipated. It had also been whispered by the wise that he was by no means valuated to make a good husband, being exceedingly violent and irritable."

"I do not say this," continued Lady St Clair, "out of cruelty to damp your expectations or form prejudice to the young man. On the contrary, I think him very pleasant and agreeable, as far as I have been able to judge. But young people are unthinking and it is right to give you some warning. You have only seen Everard Price in company, or among friends, *very* partial friends. Having no proof of his heart except by judging from your own, you can only love him for his exterior accomplishments and for fancied perfections, which after all are the groundwork of most love matches, and the reason why so many are discontented afterwards. Believe me, love, I wish you to be happy. I only wish you to have time to judge as impartially as you can and be sure of Everard's character before you trust him with your hopes of future happiness."

"Oh! the reasonable side of every question, the reality of life, how sad a thing it is!" So thought Alixe, as she retired to reflect and doubt over the *true* qualities of her earthly model. And let them sympathize who have had the same tasks to undergo.

In the meanwhile, time flew rapidly. It was now pretty generally known that Alixe had two thousand a year of her own and some few had heard that she was niece and not daughter to Lady St Clair. Without accusing young men of being mercenary, I may observe that their admiration for a young lady certainly is not lessened by knowing them to be heiresses. Alixe had attractions enough in herself to charm, and crowds of loitering, flattering things followed her steps with compliments which cost them little trouble and meant nothing at all. Captain Aimwell, now that his dangerous rival was departed, strove to make the best use of his time. And though he advanced not a step in Alixe's favour, yet he never omitted any opportunity of being at her side. How different alas! did all people and all things seem to Alixe now, how dull were all the balls, how deserted the Park and gardens! How disagreeable the discourses, which before had only appeared stupid. Alixe had too much romance in her disposition. She was too fond of making a *dreamy* world of her own to live in, to be contented with the scenes she was in. In vain did her friend Emily reason and argue and persuade. She could not convince her that there *was* enjoyment even among stupid people and in worn-out gaieties, and that people might be very happy without living in a desert island with the object of their choice and *few friends*. Alixe had been pleased with everything and everybody, as long as Everard staid. But like the beautiful and ingenious idea in Madame de Genlis's[5] portrait, the moment the artificial flow ceased to beautify the objects around, they returned to their former insipidity of colouring. She heard frequently of Everard from his sister, and his messages, half kind, half playful, were treasured up in her memory with greater care than perhaps even the writer himself could have believed. There is a wide separation, an ocean of distance between the different sort of feelings of a man who loves, and a girl who returns that love. It is the sort of disparity between the ideas of a child and a grown person. The man had probably loved many times before taking the word in its commonest sense, though perhaps the translation ought to be "fancy." When he is in love, however sincerely or proportionally, for the time he has a vague and instructive feeling that it *must end*. Past feelings act mechanically upon present airs and force on his mind the mortality of affection as naturally as the mortality of man. He is only anxious to prolong the dream to its utmost extent and, when the charm is broken, honours its departure with a sigh and turns to receive it with some other object. With a woman, the case is different. From the moment that she feels as if she were under the influence of a spell in the long bright vision of life and happiness which extends itself before her, she sees nothing impossible, nothing immaterial, nothing which she has not a right to expect. She looks forward with the firm intention "to love and love for ever!" And when time has forced on her unwilling mind that there is no Paradise on Earth, when half her life has been spent in attaining this unwelcome truth, she struggles to renew the broken fetters of her mind, and generally ends in believing, not that "bliss without alloy" is a thing not to be found, but that causes different in different situations have prevented *her* being able to find it. She feels wonder, an agonized wonder, when she finds herself no longer beloved and even when long years have past away, looks back to her first earliest passion and sighs for the witchery of its departed spirit.

Chapter 8

Alixe had plaited a bracelet of old Mrs Price's hair for her friend Emily *à son insçu*[1] and she had ornamented it with a small silver clasp and "Madre amata"[2] in silver letters. She brought it with great joy and Emily, after thanking her and expressing extreme pleasure, said, –

"How very odd; I was just bringing *you* a little present (so speedy an interchange is really like a traffic). May the one I offer you be as precious to you, as that you have given, is to me."

And Emily put into her friend's hand, a small trinket box containing a little gold harp, already known to the reader. Alixe was surprised, enchanted.

"How beautiful! Oh, how beautiful! The little crown of jewels at the top and the whole harp so exactly like a real one!"

"Promise me dear Alixe always to wear it – for my sake?"

"Oh, I promise faithfully. And the strings, they are made of your own hair, Emily, I know by the colour. What an ingenious way of giving a lock of hair," said she, laughing.

"I am glad you admire it," said her friend. "But I am sorry to say it is not my idea, nor is it my hair, though it is so like mine. The harp was made at Geneva under the direction of a person who is particularly clever at invention and has excellent taste. No doubt he chose the harp strings, as he knew it was to please you I ordered the trinket." This was said half playfully, half seriously. The crimson blood rushed to Alixe's transparent skin. Everard was at Geneva! There was a pause.

Emily, laying her hand on Alixe's arm, said "you have promised to wear it?"

"Oh yes, pour toujours."[3] And she raised her bright expressive eyes to Emily's countenance with a look of affection which made the latter sigh for the chances against her having Alixe for a sister. I have before said that our heroine was romantic, but I hope readers will not misunderstand. Alixe could not have wept over a French romance or a bad English tragedy. Neither did she sigh over love poetry, or gaze on the moon out of her chamber window, that she might be the better enabled to think on Mr Price. She had not the sickly imagination of a novel-reading miss, who requires every combination of scene, time and place to render an occurrence interesting and expects her lover to serenade her under her lattice. Her romance was the romance of enthusiasm, the hope of youth and innocence. She clothed every thing in the warm glowing colours of her own mind:

Made all a heaven without, like that within,
Too bright for sorrow, and too pure for sin.

She thought of Everard every where, at every time, even while eating her dinner. But she was neither thin nor dispirited, nor did she dream of the possibility of his changing.

At the appointed time she attended Annette Aimwell's wedding. The young lady had included Miss Price among the fashionably extended number of her bridesmaids. And the two friends came drest [*sic*] alike, with the exception that Alixe wore lily of the valley, and Emily the garden lily, in her hair. The extreme beauty of both and the extreme contrast between the light fairy form and sunniness of Alixe's style and the majestic grace and dark melancholy expression peculiar to Miss Price was the subject of universal admiration. Even the bride, drest as she was in smiles and lace, was forgotten for a moment as the entrance of the pair was observed. And Darlies, the handsome Darlies, gave a deep sigh (he had a great talent for sighing) as he welcomed them and gave one wistful look so expressive for *him*, that the carnation which so seldom visited Emily's cheek fixed there for upwards of ten minutes. The bridegroom turned to Annette. She was in the act of breaking off the outside stitch of the fan, on which was inscribed the word "souvenir" in steel dots, and presenting it to some man who received it with mock solemnity, while she said something in a pathetic tone of voice, ending by a hearty laugh. She looked at Emily, –

"Surely Miss Price has rouged today!"

"No, she has not," said Darlies, who felt somewhat displeased. "*She* never ever uses art, because she captivates without." Annette reddened and several gentlemen who were congratulating themselves that Miss Aimwell was not their wife gazed around in astonishment. "I declare," said one, "the lady he has won has inspired him."

"No," said Colonel Manners in his slow calm manner. "It is the lady he has *lost*."

The wedding was over at last, though not a few seemed to doubt much whether the lively Annette could ever be "sobered into a wife." She talked and laughed to the last minute, made the gayest adieux to her friends and at length was handed into the carriage to go to a house Darlies had taken in the country. Perhaps my reader may wish to know the uppermost feeling of the young bride separated for the first time from her family and looking forward to an unknown future? It was that her father-in-law would soon die that she might go to the family seat of which she had heard much. She departed and Pamela ruined her beautiful blue eyes, swimming in tears to her mother, who was talking to Colonel Manners about her affection for her dear girls.

"What is the matter, my Pamela?"

"Nothing Mamma, only Annette's gone," said the beauty, sobbing.

"Why my dearest love, you knew she was to go, didn't you?"

"Yes Mamma, but –"

And the years of infancy, when Annette was sprightly without affectation, and kind without being artificial, rushed for a moment over her sister's mind. The cold parting, the companionless home, all prevented her tears from stopping.

"Vraiment me chère, vous m'impatientez,"[4] said her mother. "You will quite spoil your beautiful eyes."

But Captain Aimwell was not *impatienté*.

"Thank God," said he. "Pamela at least has some natural feeling. I may console with her without being laughed at." And he stepped forward, followed by the two beautiful bridesmaids with whom he had been conversing. He spoke affectionately to his sister, and Alixe and Emily joined in the endeavour to soothe and to comfort. The effort was soon successful. Pamela dried her beautiful eyes in the French lace scarf which Darlies had presented to her as his wedding present, saying "Tomorrow will be a happy day!"

How few had found it so! Captain Aimwell felt convinced that Alixe would never change from the present object of her affections to himself. Alixe thought of Everard, of Annette. Emily sighed. Pamela wept. Colonel Manners thought no woman could love well, who did not love her own children, and turned to Lady Harriet Dure. Mrs Aimwell was jealous, Lady Townley was cross, Lady St Clair was ill. The men yawned and looked out of the window. The girls pulled the extra leaves off their orange flowers and replaced their bouquets, after declaring that the magnolia gave the headache. But even the wedding breakfast is not eternal, although it is the next thing to it. All was over. Strangers departed and the four bridesmaids and one of the two favoured gentlemen returned to dine, while during this short interval the *home* party threw themselves on sofas: "The weary to rest, and the *wounded to die.*"[5]

There was a ball in the evening at Mrs Aimwell's. For contrary to sensitive feeling and to reason and against even the corporal sensation of the whole world, a wedding day which is of all others the one of the greatest fatigue, bustle, anxiety and vexation is celebrated with an eagerness of joy which precludes all rest for body or mind. And every one, in a degree, is obliged to undergo that most abominable of all human sufferings, "forced gaiety."

Lady St Clair was too ill to accompany her adopted child, but Lady Townley, with whom the house of Aimwell stood high in favour, offered to be her chaperone. And Alixe reluctantly left her dear mother with the little table, on which stood sal volatile, hartshorn and ether, to appear in the bright and glorious scene at Mrs Aimwell's, where both sunflowers, chandeliers and wax candles were to make up for all that was wanting of enjoyment in the spectator's heart. Pamela in her mournfulness was an object of much more interest to Alixe and Emily than Pamela acting the beauty. And their kindness was gratefully felt. Timid and always thrown into the background by Annette, who considered her cleverness as giving more than an equality with her sister's personal charms, Pamela's disposition could hardly be known. Now, however, she appeared to greater advantage. What Annette had half persuaded herself and friends was silliness, was now constituted gentleness. Her want of conversation *almost* sunk into reserve and bashfulness and other qualities took a similar turn in her favour. Most of the men who had seen much of Annette preferred the younger sister and now all voices united for her who regretted the bride whom everyone else was condemning. Oh, could the lively, forward, satisfied Miss Aimwell have known and heard the observations and criticisms of her soi-distant friends and admirers, how surprised she would have been! Luckily for her peace of mind, she was some thirty miles distant.

There was to be a grand fancy ball at the Opera House in a week, that fancy ball to which Everard predicted the engaging appearance of the gentlemen of Guards and of one in particular. Great were the discussions as to the important topic – dress. Mrs Price proposed a Caucasian costume, Captain Aimwell thought they might appear as the three graces.[6] Lady Townley thought Sultana dress would be particularly becoming, and she had quantities of trinkets and beads to lend. Alixe wished to go as a French peasant. Pamela thought Flora might do for her. Both these were objected to on account of their being common. At length, after much debate, Emily Price's opinion was universally agreed to. She proposed that the three friends should go as the spirits of air, water and earth.

The morning after the ball,[7] Captain Aimwell brought his sister to sweet Alixe and Emily at the house of the latter. Miss Price and Alixe were already in consultation.

"Oh, I am so glad you are come!" said Emily. "I was afraid you had forsaken us. We must begin by settling which spirit each would be. I think there is no doubt but that Alixe should be the spirit of the air, but she has refused to decide till you have chosen."

"Oh, do not think of me. It is very kind of you to let me be one of you," said Pamela gently. "Certainly, Miss St Clair ought to be the spirit of air because she is much lighter and less than any of us."

"Then *we* must decide between earth and water."

"Oh no, Miss Price, pray choose, and the one that is left –"

"No, no, you must tell me which you prefer. Stay, I have made little sketches in the costumes I fancied would be most appropriate. I will show you, and then perhaps you will be better able to judge." And Emily took from a small drawer three little painted figures and laid them on the table.

"How pretty they all are," said Pamela, "and the spirit of air is really like Miss St Clair. I think," continued she, looking doubtfully at Emily, "I should prefer the spirit of earth, that is if you have not fixed on it."

"Oh no! If you knew how little I cared about these sort of things now," added Emily, as she saw Pamela's soft eyes still anxiously watching her countenance.

"Then you will be the spirit of water. It is a very pretty dress indeed. How pleased Annette would have been. Poor Annette, she cared very much about all balls – and fancy balls in particular."

Alixe during this discussion had been gazing at a miniature which lay in the open drawer from which the figures had been taken. Her eye was caught by the sailor dress in which the young man was painted. He seemed very young, almost a boy. He was not extremely handsome, but there was a bright, happy, ingenuous look which put her in mind of Charles, and his neckcloth was tied the same way. She looked up at last, intending to ask whose portrait it was. But her eye met Emily's and there was something in the countenance of the latter which prevented the question. Miss Price moved forward without speaking, put the sketches back and shut the drawer. Alixe had some curiosity, but she had more feeling. She thought it might have been a brother Emily had lost, particularly as it was like Everard when in high spirits, though much lighter. Underneath was written "my dear Henry," but there was no surname.

At length, the fancy ball took place. The party met at Lady Townley's, who approved highly of all the dresses, and many were the praises lavished on Miss Price for her ingenuity. The fairy Alixe was drest in white gauze with blue and silver flowers round her gown, and in her hair a scarf of the palest sky blue with a light silver fringe and silver wings. Certainly, had she suddenly fluttered round the room and settled on the piano, no one would have felt more than a momentary surprise. Pamela's dress was perhaps less remarkable than the others, but it suited her particularly. She was loaded with a profusion of flowers, with a gold basket on her head, out of which peaches and peach blossoms peeped promiscuously. Miss Price was in white with trimmings of coral water lilies and green reeds. And the same in her hair, with a long silver tissue veil and necklace and earrings of pearls.[8] Colonel Manners was there as King of Clubs, Lieutenant Brownlow, the gentleman whose description of the wreck of the Calliope had so affected Alixe, as King of Diamonds, and two other gentlemen filled the remaining court cards characters, while Lady Townley, Mrs Aimwell, Lady Harriet Dure and Lady Louisa Whittaker acted as their several queens. Lady St Clair was the Queen of Scots. Mr Whittaker wore the costume of a young Mohican chief; and Emily Price remarked to Alixe how completely and exclusively Lady Louisa's attention and admiration were bestowed on her husband, in spite of the compliment of her King and the rest of the party present.

"She so seldom goes out," continued Emily, "that it is quite a fête to her friends, her appearance tonight. And I dare say she would rather be at home, hearing Conrad Whittaker read Shakespeare, than be where she is, surrounded by admiring strangers. She is kind, so perfect, and before she married, you cannot think how gay she was and how she loved going out."

"She is just the sort of wife, I think, you would make, Emily," said her friend smiling.

Emily sighed, "No, oh no –"

"Who is Lady Louisa's King?" continued Alixe. "He is very handsome."

"Do you think him handsome? I do not, but perhaps it may be prejudice. His name is Lord Ainslie. I have heard him reckoned like Everard. God forbid the resemblance should even extend further than in person."

"Dear Emily, why do you dislike him so? He looks kind."

"He *looks* kind, he does indeed. Ask those who have been in his power what they think of his countenance. Oh, he has a serpent's heart. I heard a great deal of him from a friend who was under his command on board the *Britannia* and every thing I heard made me dislike him more. So unlike a sailor, so coldhearted and revengeful."

"You seem quite furious against him, Emily? I am afraid he ill-used your friend. Who is he? Let me know, and I will ask him about Lord Ainslie."

"You cannot ask him *now*," said Emily, and her eyes filled with tears. Alixe was much moved. Miss Price was so little addicted to sentimentality, she so seldom showed outwardly her feelings that they made a double impression. At this moment the orders were issued for departure and the two friends departed for a short interval. The ball was beautiful. It only wanted Everard to have been perfect in Alixe's eyes. Lieutenant Brownlow, to whom General Koss had explained who she was, under promise of secrecy, was attentive and kind beyond measure. He talked to her of the place where she had spent her infancy. Of Charles, of her father, he told a thousand little anecdotes of his goodness and Alixe felt she should love him very much. He would be such a good friend to Charles. His manner was animated and pleasant and every thing he said showed goodness of heart and generosity, or so Alixe expressed it to Emily:

"He was a *real* sailor." Of all classes, of all professions of men, in spite of the charms of rich landed proprietors, the glory of a title and the boasted superiority of spurs and red cloth over a woman's heart, the man most generally loved and (be it said without prejudice) the most deserving to be loved, are sailors. There is an honesty, an openness of heart, a feeling for others' sufferings, arising from having suffered with others in the hours of danger and distress. And above all, there is a love of Home: the first feeling of his heart, the last that perishes with him, which endear a sailor beyond other men to those connected with him. Without vanity, without extremity, free from the coolness of heart which characterizes men of the world, he returns to [the] bosom of his family, to be loved "for the dangers he has past" and to be glad with them till again summoned to the uncertain home on the wide waters, where he links his heart and his hand with his brothers of the sea to support his beloved country on her ocean throne![9]

From this description Lord Ainslie must be excluded. Lieutenant Brownlow spoke of him with contempt and indignation and Alixe began to dislike him even before she had heard him speak. He requested to be introduced to the trio in the course of the evening. Lady Louisa accordingly presented him to her young friends: Pamela, Alixe and lastly to Miss Price. There was something in the latter introduction which struck Alixe as uncomfortable. First, instead of the formula of "Miss Price,...Lord Ainslie", Lady Louisa said, –

"Lord Ainslie, I believe you know Emily Price?" Alixe was not well-read in countenances, but she saw Lord Ainslie was surprised and, she thought, startled. However, he said with a smile:

"Miss Price, you will excuse my forgetting you. You were such a child when last I saw you, and you are so altered. I hope your mother is well?"

Emily answered. There was nothing particular in her tone, but she was excessively flushed and she stepped back when she had finished. Lord Ainslie did not seem to notice her reluctance to speak. He asked Alixe to dance. She coloured and looked at Emily. Her partner looked displeased.

"If you are engaged, Mlle de Fleury?"

"No, I am not engaged." They then walked forward.

"Where will you stand?"

"Oh, anywhere," said Alixe, who was thinking more of the oddity of his calling her "de Fleury" than of her place in the quadrille. This mystery was soon explained. The first words that broke the long silence were, –

"I heard a great deal of you where I have been staying, at Sir William Marwood's. They seem very fond of you." After a short pause he added, "I knew your father, he was in the navy. I suppose you don't recollect him?"

"Yes," Alixe did recollect him. She recollected the pale countenance, the kneeling figure, the last struggling effort to brave the roaring waters. She thought it cruel of the Marwoods to have pointed her out so unnecessarily. She had begun to feel what it was to be a natural daughter. Lord Ainslie paused.

"The Marwoods called you 'de Fleury,' but I think Lady Louisa introduced you as Miss St Clair, did she not?"

"Yes," said Alixe, "since I came to town, I have been called St Clair. It prevents the long explanations which could follow otherwise, and which are both painful and needless with strangers." And she laid a slight perceptible emphasis on the last word. Lord Ainslie affected not to observe it.

"Then I shall call you Miss St Clair, if you please." Alixe was grieved and confused; her partner was out of temper. As they walked back, Cecil Brownlow met them. He turned and accompanied Alixe to a seat near her mother.

"Brownlow, who are you going to dance with?" said Lord Ainslie.

"With Miss Emily Price." Either the words or the expression which accompanied them displeased her partner. And Alixe relinquished her hold on his arm with a half start at his change of countenance. He observed it, looked at her for a moment with a smile – but such a smile! – bowed and passed on to Pamela, to whom he devoted himself for the remainder of the evening. Alixe was once more with Emily.

"Well, dearest, I have been watching you while you danced and you do look so very lovely as a spirit, that I have thought of a little plan to exhibit you again." Alixe laughed. "Listen, the twenty-sixth of June is Everard's birthday. He will come home for a week *then*, instead of the time he spent before, and Mamma means to have a ball. Now I do purpose that it shall be a fancy ball. Do you approve?"

"Oh yes, and he will not come till then?" said Alixe, with a sigh.

"No, he cannot. Indeed, it is inconvenient to him to return at all." But Mamma wishes it so much. He was away last June, and she was so melancholy all day. Captain Aimwell came up at the moment and begged Alixe to valse. She rose and Emily and Cecil Brownlow followed.

The three spirits were excessively admired and Pamela was informed of the arrangement made for the sixteenth. She was all joy. After some moment's reflection, she said, –

"It is the 24th of May tonight. Annette will go out *then* will she not?"

"Certainly, if she wishes it."

"And may I write and tell her of your ball?"

"Oh! yes pray do. And petition her to come, and Mr Darlies too."

The night passed, the morning broke, the rouged chaperones fled into the carriages, the wearied girls took their last glance at the favourite partner, who handed them in, and sank back to muse on their past delights, and the men went home. It was past five when Alixe got into Lady Townley's carriage. Captain Aimwell carefully helped her in and shielded her silver wings with his hand from injury. A murmur of admiration ran through the crowd, assembled to see the departing costumes. Perhaps they made the same reflections as Lady Townley, who said, smiling through all the fatigue, "A very handsome pair you would make."

Alixe coloured and looked out of the window. Captain Aimwell was standing gazing at the carriage. He kissed his hand and they drove on.

Chapter 9

More than a month before Everard would return! Such were the reflections passing through Alixe's mind as she watered the moss-rose tree which Emily had given her, and which was allowed a place in the greenhouse. She was still occupied arranging and dressing the flowers, when she heard her mother's voice from the drawing room. She put down the watering pot, skipped up the few steps which led into the room and advanced to her mother. Lady St Clair looked grave. She had a letter in her hand.

"Is anything the matter, dear Mamma?"

"No, my love, only you must consider attentively what I am going to say. But first read this note which is enclosed for you." Alixe read it:

Grosvenor Place
May 27th

I have been some time mustering courage to address you. But it is better to be sure of one's fate than to hang on in suspense, as I have done for some time past. I have no eloquence at command, particularly at this moment. But if the sincerity of attachment can make any amends for other defects, it will be my excuse on the present occasion. By enclosing this to your amiable mother, I hope not to offend you or her and may I hope that her voice will plead successfully for me? I have a fortune, I have friends. With you, I shall want nothing to make me happy. Believe me, the whole study of my life would be to make you equally so. If you could hear my feelings at this instant, you would pity me.

Yrs devotedly, Alfred James Aimwell.

Alixe stood unable to raise her eyes. The note dropped. She stooped for it and her mother broke the silence.

"I know, my dear girl, you have a partiality for another, but for reasons I have already given you, I would have you weigh well your feelings with regard to him. Everard has made you no decided offer. He is bound by no promise and I am sorry to say young men have said more and yet ended up doing nothing. Captain Aimwell is a suitable match. He is an only son and an amiable man. May you never live to feel bitterly that such men make better husbands than men of talent, of the world. Act for yourself, judge for yourself. Only believe me, if Everard Price were to marry you tomorrow, you would never be so happy with him as with your present admirer. Everard Price would never be domestic."

Did Alixe believe her adopted mother? We know not, but Captain Aimwell was refused. Pamela was now become the constant companion of Alixe and she loved her, though not then so well as her first friend Emily. Pamela Aimwell was beautiful and gentle and she was grateful and good-tempered, but she was silly. And Alixe, who admired with enthusiasm the talents and dignity of character belonging to Miss Price, looked down from an imaginary height on the bending, wavering, affected beauty who gave way to every feeling, as the reed inches before the wind that ripples the water under it. She told Alixe in confidence that Lord Ainslie said he loved her and she asked her advice. Alixe was startled.

"You had better ask your Mamma, my dear Pamela."

"Oh, not Mamma, she would laugh at me, or scold me. I could tell her if he had proposed. But now –"

Alixe did not know what to say. She did not like to tell Pamela anything against her lover. She could not plead for him.

"Wait then a little while. I dare say he will soon propose." And the matter rested for the present.

The time drew near for the day of rejoicing. Emily was active in preparation. Mrs Price was quite happy. Alixe was in transport, but in the midst of all, a letter came which dampened their hopes. Emily brought it to Alixe. It was from Everard, stating that he was at Paris, having had a serious inflammation of the lungs, but that he was getting better. It ended, –

"If I *can*, I will be with you on my birthday, for my dear mother's sake. Pray do not tell her I have been ill till I am quite recovered, and let nothing be stopped. Love to my Alixe, Yr affect brother, Everard."

Emily wept. Alixe was thunderstruck. "If he *can*," – the words were vainly repeated a dozen times.

"Oh, if you knew how my mother loves him. And my brother Albermarle died of the very same thing, years ago. And Everard makes so light of illness in general."

And his sister wept again.

At length the day came. And with it a letter heralding the adored Everard's arrival. Again all was joy. The spirit of the air was deposited at the door of Mrs Price's and went upstairs. There was a confusion of lights and flowers and people and dresses. But she saw Emily at a distance and begged her mother to proceed. At this moment someone closed her wings. She turned round, saying, –

"Oh, take care!" and beheld Annette Aimwell, in a superb dress of scarlet tissue with wavy lines of gold, a crown of scarlet feathers and a palely greyish scarfe with gold trimmings. She looked handsomer than Alixe had ever seen her.

"So, my fellow spirit, you did not wish to recognize me."

"Spirit, what spirit are you?" said Alixe.

"The spirit of fire certainly and this is my smoke," said she, shaking her scarfe. "We ought to be called the four elements, but where is Miss Price? Oh, I see. Come, I am a chaperon now. Will you trust yourself with me?"

"If Mamma will let me," said Alixe. Leave was granted and they made their way to Emily, who was going through the fatiguing honours of the mistress of the house.

"Here is our fourth spirit," said Alixe. "Mrs Clifton Darlies is the spirit of fire." The dress and the taste of the wearer were complimented.

"But where is Mr Darlies?"

"Oh, he is gone to see his father who is quite dying. He would hardly let *me* come, much less come himself. He is so particular about his father and so angry if everyone does not guess the old man's wants and wishes. But after all, it is kind-hearted of him."

Alixe *looked* at Emily. She answered the look, –

"Yes, Everard is come, but he was so tired that he was obliged to lie down before he can appear here. He is looking ill and thin, and I am vexed and fagged to death, but my poor mother is so glad to have him with her today. She says she is sure it is the last birthday he will spend with her. I will go and tell him you are come."

Alixe waited in beautiful expectation for about five minutes. She heard his step, the well-known step of the graceful Everard. He came in and held his hand out. But Alixe could not take it. She had raised her eyes as he entered and that one glance showed him so changed, so languid, so like the ghost of himself, that she burst into tears. Emily took her hand. Everard leant against the marble chimney piece.

"Alixe, my dearest, don't. I cannot bear it. I have been very ill. But I did not think my appearance would have startled you so. Dry those sweet eyes or someone will see you." Alixe obeyed the command and they sat down.

The people were nearly all come and Emily, weary as she was, tried to raise her brother's spirits and prevent Alixe from seeming to feel how ill he must have been. In the midst of their conversation, Annette Darlies came up. Everard smiled languidly and rose. His former love started, –

"Dear me, have you been ill, mon idole?"

"Yes, I assure you. I hardly thought to see England and its fair ones again. But I am come to lay my bones among you. Will you take care to have me decently buried?" Annette looked mournful. Alixe sighed. Emily turned to a large Camalia Japonica.

"I think," continued Everard, "my coffin should be mahogany, well-polished, with silver nails. A plain marble slab should decorate my tomb with the epitaph 'Here lies a *heart*' to commemorate my having been able to carry it away from the London ladies."

"Ah, mon idole!"

"Now, that is naughty. You must not call me 'mon idole' *now*. Because you know Darlies is your idol. But I must go and speak to my mother. And then I shall expect to take you to the dancing room, young ladies. I see only chaperons here." And he rose and walked away. There was a deep silence. Alixe noticed his altered step. Annette regretted – no matter what. Emily broke the silence, –

"Suppose we all go and see my mother? She does not come out of the drawing room."

This was gladly agreed to and they went to Mrs Price. She had eyes and ears for nothing but Everard.

"Do not exhaust yourself, dear boy," said she tenderly.

"My dearest mother, I am quite well. I am just going to valse with Miss St Clair."

"Well, take care of yourself. Emily, he is so untameable, but you will look after him." And the young party proceeded downstairs. As they past Emily's boudoir, which was beautifully furnished with pale rose-coloured silk, Everard's quick eye caught the figures of Pamela Aimwell and a gentleman standing by a marble table.

"Pamela," said her sister, "are you not coming to the dancing room?"

And Pamela followed with Lord Ainslie, her companion. They reached the landing place. Everard turned to say something to Pamela. His smile vanished, –

"*You* here Ainslie?" There was contempt and anger in his countenance. Lord Ainslie was not slow to reply, –

"Do you think it extraordinary, Sir, that when your mother invited me, I should come?"

"I do not think it extraordinary that my mother invited you, for she is an angel. But that you should come, yet that is not extraordinary either, for *you* are –"

Everard had spoken eagerly and hurriedly. He paused. The brow of Ainslie fell darker than a thunder cloud. His lip whitened.

"*What* am I?" said he, in a tone of defiance. But Emily was by his side. She even laid her hand on his arm as she spoke, –

"For God's sake Lord Ainslie, do not answer. Agitation may cost Everard his life. We have long forgiven, I mean we have nothing to complain of. Only he is ill."

The tears stood in her eyes and for a moment the harsh cold heart seemed moved. He turned to Everard, made an effort to say something polite and held out his hand. Everard gave his, but as he did it, he said emphatically, –

"This is my own house," as if to excuse the action to his conscience. This past in less than three minutes. The terrified and agitated girls proceeded onwards. Ainslie's look and voice resumed their softness and all was tranquillity. Everard said as he entered the dancing room, –

"It is too hot here. I must return upstairs. Come to the boudoir as soon as Emily can accompany you. Poor Emily! You know all about Henry and Lord Ainslie, I suppose, being such a friend of hers" –

"No, Emily never said anything further than that he was a bad man."

"'A bad man'? God knows he is. Ask Brownlow. I would tell you myself, but I am not equal to it tonight." Alixe, accordingly, appealed to Brownlow.

"I am hardly sure of the story myself," said he, "and yet I have heard it from a great many different people. I know Miss Price was engaged to a cousin of hers almost from infancy and she was very fond of him. His name was Henry Stanmore and old Mrs Price liked the thought of the match excessively, but they were too young to marry then. Henry had little or nothing till his father died and they sent him to sea. He did very well for a time, although under Lord Ainslie's command. And his friends thought it was better his captain should be strict, and told him so. But the poor fellow was not contented; he was of a sweet disposition and bore everything without murmuring. But he used to tell his Emily many a little anecdote of oppression and cruelty to himself and others which would have prejudiced any mind against Ainslie. I saw Henry Stanmore once. It was when Emily was about sixteen and he was perhaps three years older. She was not at all what she is now and was a gay lightsome creature – very bright and lovely, and slight and girlish looking in the extreme. He was sitting on the floor by her mother and she was playing the harp. When I came in, he rose and gave me his hand, saying 'we sailors are all brothers, you know.' Poor fellow! Ainslie saw Miss Price and heard she had a fortune. He knew her father had been immensely rich and he made love to her. Emily refused him and gave as her reason that she had been engaged to her cousin for some years. Ainslie took his dismissal very well, but bitterly did he make Henry rue being the cause of it. The *Britannia*[1] was bound for the West Indies and during the long voyage every species of petty torment, every denial of little indulgence, all the seething of malice which make the insupportable whole, were heaped on his victim. Henry, however, was not the man to be cast down at a little [setback, but] the climate disagreed with him and Lord Ainslie, who had always promised his father to treat him as his son, endeavoured by every means in his power to augment the evil. He had a nephew, Barry, a little midshipman to whom Henry had been very kind. Barry loved his friend and braved many a sharp word or blow to serve him.

On the voyage home Henry heard of his father's death. His mother died in his early infancy and he worshipped his surviving parent. Deeply grieved and being besides previously ill, he became too weak, and too melancholy, to go about his tasks with his accustomed alacrity. Threats and punishments had no further effect than to make him rebel against what he thought cruelty and injustice. He was confined to his cabin, and when the period of his liberation arrived, he was too ill to avail himself of it. During a long fever which followed, Ainslie never once went to see him, never sent a kind word to comfort him. Little Barry used to read to him and write for him, till one day when Ainslie said, 'is not that boy dead yet?', the boy answered, 'Uncle Ainslie, you are worse than a savage!' For which disrespect he was mastheaded[2] and forbidden to see poor Henry, who was now actually dying. When warned what would follow his disobedience (for he still paid a visit when he could) by an anxious associate, the undaunted boy answered, 'Uncle Ainslie can only kill me and I should not mind dying, for when Henry is dead, all those I love will be in heaven.' Ainslie's first visit to the cabin was paid on Stanmore's last day. Barry was with him then and he declared solemnly that there was a letter and a journal directed to Emily lying by Henry, which Barry was to have delivered. But after Henry's death, they were never found. He died in the course of the evening and Barry assured me that several of the sailors sobbed aloud when the corpse was flung into[3] the sea. Poor little Barry was shot some time after. He came alone to Mrs Price's when they reached England and gave Emily a ring and a silk handkerchief Stanmore had worn. He told me the story of Henry's death and cried bitterly when he saw Emily and her mother.[4] *He* did not lose much by quitting this world, for Ainslie was the only tie in it.[5] You have now the story as I heard it. It is difficult to know exactly the rights of it, hearing it only from strangers. But this much is certain: that Everard looks on him as little better than an assassin and I only hope they will keep out of one another's way."

"And Emily, poor Emily?"

"She never speaks of it, not even to her mother and does all she can to soften her brother's mind. But she has never recovered [from] it though it is four years now since Stanmore died."

Alixe sighed and returned with Brownlow to the boudoir. Emily joined them a few minutes afterwards with her brother. Everard sat down.

"You look pale love, are you tired? Do go to bed, now pray do."

Everard smiled. He had first raised his eyes and perceived those of Alixe fixed with such mournful anxiety upon him that he was going to rally her, when suddenly, grasping the arm of the sofa, he fainted. Alixe gave a short subdued scream and Emily knelt by his side and chaffed his temples. He soon recovered, and when Brownlow brought a glass of water, he proposed dividing it between his sister and her friend, in both of whose eyes the tears were starting.

"Did you ever see so pretty an illustration of the lily and the rose in the evening, dear? I will write an ode on the subject, but meantime I will take Emmy's advice and go to my pillow." So saying, and pressing Alixe's hand, he walked slowly away, Emily following. Alixe was roused from the melancholy reverie into which she was falling, by the observations of two deeply rouged and blonded Dowagers, who had watched Everard's progress thro' the rooms and up the magnificent marble staircase.

"That young man won't live."

"Do you think not? Oh, depend on it, he will get over it. Young men do not die so easily."

"I beg your pardon. There is consumption in the family. I remember his brother Albermarle, [a] fine stout creature with as high colour, which Mr Price *never* had. And yet that lad pined away and coughed till he died."

"It's a great pity."

"Yes, it is. For it is a very pretty property and heaven knows who it will go to."

"And the poor old Lady too."

"Oh, she will never live to see it happen. But come, shall we look for Louisa & Caroline? They must have finished waltzing by this time."

"Won't live!" repeated Alixe, almost mechanically. And the sound of his light happy laugh rang in her ears. And then she thought over the scene that had just taken place, till flinging herself on the sofa, she wept. Some people coming towards the boudoir made her start up. And to avoid being seen, she went out on the balcony which looked out onto the road. The daylight was breaking and the carriages were nearly gone. Mrs Aimwell was just getting into her carriage. She said something, which our heroine's anxiety, rather than her ears, interpreted. And the slow musical voice of the serpent-hearted Ainslie answered, –

"I hope not for his poor mother's sake." He turned, and Alixe drew back, that he might not see her as she past. But he did not pass. He came and stood for a few moments under the boudoir window with his arms folded and then in a tone of anguish, he exclaimed half aloud, "Oh Emily, Emily!" Then, hastily turning away, he departed. Ainslie had, as we have before said, a very sweet voice. Whether this had its due effect on Alixe, or that she felt deeply the opinion expressed by the first of modern poets, that "none are *all* evil,"[6] certain it is that she was touched by his ejaculation and, as she leant back silently in the carriage that conveyed her home, she attributed many a secret feeling of regret and softness to the late object of her honour and the cause of her friend Emily's unhappiness.

Chapter 10

Lady St Clair was vexed at the oppression of spirits which her adopted child vainly endeavoured to conceal or repress. Everard grew daily weaker and at length his anxious mother persuaded him to allow them to accompany him to Hunsden, his country seat. Accordingly, they all left town and, in spite of constant bulletins from Emily, Alixe's dejection visibly increased.

At length they left Hunsden for Lady St Clair's cottage,[1] but the occupations which had given Alixe such pleasure six months before had ceased to interest her. Her doves were still allowed to be fed by the gardener. Her flowers withered without being seen and the only walk she liked was a narrow green lane up which the village postman was wont[2] to come by way of a short cut, and by constantly waylaying him she managed to get her letters 10 minutes sooner. One sorrowful day this slight gratification was the cause of alarm and anguish. She met old Jenkins as usual. He had no letters for her, but there were two for Lady St Clair.

"Take them up to the cottage," said the anxious girl in a disappointed tone.

"I'm afeard, Miss, that one of 'em has bad news in it," and so saying he displayed a letter whose broad black edge and seal swam in Alixe's sight for a moment, and then became more and more indistinct. She fell to the ground.

"Oh Lord, Oh Lord!" said the poor old man. "She's swooned or dead may be, and it's all me, it's all me." But the fresh air prevented Alixe's deadly sickness from turning into a fainting fit. She sat upon the bank and leant her head against a tree.

"Shall I send any one down from the Cottage Miss? I'll run directly."

"No, no, I beg you will not. I had rather not. I am quite well, – it is so hot." He rose and returned to the garden and, going to the little summer house Charles and she had built years ago with the gardener's assistance, she wept incessantly from noon till dinner time.

And he was dead, Everard was gone! The heavy gravestones would cover him from her sight, the cold earth would be thrown over him and his name was now an empty sound to which nothing living lay claim.

"Everard! *My* Everard!" repeated she, as she clasped her trembling hands together. He could never answer to the call again, never beg her to say "*dear* Everard," never go with a kind farewell to return again. No, he was gone – gone, to a land whence there was no return. Weary and sick with weeping, she gazed on the blue sky without tears and almost without thought. Her maid came to inform her that her mother had sent for her.

"Now," thought Alixe, "the dreadful moment is come. It will soon be over." And she walked slowly to the house. She had hardly the strength to open the drawing-room door, where Lady St Clair sat. The broad, black-edged letter was visible and as her adopted child entered she wiped away her tears. Alixe walked feebly forward.

"Sit down my love. I have had news from Hunsden. Emily does not write herself because – But what ails you? Speak Alixe! My child!" said she, as Alixe laid her head with convulsive sobs on her arm and leant against the table for support.

"Forgive me, dear mother. I know – I grasp it all – he is dead. I do not wish to hear any more."

"My dear Alixe, what has happened? Why do you grieve so bitterly? *Who* is dead?" The weeping girl gave one bewildered gaze at her adopted parent and tried to answer. The words died on her tongue.

"There is some mistake Alixe, as I cannot suppose you would grieve so bitterly for your unhappy little cousin. Have you had any letters?"

"No, no, but I thought, I felt sure that –" She paused, and throwing herself on her mother's neck, she wept again. Lady St Clair partly grasped what had happened and had time to relieve her mind.

"My love, Everard Price [is] better, much better. The letter from Hunsden [is] to request we will come there as Mrs Price is much indisposed and wishes to see you. Emily fears that two invalids requiring constant attention will be more than she can manage."

"Mother, dear Mother!"

"My love, I am sure no observation is necessary from me to make you feel how weak you have been. Try Alixe, oh try, not to hope and fear as you do, always in extremes, or you will not be as happy as I think my child deserves to be. This other letter I own has distressed me." She gave it to Alixe, who read as follows:

Dear Madam

It is my painful duty to inform you (as one of the kindest friends of its unhappy parents) of the death of the infant son of Sir W. and Lady Marwood, a loss aggravated by the shocking circumstances of its death. Lady Marwood and her husband had been for some days at the seat of a neighbouring baronet and the child was in perfect health the day before they returned. That evening, however, the servants had a supper and the nurse, having washed and undressed the baby, left it asleep in its crib. Some time after, they heard the baby cry, but the nurse was persuaded to sit still on the plea that "it would soon *cry itself to sleep.*" The noise in the servants' hall increased and they thought no more of the child. Some time elapsed before the party broke up.[3] The moment they quitted the room they were in, one of the housemaids declared she smelt fire.

The nurse instantly exclaimed "My God – the child!" and rushed upstairs, followed by the whole household. Their fears were realized. The lighted candle had fallen from the chimney piece into the crib and set fire to it. The unhappy babe was still alive, though dreadfully disfigured, and continued testifying its existence by feeble moans till the next morning. When the returning carriage was heard, the nurse started up, saying "I cannot see *her*," and left the room. Lady Marwood, who had interpreted with a mother's feelings the looks of her servants, rushed up in time to hear the last moan of her miserable infant and gaze on its disfigured corpse. I never saw so horrible a sight. The surgeon wept bitterly while he held the mother's hands, vainly attempting to make her hear him, while she stood by the bed, gazing on its face and repeating in a listless tone, "my *pretty* child, my boy, my beautiful rosy boy!"

And his miserable father hid his groaning head, that he might be spared the sight of the infant he had been so proud of. Lady Marwood is still delirious. Her mother and friends are with her. The wretched woman whose carelessness caused the event drowned herself that day. Sir William requested I would inform you of the circumstances and likewise to say that it will prevent his receiving his friends as usual this autumn, though he hopes you will visit Lady Marwood as soon as she can see anyone.

With every sentiment of respect & esteem
believe me dear Madam
Yours truly
Charles Philipps

Holmwood July 13th

Alixe felt a sick thrill of horror as she perused the letter, and for some moments neither she nor her mother spoke. She thought of the many times she had played with the poor child. Its little engaging ways, even the tone in which it endeavoured to lisp his name came fresh to her memory. And tears of pity stole from her eyes. But Everard was better, and she was going to Hunsden. That was a consolation, which would have superseded many a misfortune. She counted the hours which would elapse before they could arrive. Hunsden was in Derbyshire. She calculated that two days and a half would bring them to this paradise. On the evening of the third day, Lady St Clair and her adopted child drove up to the door of Hunsden House, and in a moment Alixe was in the arms of her friend Emily.

"How is your mother?"

"My poor mother is rather better. I think her recovery depends very much on Everard's. I am convinced that anxiety only has been the cause of her illness. She is asleep, and if you are not tired, we will walk round the grounds. I dare say we shall meet my brother, who is enjoying the summer air for the first time since he came down. Or perhaps you are tired with your journey?" Lady St Clair was, but Alixe was quite equal to the walk. Emily ushered the former to her room and returned to her companion. The grounds were beautiful, the lawn sloping down to the sheet of water in front, the long shrubbery with its many windings and turnings, the beautiful view in the distance, which the setting sun improved, according to custom, – all filled Alixe with delight.

"There," said Emily, as they came to an opening which afforded a full view of the house and distant hills. "This is my point de vue and that little hill covered with trees is my favourite walk. The grove was planned and executed by my grandfather, and in a most curious specimen of ingenuity, being a sort of labyrinth with a hundred little green seats on different corners."

"Dear, how delicious," said Alixe

"Yes, it is very nice, but I cannot take you to the mount tonight," added Emily laughing, "tho' I see you long to go. Tomorrow, however –" Everard's appearance put an end to the conversation and the three returned to the house. As they past under the portico, Everard twisted off a rich branch of jasmine.

"There! You are to keep that long after it is faded, in the most romantic way, in memory of Hunsden!"

It *was* kept in the most romantic way, long after the master of the beautiful tree had forgotten his gift. Alixe wore it in her hair at dinner time and then placed it with many other treasures in a little box sacredly kept from human eyes.

For a short time, Mrs Price continued gradually mending, and those days were the happiest in the life of our young heroine. There was not a moment which was not employed delightfully. She went the rounds with Emily in the little village of L. about two miles beyond the Park Gate. She worked for her pensioners, wrote out her lists and became interested about every sick old woman and rickety child in the parish. She had employment in the garden, put goldfish in the fountain and helped to construct a root house.[4] Sweet sunny days! How soon they seemed over! And the moonlight walks, in which the whole party, even old Mrs Price joined, the resting place where they sat down to look at the pale clear sky or the slow light clouds that passed over it; all too delightful to last. Even Alixe, with all her natural gaiety, felt this instinctively. One lovely starlight evening, when they had been haymaking with the villagers, Emily and her brother and our heroine came round by the mount. They sat down on one of the many rustic benches and gazed silently on the starry sky. Everard broke the silence by repeating those beautiful lines of Sir Henry Wotton's:

> Ye meaner beautyes of the nighte
> Which poorly satisfye our eyes
> More by your number than your lighte
> Like common people of the skies
> What are ye when the moon dothe rise?[5]

Alixe sighed and turning to Emily said, –

"I am afraid your poetry makes me melancholy, for this morning when I was reading the lines on this tree beginning 'Oh happy days!', I sighed to think that happy as those are I spend with you, they must soon be over. I know it is fancy, but one's 'happy days' all *seem* to be shorter than others." She paused, for Everard touched her arm, and Emily sobbed aloud.

"Emily! dear Emily! what have I done?" said the terrified girl.

"My dearest love," said her friend, taking her hand. "It is weak of one to say it thus, but the lines you allude to were written by a dearly beloved cousin, since dead, when we were both *very* young and *very* happy. We used to walk here together many a summer's night. And now when I come to Hunsden and sit in the same spot to look on the same sky, I feel melancholy, *foolishly* melancholy, for I know my Henry is in heaven – and happy. And when I come here alone in the still night to his favourite seat, over which he has nailed those verses, the sound of his clear cheerful voice startles me and I can hardly persuade myself. I *am* indeed alone. I am afraid the kindness of my friends has spoilt me," added she, smiling sweetly at Everard, "for every one has so carefully avoided his name and everything connected with him, that the mention of such subjects, is now a painful surprise. But I do not mean to be weak anymore, but to speak of Henry Stanmore and make you love his memory."

And they rose and went to the house. Alixe read again the verses which had struck her, and as she liked them we offer them here:

> Oh happy days! Oh sunny hours!
> How bright and swift ye pass along
> How soft the breeze within these bowers
> How light and sweet the blackbird's song!
> The shade is o'er your splendour thrown

Save such as darkens your clear rill
Which makes a space so green and lone
That all beyond looks brighter still.

Oh happy days! And can it be
That they must pass away for ever?
Alas to shield the fading tree
Would be a wild, a vain endeavour.
The flowers must droop – the scene must change
The joyous summer *must* depart –
But ye shall live wherein I range
Dear happy days, with my heart!

Henry Stanmore was no poet, but poetry depends much more than the writer is aware, on the previous feelings of the reader, and *his* simple lines struck home to the heart of our young and innocent heroine.

Chapter 11

The quiet enjoyment of the society of her friends, which had hitherto been the position of our heroine, was interrupted soon by the arrival of a favourite companion of Everard's. Harry Dunstan leaped lightly from his cabriolet, gracefully entered the drawing room, shook hands with a glad smile with all the Hunsden party, bowed courteously to Alixe and her mother and sitting down conversed in the most agreeable manner. What there was in all this to displease Alixe we know not, but she felt an instinctive aversion for Captain Dunstan, of which he was far from being aware. He was handsome, gay, rather clever and was moreover a Captain in the Blues and much admired in general. But to this rule, Mlle de Fleury was the exception. However, a few days almost reconciled her to his presence. He was so prévenant,[1] so attentive to old Mrs Price, so jokingly fond of Everard. And though it would have been pleasanter certainly to have been only with the Prices, yet it was unjust to dislike him and think him an intruder.

Another arrival caused great pleasure to Alixe. It was none other than General Koss, the friend of her mother and the indulgent playmate of her childhood. After dinner they were taking their usual midnight stroll, when General Koss abruptly said, –

"Well, and how do you like Captain Dunstan?"

"Oh, I like him very well *now*, he is very agreeable very pleasant and apparently kind."

"*Apparently*, yes. I asked you what you thought of him because I thought him a perfect specimen of a *real man of the world*, and in *this* case, I thought you would judge more impartially than you are in the habit of doing of those sort of people – of that sort of person," added he, after a moment's pause, half smiling. Alixe blushed and answered eagerly, –

"Oh, but they are not all alike. There is a difference, a great difference."

"Not a *great* difference, there is some certainly. Different contemplations will produce difficult feelings – and where there are fewer incentives to evince, the outward subjects of [a] corrupted heart will be fewer. But in the groundlessness of character, they are all alike: selfish, unprincipled, heartless and unfeeling. Their lives are spent in rebelling against the laws of God and trampling on the rights of man. Pardon me, my dear young friend, if my expressions appear violent. The interest, the intense interest, I take in your welfare has prompted me to speak. You are young and romantic and your adopted parent is (forgive me if I say it) too indulgent. She has all the self-imposed tenderness and watchful care of a mother, without her natural authority. Alixe de Fleury, your life is bright before you. Your eyes are dazzled. Oh! do not think the friendly hand cruel. That future will be a stormy one, unless you are warned in time. Do not, oh! do not, trust your happiness with a man who has no principles but those of worldly honour to depend upon, no guide but passion, no excellence except in nurtured advantages and accomplishments which may 'win the eye but ought not to charm and

[At this point in the MS there is a missing section of 15 folio pages, from which we can deduce that Alixe learnt of unacceptable conduct by Harry Dunstan prior to his appearance in the novel. She is shocked to discover that Everard still considers him a friend.]

[…] all, the warm friendship testified by Mr Price for his unworthy companion alarmed and surprised her. Was it possible he could be ignorant of his previous history? Or was Everard, *her* Everard indeed, so much a "man of the world" as to look with calmness on treachery and heartlessness? She turned away from the window, where she had been reflecting on these circumstances, and sat down by Emily, who was working. Alixe soon engaged in a similar employment. But the needle dropped from her hand and again she became wrapt in thought. Everard and Dunstan were at a little table playing cards, more eagerly than Alixe thought at all necessary or proper. Before Henry Dunstan came, their evenings had been spent so much more rationally, so much more pleasantly. Music, reading aloud, settling a thousand little plans for the good of the villagers under Emily's care had occupied them. But Harry Dunstan didn't care for reading, liked cards better than music and appeared to exercise a greater degree of influence over Everard than was natural, considering the superiority of the latter. Our heroine watched them, as the varying fortunes of the table partially showed itself on the countenances of the players. Harry Dunstan indeed was little moved. Now and then, when Everard bent over his cards with a perplexed look, Captain Dunstan smiled and his smile was not an agreeable one. It was triumph concealed – and perhaps malicious. Everard Price was evidently anxious and when at length he rose with a flushed countenance, it was with ill-concealed vexation that he said, –

"You will ruin me in a week if this goes on, Dunstan. I can't conceive why you always win, I am in general a lucky dog." A cloud passed over Dunstan's brow but he laughed and replied slightly. Music was proposed and Alixe sang with Everard and afterwards alone. She chose "Auld Robin Gray."[2] It was a favourite of hers, that is, ever since Mr Price had approved of it one evening.

"Thank you, thank you," said Captain Dunstan. "You sing that with true feeling, Miss St Clair. In the poet's spirit," added he, smiling. Then, turning to Everard, he said, –

"Do you know I never heard anyone sing it so well, except poor Minny, and she was very fond of it. I think you heard her one night at Sir Samuel Repringer's. You need not feel jealous Miss St Clair –" Harry Dunstan stopped. Alixe, unaccustomed to conceal her feelings, gazed with a mixture of anxiety and wonder on the countenance of her lover and gave one glance of abhorrence at his friend. Dunstan looked as if he would have read her soul. His deepset eyes actually flashed from beneath the dark eyebrows above them. It was a momentous mutual understanding. Dunstan coolly turned away and Alixe shrunk back by Emily.

Alixe de Fleury, when she retired to her room at night, thought sorrowfully of the events of the evening. Everard a gambler! A man of the world! Yes, he evidently knew Dunstan's story and to be the friend of such a villain! She was startled from her reverie by eager voices in the next room, which was Captain Dunstan's. It was impossible not to hear them and tho' Alixe, after her first surprise, coughed two or three times to warn them how easily they might be overheard, they continued without appearing to have caught the sound.

"I tell you Everard, someone must have been mischief-making. I can read countenances, as well as most men, and your little Miss St Clair's was no loving look, I promise you. Pray, have you any serious thoughts that way?" The answer was inaudible but appeared to be given in the negative.

"I thought not. I said you could not be such a fool, you who are the favourite of all the married ladies in England and France, to think of being taken in by a little lovesick girl. Nobody even knows who she is, and if you ever marry, money is not what you ought to think of, if indeed two thousand a year is any consideration. *Family*, family my good fellow, is what you ought to look for and that only. Lady Barbara Lavington, you know, would marry you tomorrow. Not that I advise you by any means to marry, for I declare to you, and I must be disinterested, that it is not a happy state, at least unless both parties marry from very different motives, than is either common or prudent."

"There is but one woman at this moment I would trust my happiness with, and you know who she is – yes, my sister. But before you advance there, Harry, I should wish to see you more steady. Between you and I, almost all the money you have in present possession has been won from me, and though I am partial even to your faults, you behaved very ill to that poor girl who died."

"There, my dear fellow, you are out. *I* behaved very well. If the girl was a fool, and married merely out of vanity, all the time regretting her shepherd of the hills, it was her fault, not mine. But this is a subject on which we can never agree. I would rather think of your future, than of my past follies. You do not then intend to marry Miss St Clair?"

"Intend? Dunstan! How can I settle my plans when you of all men ought to know how embarrassed I am? What with the improvements here and that cursed gaming table, I really believe," continued he with a forced laugh, "that my fortune will change hands and that you, Harry Dunstan, will possess all the Everard property. You will then realize your views about Emily with great ease, and as to Miss St Clair, he will be a happy man who does marry her." So saying, he left the room.

Perhaps if Miss St Clair could have heard the mingled pain and tenderness with which her name was repeated after his step had died away along the corridor, it would have helped to still the painful feeling that swelled in her heart. But she had not that consolation. Bitter tears rose in her eyes. But woman's pride checked them and after a long mental discussion, in which she began by settling a plan of indignant conduct towards Everard, and ended by making excuses for him, she fell asleep.

When Dunstan so boldly proclaimed himself disinterested on the subject of marriage, it is not to be supposed that he told the truth. Accustomed to rule, Everard by means of his failings, to stand like Mephistopheles and urge him on to vice, having made him useful on various occasions either by making his purse or his word pass instead of his own, and having moreover, as Everard hinted, plundered him (how fairly we shall not pretend to judge) of a large part of his property, Harry Dunstan felt that to let his victim escape, to allow him to give way to the better feelings of his nature, to settle into regular habits and learn to love home for home's sake, would be a failure in schemes laid for years and practised with equal earnestness and duplicity. Everard's principal failing was vanity and there never existed a more adroit flatterer than Dunstan, or one who could point with more power the shafts of ridicule. Habit, the remembrance of their college hours, where Dunstan was reckoned the most agreeable and obliging of his companions, and gratitude for the real or imaginary favour of having stood by him thro' thick and thin, had made the society of his friend almost necessary to Everard. It never once struck him that the pliancy which thus stooped to please all was anything but a fine trait in Dunstan's character. Or that the young lad who encouraged his follies, while others blamed, argued on his side from motives of self-interest: the rich, handsome and fashionable Mr Price was to Dunstan what the substance is to the shadow, and once linked, he took care to rivet the chain that bound him.

Alixe had taken very much to heart Captain Dunstan's description of her as a *lovesick* girl. She resolved to conquer her feelings, not only to *seem* but to *be* totally indifferent to Everard. There was an indelicacy in persisting, in giving way to an affection for a man, who if he was not unworthy of it, had at least denied any intention of marrying her. Nay, had coolly talked of seeing her happy with another. She would cast him from her thoughts and tho' certainly could not love any one as well as she *had* loved her Everard, yet she would think of anyone rather than of him. In pursuance of these wise resolutions, she began by being indifferent, studiously so, to Everard's little attentions. But her flushed cheek betrayed the vain struggle and the tremulous sound of her voice agreed but ill with her careless answer. Emily watched her and was surprised. In the evening, when they were as usual taking their moonlight walk, she said, as her brother and Alixe walked silently by her, –

"I cannot think what you two have quarrelled about? Pray tell me, and I will endeavour to mediate between you. What is the matter, Everard?"

"I am sure I do not know what Miss St Clair is displeased at," he sighed, and the sigh almost reconciled him to Alixe. She stifled the sob that rose to her throat and said in a low voice, –

"I am not displeased." But conversation did not flow as usual, and at length Everard left them, as he said, to see his mother, who was not so well that evening. Twenty times, during the half-hour he had been with them, Alixe had longed to speak to him as a friend, to warn him against Dunstan, to supplicate him not to gamble. Twenty times the first sentence was on her lips, but each time the thought obtruded itself. By what right was she to lecture him [on] his avowed affection for her? He had denied it to be serious. Should she supplicate him for *her* sake? He would laugh at her. For his own [sake] why should she interfere? Grieved and perplexed, she at length came to the determination of confiding in Emily. The conversation of yesternight she did not think herself at liberty to repeat. But all that she could say, she did, and earnestly begged Emily to use the eloquence of affection with her brother. Emily promised. And Alixe, relieved in some measure, returned to the house.

Mrs Price was not all well, worse than she had been for many days, and the evening was a sad one. In the morning, Alixe, as usual, descended to the breakfast room earlier than the rest of the party, Emily being in attendance on her mother. She had proceeded a few steps forward, when she saw Everard in the window. It was the second time she had ever been quite alone with him. He did not seem to observe her, and for a moment she looked irresolutely round, equally unable to advance or retreat. She had half resolved upon the latter, and had turned to the door, when Mr Price gently prevented it and saying with a smile, – "this is the second time you have stolen upon me unawares," he led her to her usual place at the work table. Alixe mechanically took out her work, while Everard after a pause rapidly and energetically explained his feelings, his plans and his hopes, confessing that Emily had made him ashamed of his follies, and finally conjuring her to let him look forward to the future with hope, that when his present embarrassments were settled, he might be happy as her husband. The first gentle kiss was printed on Alixe's forehead, as she bowed her beautiful head on his shoulder and swore never to be the wife of another. There was a moment of breathless silence. A wild and fearful shriek broke it and Everard's name was repeated twice in an agonized voice. He flew out of the room and Alixe stood trembling. She had not long to wait. Lady St Clair entered the drawing room.

"Mrs Price is dying, Alixe, and she wishes to see you." They ascended the stairs and entered the sick room. It was with difficulty they made the poor old woman understand that her "bright favourite" was come to bid her adieu. As the weeping girl knelt by her bedside, she placed her wan withered hand upon the rich curls which adorned her head. Then clasping her hands with one long look of love at her son, she appeared to murmur a prayer. The hands slowly untwined and sank upon her breast, and there was one living being less in the apartment of Death.

Chapter 12

When all was settled after poor old Mrs Price's death, it was decided that Everard and Emily should go to Geneva, Emily's spirits and health having received a severe shock in her kind mother's death. Captain Dunstan had departed the first day, grumbling at the ill-timed decease of his friend's remaining parent. Alixe and her mother made their melancholy adieus and returned to the cottage. Here, Alixe speedily recovered her spirits. The bright side of the picture was constantly before her and with the sanguine disposition of youth she foresaw no obstacles now that Everard had explained himself. His impassioned tone rung in her ear when she was alone and she conjured up plans innumerable for the future for Everard's happiness and advantage. Sometimes indeed, the shriek which had interrupted their interview weighed on her spirit and appeared like an evil omen to secure her from dreams of happiness. But the cloud soon past away and left all sunny as before. It was at this juncture that Charles St Clair returned and our readers have already been informed of the events which followed. When made acquainted with the outline of Alixe's history since his departure, by means of her journal, he generously resolved never by word or look to remind his adopted sister that he had ever wished to be other to her than a fond visitor. His love was too pure, too perfect, to allow even in his solitary hours all the bitterness of his regret.

"After all," would he say, "ought I not to prefer Alixe's happiness to my own? Is it possible I was selfish enough for a moment as to reproach her for a natural feeling? If she is happy, that is all I desire and I think. Nay, I am sure, I could rejoice with her and love those she loved." Sometimes his heart would ache, in spite of his resolutions, when he thought of Everard Price, whom he endeavoured to clothe with perfection to make him worthy of Alixe. And as the day drew nearer for their departure for town, he almost wished himself at sea again. But at other times he felt that he should be a protection to his fatherless sister, and his generous heart swelled at the thought that it was in his power at least to see that she was not wronged, if indeed anyone in cold blood could think of wronging his "fairy," Lady St Clair had also a mother's feelings on the subject and as she gazed fondly on the open animated countenance and graceful manly figure before her, she sighed as she thought, –

"Can it be because he is my son, my one son, or is it not in reality strange that the cold, vacillating Everard should take [the] place of Charles in Alixe's affections? Surely, surely my boy is more worthy to be loved?"

And she strove to feel what she had always said, that Alixe had a right to make her own choice without being prejudiced, and consoled herself by thinking that after all Charles might be happy with another. Or that circumstances might make his marriage with Alixe still possible. As to our heroine, she was quite happy, confiding with all a woman's faith in the steadiness of Everard's attachment. Attributing every thing like error in his conduct to the influence of circumstances over which he had no power, and contented that Charles was again as he had been, all was to her a source of sunshine. She neither saw the fond anxiety of her adopted mother, nor the struggles in the heart of her son, but indulged in bright visions of happiness, which a few years back she would have deemed solitary, since it depended not on the society and endeavourments of the friend and companion of her childhood.

With a beating heart, she looked forward to the fast-approaching day which was fixed for their removal to town. The day came, the 1st of April, as lovely as heart could wish it. And as the warm rays of the sun shone in at the carriage windows, Alixe almost sighed to leave the perfumed air of the country; to exchange the pale, green buds of the young trees and the violets and primroses of the cottage for the whirling dust and noise of the gay metropolis. Charles sighed too: more deeply, more sincerely; he had nothing to look forward to, but to watch Alixe's career of temptation, to see himself cut out by men who knew more of the world. A man of the world – magic sound! What is there in the inspiring title which proves such a charm to woman? Why does she prefer to all others, the one of *his* sex who has deceived most of hers? Why does she shrink from the thought of sharing an undistinguished lot with one not the less amiable, for being unaccustomed to place his chief pleasure in the vanities and his chief glory in the views of the world? A woman's sphere is, however, the scene of her joys and sorrows. Her smiles and tears are confined to that narrow spot. Let those women whose lot is it had been to love such,

> And to make idols – and to find them clay
> And to bewail that worship[1] –

answer whether their firesides have been happier, or their homes brighter, because their husband's name was [a] familiar sound in the ears of the light and vain. Who is there, who driven by their own melancholy restless thoughts from the domestic sphere, who even while their rounded necks are glittering with ornaments and their eyes sparkling with light as false and cold as the mock daylight thrown from the lamps above them? What woman is there, I ask, with a soul to feel, and reason to appreciate, the reality of happiness, who does not sometimes sigh even with the smile on her lip for a *home*, a home where fond confiding affection would make its inhabitants look on the world as on a hollow bauble, and pity the aching hearts whose owners' "strut their little hour upon the stage"[2] and return to their abodes weary and disgusted, to fling off their gaudy trappings and weep; a home to which they would come back with redoubled pleasure as the only spot where their thoughts and feelings, always linked by the same chords, may be poured reciprocally into the fond and faithful bosoms, which share all even to their sorrows.

Lady St Clair and her young companions arrived at their journey's end without accident. One evening was melancholy, for Charles and his mother had their own thoughts to occupy them and even Alixe felt a degree of sadness at the prospect of meeting her friend Emily, with whom she had parted on so awful an occasion. The next morning Lady St Clair, who had affairs to arrange, proposed that Charles should accompany his adopted sister to her friend's house. Charles assented without looking up. They arrived at Grosvenor Place. Miss Price was at home. She was ushered into the same drawing room, so dear and so familiar to her. There stood poor old Mrs Price's chair, empty and deserted. There hung Everard's picture and that of his departed brother, Albermarle. Alixe felt extremely melancholy. She walked to the superb harp. It was out of tune to the piano. It was locked. The music was settled in precise order. No loose songs carefully scattered on the rosewood lid proved which were the present favourites of her friend. In a few minutes Emily entered. She walked up to Alixe and attempted to express her pleasure at seeing her again. But the words faded from her lips and with a gush of tears she said, –

"Oh! Alixe, if you knew how you're being here puts me in mind of last year!" Alixe spoke of the future and the present, and in spite of the confusion of her consolations, her friend became quite composed. Charles was introduced and they began to talk on general subjects. Emily told all that had happened at Geneva that she thought would amuse Alixe, and what had become of several people she had known the spring before. Everard was at Lord Darlies' place in the country, the old Lord being dead, and Annette Aimwell at the height of her ambition.

"And now," said she. "I have nothing more to tell you, except that Louisa Whittaker has another baby and that her uncle has forgiven her and they are all living together now and she will have his fortune. I suppose you have heard all about poor Pamela Aimwell?"

"No, I have seen none of my town friends since last summer."

"Oh, it is the most melancholy thing! You know she was in love with Ainslie? Well, after paying her great attention both before and after she left London, he proposed to her one night[3] at a ball. And he was to have come to Mrs Aimwell the next morning. And would you believe it, he never came at all. And the next Pamela heard of him was that he was gone to Paris. Poor little thing, she was so ashamed and shocked at her own folly in not before applying to her mother that she told no one, but she grew more and more melancholy. And at last she became seriously ill and Mrs Aimwell was advised to take her to the South of France. But when Pamela heard it, she was excessively overcome and kept repeating, 'Oh! not to France, not to France!' And at last, her secret was wrung from her. Mrs Aimwell went into hysterics, Captain Aimwell was furious and he went to Paris and challenged Ainslie. And when the latter requested and received an explanation, instead of fighting he declared he was willing and ready to marry Miss Aimwell whenever her friends thought proper, and that he was at Paris on indispensable business. In short, to the surprise of everyone, they were married, and tho' he was anything but kind, she was dotingly fond of him and divided her time between weeping when he was absent, and endeavouring to smile when he was present. All this did very well till about a month after they were married, when Mrs Aimwell received some strange letter, evidently alluding to a former one which had never been received. It ended, –

'I repeat my warning: If you marry your daughter to Lord Ainslie, you ruin her. You have not replied to my last letter. Beware how you suspect me of imposture. For my children's sake, I will make my title good. I pretend no affection for Lord Ainslie. Woe to the woman who feels any, for she cherishes a serpent. I shall appear, tho' he thinks I cannot, and in the meantime preserve your daughter.' Captain Aimwell was not at home. Mrs Aimwell was staying with the Ainslies at Taly Castle. She had the precaution for once to spare Pamela and took the letter to Ainslie. He affected so much surprise, and then laughed so heartily that her suspicions were quite lulled.

The day however came when the thunderbolt fell. Ainslie was out hunting, Pamela, who was not well, was loitering about the park. A woman apparently of the middle class came up the avenue with two children. The extreme beauty of one of these struck Lady Ainslie and she stopped and spoke to the woman. The latter instantly grasped that she was speaking to the mistress of the castle and communicated to the unhappy girl (who heard for the first time that there existed such a person) that she was Lord Ainslie's wife and was come to prove her son's right. Wild and emaciated in her appearance, proud and almost menacing in her manner, Pamela thought she must be some maniac. For a moment she stood bewildered. And then summoning all her strength, she ordered the woman to follow her to the house. Lady Ainslie reached the threshold and fainted. To shorten her melancholy tale, the marriage was proved. Captain Aimwell is expected home every day and has challenged Ainslie. Pamela is in town with her mother in a delirious state and the woman who calls herself Lady Ainslie is at the lodge of the castle."

"Heavens, how horrible!" exclaimed Alixe. "What a villain Ainslie must be!" added Charles. "Poor Pamela, poor thing, and yet she is happy to be spared the horrible suspense of the duel."

"Oh yes! But how can it end? She must be miserable either way." Emily only answered by a sigh, and they parted. As Charles and Alixe returned home, the former expressed great admiration of Miss Price's manner and disposition, as far as he could judge. But he did not admire her beauty as much as Alixe expected. She certainly was handsome, – "But it was not the *style* he liked," and he unconsciously raised his eyes and cast them on the bright face of his companion.

"She is certainly pale," said Alixe, "and looking very ill and very grave, but that you know is only temporary."

"Perhaps," said Charles who was evidently thinking of something else. And they arrived at Lady St Clair's, to whom they hastened to repeat the fate of the unhappy Pamela.

Chapter 13

Lady Townley embraced the first opportunity of giving a ball in honour, as she said, of Alixe's arrival, though the latter was rather surprised that she should think of gaieties when her favourites the Aimwells were in such distress. She had to learn that in the world, friendship is little more than a name; and that the same people who flatter and caress you one night, would if you were dead, reconsider the accident at the next ball, in the same breath, with a description of the week's amusements, and *chassée* [*sic*][1] forward with the utmost composure after they had finished. Alixe was reflecting painfully on this circumstance and wondering why all Pamela's professed friends danced so gaily, and seemed so merry, when she saw Everard standing in the middle of the room. He did not see her for a minute or two. He was talking eagerly and laughingly to someone she could not see. Charles St Clair, who was standing close by Alixe and had just begged her to dance the first dance with him, as he knew no one, saw her raised colour and open eye and an instinctive feeling told him that Everard, the dreaded Everard, was in the room with him, probably within a few yards of the place where he was standing.

In a moment after, that interesting individual came forward and greeted Alixe with great eagerness. He asked her to dance and offered his arm as if he knew there could be no refusal.

"Alixe, you are engaged to dance with *me*," said Charles in a tone he intended should be playful. Everard started and fixed his eyes on the speaker and then turned to Alixe.

"I beg your pardon Charles. Mr Price, my brother, Charles." Everard extended his hand with some slight compliment. Charles St Clair took it, and if his pulse was quick and his hand feverishly hot, Mr Price could not tell that a few moments before, those symptoms were not visible.

"Well," said Everard, smiling, "I aim to resign you to Mr St Clair." Charles, who was "himself again," begged he could not consider it an engagement, adding that he believed it was not the fashion for brothers to make partners and that perhaps Alixe would give him some other dance in the course of the evening. It ended with Mr Price's arm being accepted and Charles was left alone to watch her through the dance. How beautiful, how very beautiful he thought her! Her steps seemed winged with happiness, her bright eyes and her cheeks burned brighter even than usual and the rich golden curls that escaped above and below the favourite wreath of convolus [*sic*][2] made her altogether seem (at least to the partial eyes of the adopted brother) a fairy creature. Everard remarked his watchful and almost mournful countenance, –

"Your brother never takes his eyes off you, Alixe!"

"He knows no one here," answered she.

"He is very handsome, but rather too grave!"

"Grave! He is the gayest creature possible, at least generally. He has indeed been rather grave lately." And Alixe blushed, for she could not help feeling that if he *was* sad, it was for her. Charles saw the blush, but did not have the accompanying words, and he turned away and went to his mother. Others beside Everard had remarked Charles St Clair's strikingly handsome appearance and his fond mother was receiving compliment[s] upon him at the moment he came up.

"I thought you were dancing with Alixe?" said Lady St Clair.

"Mr Price has asked her."

"Is Emily Price here?"

"No, her brother says that she did not like to come out because of the Aimwells. You know, Lady Ainslie's brother is returned and they are hourly expecting news of the duel."

"Heaven forgive them," said Lady St Clair, "and spare their lives."

"Amen," said Charles solemnly. Everard Price had finished his dance and was bringing Alixe back to her place.

"Stop," said he, "will you let me present you to a very charming foreigner, whom I met at Geneva, the Baroness de Valcone."

"Any friend of yours –", said Alixe, raising her bright confiding eyes to his.

"Here she is!" The lady in question extended her hand and greeted him with an exclamation of delight. And as she continued for some time to interrogate him in a mixture of French, English and Italian, Alixe had ample leisure to observe her. She was short and as round and plump as possible without being clumsy. Her mouth was rather large, but her teeth were dazzlingly white. Her large black eyes had more of restlessness than animation in them and now and then a flash fiercer than female eyes generally emit broke from them. Her eyebrows were jet black, but her train was several shades lighter and seemed as if no hairdresser had ever been allowed to interfere with its arrangement. There was to Alixe's eyes a studied negligence, a *pretension* to charm, but perhaps it was prejudice. At length, there was a pause and Everard concluded by some speech about his having lived on the hopes of seeing her for the last two months.

"Il suffit ti voilà!"[3] said the Baroness, twisting her fingers through one of the glossy velvet curls that hung on the left side. Everard presented Alixe. Mlle Valcone smiled –

"Are you his sister?"

"He? Oh no –"

"His cousin, perhaps?"

"No."

Everard caught the question,

"She is a charming Englishwoman, Baroness, and I thought it would be meritorious to bring the perfection of each country together."

"Ah!" said the half-satisfied Baroness. And she turned and made her way through the crowd to the other end of the room.

"What do you think of her?" said Mr Price, as they again walked forward.

"Oh, I think she is a very handsome little woman."

"I have just danced with her," said Colonel Manners, who just joined them, "and I think her a handsome little devil. Excuse me, Miss St Clair, but really when I looked round after a pause and met those large flashing eyes expecting me to talk, and utterly depriving me of the power of speech, I should not have felt the least surprised, if transparent black wings had sprung from her shoulders."

"Colonel Manners is pleased to be severe tonight," said Everard. "But say what you like of the Baroness de Valcone, she is too perfect for criticism." It was now Charles's turn to dance with Alixe. Everard joined the beautiful Baroness. Just as they were finishing their dance, Alixe's quick eye caught the form of Dunstan making his way through the crowd.

"There is that wicked Captain Dunstan," said she. Charles looked eagerly. Dunstan whispered something in Everard's ear, which brought a momentary flush into the pale cheek of the latter. Alixe, who always connected Dunstan with horrible scenes, was alarmed, but Mr Price turned smilingly to Madame de Valcone and appeared to wish her good night. Then taking Dunstan's arm, he walked to the door. When there, he suddenly turned back and coming up in a hurried manner to Alixe, he said, –

"The duel has been fought and Ainslie has very few hours to live. Aimwell is wounded in the arm and has set out for the continent.[4] Ainslie has sent for me. Good night. I hope you will come to Emily tomorrow."

Alixe found the ball very dull afterwards and they returned home. She longed to ask Charles what he thought of Everard Price, but she dared not. Her adopted brother, however, gave his opinion unasked, –

"Mr Price is very handsome, Alixe." A pause. "He is rather conceited, don't you think so, Mother?"

"A little, he has been spoilt and flattered and has many personal advantages."

"And he is clever," said Alixe almost interrogatively. Lady St Clair smiled, – "Yes, he is clever." And the subject [was] dropped.

The next morning Lady St Clair said she was anxious to hear about Lord Ainslie and his unhappy wife and they accordingly proceeded to Grosvenor Place. Emily was sitting alone. She was very pale and looked as if she had been crying. She rose as they entered.

"All is over now," said she. "Ainslie is dead, and he has confessed everything. Everard will be here presently and will tell you all." There was a pause. Alixe broke it by saying, –

"Oh, there is something, I wished to ask you about. It is the Baroness de Valcone. Your brother introduced me to her last night. Is she a nice person?"

Emily sighed.

"Yes, she is very fascinating, very clever and her story is rather odd. Her father was a French officer with a small patrimony and dreadfully in debt. And when he took her from the convent where she was educated, the Baron de Valcone saw her and fell desperately in love with her. There was an agreement made that he should pay all the father's debts. And as he was very rich and of a good family, the old man was enchanted. He was very fond of his daughter however, and as he could not help seeing that the Baron was a fool and had moreover *English* ideas of marrying his daughter according to her own choice, he was some time before he mentioned it. Honorine de Valcone received it, however, with the utmost composure and agreed to become the wife of a man she had never seen. The father died soon after. Whether she had since repented her marriage, or whether the baron is become more odious, I do not know, but she pays him *very* little attention and talks of her unhappiness to all the young handsome men who are caught by her beauty and wit. She has one lovely little boy, having lost two babies, and of their child she is dotingly fond. She was very kind to us at Geneva, but –"

At this moment the door opened and a little fat woman waddled into the room, followed by Everard who looked exceedingly *impatienté*.

"How do you do Lady St Clair! Lady St Clair, – my Aunt Miss Herbert!", was all Everard was permitted to say, for Miss Herbert, having once opened her mouth, was in no hurry to close it. At length, she paused to take breath and a pinch of snuff. But just as some one of the party had commenced an enquiry, Miss Herbert began with renewed strength.

"Now Aunt, if you will allow me," said Everard, half provoked, half laughing.

"Oh, let me tell them one thing more. Have you heard Miss Emily? Do you know, Lady St Clair, our Everard is to be a parliament man?"

She stopped one second to enjoy the ejaculation of surprise, which burst from the lips of some of the party.

"He is indeed, and you see that's what he had been wishing and wanting this many a year. The Earl of Sunderland[5] is to put him in, as he says, for his beautiful conduct about that wicked Lord Ainslie."

"My dear, dear Aunt, what confusion you do make," said Everard, now laughing heartily.

"Well," said Emily, "but let us have an explanation."

"Certainly, my good sister, and if my Aunt will grant me twenty minutes, I will begin at the beginning. Last night I went straight from the ball to Lord Ainslie's. I found him evidently dying. He was aware of it and holding out his hand said, – 'I dare hardly ask you to forgive a dying man. I have need of someone I can trust. I know you to be a man of honour. To your sister, to poor Emily, take those things – they belonged to Henry Stanmore – and say that if the knowledge of the many bitter hours they have cost me can be any satisfaction, he has it. Many times I have walked up and down on my sleepless nights with that small packet in my hand, endeavouring to muster courage to return it the next morning. But the long delay and the lingering hope I still cherished. Forgive me Emily," said Everard, interrupting himself, "I will spare you that. Lord Ainslie continued to speak at intervals, for he grew very feeble from loss of blood. He said that Ellen Morehead was his wife, but he swore solemnly that he did not believe the marriage was binding, till he received a letter just after he had proposed for Pamela. It was what is commonly called a Scotch marriage and he had not even lived with the woman after the first two years, and considered her as an inconvenience he could shake off at pleasure. She had at first been very fond of him and followed him to America, in the hope of moving him by the endearments of his boys. But her pertinacity only served to enrage him and she was so struck by his coldness and want of heart that she desisted from her useless task, and after having vainly solicited money to take her back to England, she sat down to brood in silence over her wrongs and watch the sight of her children for whom alone she lived. When she heard of Pamela's expected marriage, she wrote to Ainslie and at the same time to Mrs Aimwell. Lord Ainslie obtained possession of that letter and burnt it. It was too late as a warning and he trusted partly to what he thought the impossibility of her proving her marriage, and partly to her weak health and want of means.

There was one other feeling, a disgraceful one. Embittered by Captain Aimwell's conduct at Paris, he thought in the first rage of his heart, that whatever happened afterwards, they might thank themselves for having forced him to a marriage for which he showed reluctance. The unexpected assistance afforded to Ellen Morehead by an American merchant, to whom she told her story and showed Ainslie's first letters, enabled her to come to England. The agitation, however, and fatigue of the journey, and the agony of the scene she had to undergo with her faithless husband, were too much for her shattered constitution and she expired the second week after her arrival. 'A few weeks delay,' said the unhappy man, 'and all this would have been spared. Pamela would have been spared me. But perhaps it is well, my boys! I am growing faint but you must remember, my boys!' And he raised himself in the bed and stared wildly round him. 'Go to my uncle, Lord Sunderland. I quarrelled with him when I grew up, but he was fond of me when I was a lad. Give him this ring. It is my mother's hair, his only and dear sister. Tell him the wayward boy, the headstrong youth and tyrannical heartless villain perished, perished *too soon*. Tell him that I support him and yourself, if you will. Accept the office for my boys' sake, as their guardian. Make them as unlike their father as possible. And for God's sake, do not give them over, as I was at an age scarcely past childhood, to the mastery of their own passions.' He spoke feebly afterwards but I could only make out a word or two. It seemed but a repetition of what he had already said. He died as morning was breaking and said, looking towards the window, 'my last glimpse of daylight!' His last words were 'God bless you' and 'my poor Pamela, poor thing, poor thing,' and he died."

Chapter 14

Everard's visit to Lord Sunderland had been productive of much good. The old earl was lonely in his declining age and embraced with ardour the prospect of becoming the protector of his grand-nephews. He sent for them immediately.

"Poor Ainslie," said the compassionate old man, "with a good education he might have made a very different man. But he was left an orphan so early and was so flattered and indulged, that his mind became ruined." Everard did not reply. He felt he could not speak in favour of the departed and all feeling of anger had long since left his mind. The story Miss Herbert told so confusedly was true in the main. Lord Sunderland had been wavering among several of his young friends, to fix who he thought most worthy of the borough of M---, which was vacant by the death of the last occupant, a nephew of his own, and who would eventually inherit the title. The younger brother of this nephew was abroad and was too wild to think of depending on. Everard's political ideas happened secretly to coincide with those of Lord Sunderland and the feeling with which he spoke of Lord Ainslie's death and his children wrought on the heart of the old man. Everard Price had besides, in spite of his worldliness in little things, an enthusiasm and hopefulness of spirit, which is in itself a merit to the aged.

Everard's dream when he was a very young lad was Politics and if in after life the little expectations he saw of realizing his hopes, and other perhaps less worthy occupations, deadened the feeling, it returned with redoubled force now, when a sudden vision opened upon him of the consummation of his wishes, like a fairy gift, without any trouble on his part. The only cloud in this brightness was that Dunstan – Harry Dunstan, his old familiar friend, was to be his opponent. He would rather it had been any one else; even as it was, he could not help evidently wishing for success.

Easter Eve saw Alixe and her two friends together for the first evening since they had parted in the country. Lady St Clair saw that Emily Price's spirits were very low and she endeavoured to fix her attention on the things most likely to interest her. There was an affectionate solicitude in all to amuse her and make her happy, which could not but be grateful. And as they all sate at Lady St Clair's, even Emily seemed gayer than she had been for some time. The evening past away as usual and at the close of it, Alixe and Charles sang an Easter hymn. Everard was particularly struck by it and remarked that he had never heard a hymn sung, except in church, and begged it might be repeated. Charles looked incredulously at Everard and then glanced at his sister. He caught the look and said, –

"Oh, I dare say Emmy sings them, but I never happened to hear her. I am not often enough at home of an evening." Charles silently turned again to Alixe and their rich clear voices rose once more to Heaven. The last humbling sound died away and there was silence, a solemn silence, and the "Good night" had more true feeling and less gaiety in it than it ever seemed to have before. Many a day afterwards that hymn rung in Everard's ear and forced a sigh from his inmost heart. The air was the one belonging to the psalm, the words [of] which were written by a young clergyman of the village in which Lady St Clair lived, and who died afterwards of a consumption, were as follows:

> The joyous spring is come again with all its living flowers
> And earth gives forth its grateful dew in pure and blessed showers.
> And all is bright within the vale and in the mountain sod,
> As if all nature rose in joy to praise the mighty God.
>
> Yet man, while gazing on a scene so beautiful and bright
> Feels working in his soul which dims that outward light.
> Forms that are gone come round his path and woke silent tear?
> Where are ye flowers and voices, of the lost and vanished year?
>
> Ye who slept within our bosoms, the beautiful and brave!
> Ye who are mutely sleeping *now*, within the cold dead grave!
> And each silver voice seems answering in heaven far away
> We are waking with the Lamb of God, who rose on Easter day!
>
> The flowers of earth are blowing to fade away again
> What *we* are where no change can come, no sorrow and no pain,
> High in our glorious home above, to contrite sinners given
> With him who died and rose but once the Pascal Lamb of Heaven.

Easter was over. Those who had gone into the country returned and those who could not afford to run in and out of London emerged from the garrets and dark lodgings where they had shrouded themselves. Gaieties poured in abundantly and Alixe was prepared to enjoy them as much as she had done the spring before. But there was a change, a change in Everard Price! His manner to *her* was still the same, perhaps even more kind and gentle than formerly. But his time was not all devoted to her. His eyes did not follow her as they used to do. She could not explain, but she felt within herself that his feelings were altered. The half playful, half affectionate sentences, which used to be so clear to her, were again lavished upon the many, or given to the beautiful Baroness de Valcone. Some time before, Alixe would have laughed at the idea of being jealous of a man who had sworn affection for her and listened with incredulity and horror to anyone who hinted at a married woman as an object of rivalry but a year in the world; that world, the corruption of the gay and innocent in which, teaches us to distrust even those we lose; that world which deadens the two most blessed feelings of the human heart. The hope and confidences of our first years had made many things seem natural to Alixe, which were before incredible. And tho' she did not whisper it even in her own chamber, she felt a secret fear that Everard would transfer his affections to the Baroness. But the latter disarmed all prejudice. Her fond caressing manner was the same to Alixe as to Everard. She even slightly and smilingly alluded to a suspicion of their affection. She never seemed to wish to detach, even for a moment, Alixe's lover. Her own heart seemed set upon her little boy and if she was not respectful to her husband, few people could have been; and she was kind and coaxing even to him. Then she was so beautiful and such a strange wild sort of beauty. She sang such gay French romances to her guittar, and now and then, but *very* seldom, after carelessly striking some slow minor chords, she would breathe some rich melancholy Italian air with such languid melody of voice, that her auditors felt their pity and their admiration so mingled it was difficult to tell which feeling had the preponderance. There was the same strange attraction in her conversation, the same *striking on minor chords*, a mournful word, a half sigh over some picture of perfect happiness. And then the same wild gaiety, the same flashing of her playful wit and large bright eyes, which like the dancing of the waters seemed only to cover wrecks. She loved to have Alixe with her and seemed constantly wishing to show her off to the best advantage. Secure in her own beauty, she never had a feeling of envy towards other women. She sang with her and would sit to hear her sing for hours.

"Your voice is so like a bird's," said she one evening, "so like a bird that has never been caged. It is the freshest, the truest voice I ever heard." Alixe smiled at her manner of expressing herself. Charles, however, warmly approved of the description and so did Everard. Said the former, –

"Sing 'Azium's Lute.'" Alixe took her guittar and sang accordingly:

My childhood's home is standing fair
Midst cosy flowers and purple fruit
And sweet to me when I dwelt there
Were Azium's love and Azium's lute
He had a hero's soul – And fought
The foes who dared his sword to meet
But ere he went his lute he brought
And laid it sighing at my feet!

"Take it" – he cried and when I die
On some unknown and distant shore
T'will bring thee back thy Azium's sigh
When Azium's lips shall breathe no more!
How shall I tell my tale of woe?
My father urged the sultan's suit –
I left my childhood's home – and oh!
I left behind me, Azium's lute!

They chid me for the falling tears –
They gave me jewels bright, in vain –
My yearning heart still wished to hear
The sound of Azium's lute again. –
They brought a harp – Alas! the sound
Was harsh and strange – with trampling foot
I spurned its chords upon the ground –
I *knew* it was not Azium's lute!

I bid them seek it in that home
My weeping eyes no more might see.
I bid them ever wandering roam
Till they brought back that lute to me.
They brought it – but the sighing strings
Lay soundless all – and coldly mute –
It matters not what sorrow brings,
My heart is broke – like Azium's lute.

Alixe paused. The Baroness was leaning over her and our heroine felt her warm tears dropping on her shoulder. Startled and embarrassed, she sang the last two lines tremulously. It perhaps added to the effect of the song, but she felt uncomfortable. She hardly dared look round. When she did, Madame de Valcone's large dark eyes were mournfully fixed upon her.

"It is strange," said the Baroness, "what power sounds have over the soul, how a single chord will bring so very many recollections to one's heart. It is such a natural idea, that Azium's lute. I remember in my convent I had a young friend with whom I used to make many plans of happiness and who in return confided hers to me. When we parted, she said, 'Go, but when you hear my favourite little romance, think of me.' She is in Italy now with her husband, who is not very kind. She does not write now, perhaps she has forgotten me. 'Mais si vous saviez combien ce "pensez à moi" me *pèse* au cœur.'[1]

"Oh sing it, sing it, Baroness," said the circle by the piano, "*do* sing it." And after some little hesitation, the request was complied with. After it was ended and while every one stood murmuring their applause, Madame de Valcone, shaking back at the same moment her thick curls and her tears, said, –

"Mais a quoi bon les soufirs?[2] We should always try to be gay." And the sunbeam lit her countenance accordingly. No one would have believed five minutes afterwards that she had ever shed tears in her life. Alixe looked up and saw Everard's dark eyes fixed full upon Madame de Valcone, as if endeavouring to read her real sentiments. Alixe sighed. Everard, startled, turned round. For a moment, their eyes met. He rose and seated himself by her.

"You are sad," said he.

"Oh no, indeed. I think, like the Baroness, one should always try to be gay."

"Now I think forced gaiety an odious thing. It is either done for effect, or the woman must be a great hypocrite if she does it so well that no one can make out the difference."

"But a woman would be tiresome and insupportable to other people, who was constantly parading her griefs. And there is one other reason," nodded she after a pause. "In the world there are so few people who really sympathise with you or care about you, that the pride or delicacy or what you choose to give the feeling, would prevent you making all marked for confidence to strangers. And those who are really interested about you will easily read beneath the veil."

"Perhaps," said Everard. "And after all there is a great pleasure in knowing that you are the only person that can read the thoughts of another. And *that* other is willing you and you only, should read them."

At this moment, Dunstan entered the room. His eyes were more than usually expressive of bad feelings and he was unaccountably ill-tempered, even to Everard Price.

"I really wish," said the latter, laughing, "that someone would read Harry Dunstan, for his face baffles me."

"I think any one can understand the expression. He is angry and perhaps disconcerted, but what has displeased him *does* puzzle me."

"Oh I don't think he is displeased. He is perhaps anxious. You know on Thursday our electioneering business begins. His uncle, General Montgomery and Sir Samuel Repringer give him all their interest. And their power is, I believe, nearly equal to Lord Sunderland's. Perhaps poor fellow, he dislikes too, that I should be his opponent. For it must be a great object to him, from many causes, to succeed and it is disagreeable to have your friend for a rival."

Alixe did not give him credit for any such feeling, but she made no answer. Everard rose and tapping Dunstan on his shoulder, as he stood gloomy and silent by the marble chimneypiece, said with a smile, –

"You are reflecting, I suppose, on the business of Thursday. I am sorry, I cannot wish you success without being a hypocrite."

"Lord Sunderland has made reflection unnecessary on your part, I apprehend," said Dunstan, endeavouring to return the smile. And he walked forward and seated himself by Emily Price, who was talking to Charles St Clair with great interest.

"Now do, Captain Dunstan, endeavour to convince Mr St Clair. He persists in saying 'that education for the lower classes is not only useless but pernicious.'"

"I think," said Dunstan carelessly, "it only teaches maidservants to write love letters and apprentices to forge drafts."

"I do not generalize quite so much as Captain Dunstan," said Charles gently, "but I think that in general it does more harm than good. If on the one hand, heaven has given talents to the objects of charity schools, there are few instances in which they are not prevented. What they do learn merely raises them above the sphere which nature intended for them to occupy. On the other hand, if they are as heavy as the clods of the earth, they are destined to plough the smattering of everything, which they obtain by an attendance at these large schools, almost to nothing, and which only makes them discontented. I speak, Miss Price, of *public* charity schools, where the supporters satisfied with paying their own subscriptions and obtaining others, perhaps, think it unnecessary to visit in person the institutions to which they have contributed. Private schools, where, as at Hunsden" (added he, smiling at Emily), "an amiable woman consecrates herself to the improvement and instruction of her fellow creatures, are another consideration. And I do firmly believe that more good has been done where the first principles of truth and graciousness have been taught together by the meek and holy voice of a pious woman, than by half the missionaries to India, even where for a time the effects have been deadened by bad habits or natural depravity. The bread cast upon the waters is found again after many days. And on the sick or dying bed of the thief or blasphemer, the sound of those calm pure tones, the nightly prayer breathed for him and the supplication in which he used to join, will haunt his soul and wake to remorse a heart long seared by perseverance in crime. I was once an eye-witness of a similar scene. The poor man to whom I was reading gave a deep groan. I thought it was bodily pain and stopped. 'Read on!' said he. 'It does me good. It puts me in mind of the time when I and my brother held one bible between us in one class at the charity school where Miss L. taught.'"

Charles had spoken rapidly and earnestly. Captain Dunstan gazed on him with unfeigned surprise and turned to Emily with a disapproving and incredulous smile. But Emily's soft eyes were fixed on the inspired face of the young speaker and the colour had mounted into her pale cheek. Charles, who had been looking at his fairy and probably thinking of her during the concluding sentences, turned and met the gaze of his companion. At that moment he thought her beautiful. It was the beauty of soul on her features. Dunstan, who was not accustomed to consider himself as a secondary object, rose, and, whistling an air, walked away.

"I was wrong," said Emily to her companion. "I thought you condemned charity schools in general, but I understand you now." And Charles felt gratified at being understood by a person who had known him so little. Emily Price was the only London girl whom he had been introduced to, whose conversation suited him. She was unaffected and he loathed affectation. She was dotingly fond of Alixe and hers was the sort of affection you feel and know to be unwavering, even while untried. She had the same tastes, liked the same passages in the same books, as he did. And above all, she was, he knew her to be, unhappy. Naturally serious and bitterly dispirited, Charles eagerly sought the society of the only person who came next in his imagination to Alixe, uncaught by the wiles of practised coquettes, undazzled by the beauty round him and unspoilt by the admiration and flattery of marrying mothers and daughters, who had taken it into their heads that, because Alixe was an heiress, Charles St Clair must be a match. He clung to the pure and warm affection for his adopted sister and, for her sake, to the society of her friend. Emily on her side was happy with Charles St Clair. He was totally unlike the men around him. She liked him because his presence and conversation made her forget the artificial world in which she breathed. It is easy to fill a young heart with gaieties even when trifling and vain. For happy within itself, it casts brightness on the most trivial objects. But to a heart that has tasted of sorrow, the allurements of the world have no charm. Or if for a moment the emptiness of our soul is filled with their images, it is but to turn away with a renewed feeling of disgust. Charles denied that he was thinking of Emily when he wrote the following lines, which Alixe (after assuring him that she did not believe one word that he said) set to music and sang the night before Everard took his departure to the contested borough.

A weary and a wounded bird
Returning to her distant nest –
Her wailing cry I faintly heard.
The hunter's shaft was in her breast.
"Sweet bird," said I, "why moanest thou?
The noonday sun is smiling bright;
Thy nest is hanging on the bough –
Where thou mayst shelter thee at night."

"The noonday sun is shining on
But my soft nest is desolation –
The eyes that were my day are gone
The shaft hath struck my gentle mate."
"Sweet bird," said I, "new suns will rise
As bright as that which now we see –
And then mayst find in other eyes
Soft beams to light thee lovingly." –

"No other sun – no other sun –
Can be like that for ever set:
Bright they may be, but oh! will *one*
Behold us meet as once we met?
His joy was all my joy – I roam
In sadness through the glad blue sky
I will but reach my distant home
And fold my weary wings and die!"

A sigh was the tribute paid to the verses of the young sailor and the music of his adopted sister – but it was a *real* sigh and both Charles and Alixe were contented.[3]

End of 1st Volume

Volume II[1]

Chapter 15

The election came on. Alixe listened with intense interest to the accounts Emily received of her brother's success. The first day, the odds were greatly in favour of Everard. The second day, Alixe made [herself] sure he would be returned. Judge then of the sorrowful surprise with which the news was received of his failure. Harry Dunstan was member for M___! What dull senseless people the inhabitants of that borough must be. Everard returned fagged and out of spirits. His pride was mortified and the great aim of his life baffled, just within view of success.

"And that old foolish Lord Sunderland was so positive of his influence," said the disappointed candidate peevishly, as he threw himself into the chair Emily wheeled round for him.

"And the fools on whose votes I depended, gaped and hurraed and drank and fought and looked at their own cockades, till I am sure they did not know Dunstan and me apart. And there again," continued he, growing more wrathful at the recollection, as a soldier's blood warms during the recital of his past campaigns, "*there* I was to be fooled and insulted. I held out my hand to Dunstan when I met him, and drew back with air of an injured hero and said, 'Now, you have already told me you cannot wish me success and we do not meet *here* as friends, we that have been friends ever since we were boys at College and wrote themes to the tune of Damon and Pythias!' Oh it was shabby, confoundedly shabby. So I left him in a very ill humour, for then he did not seem to have a chance of success."

"Yes, the tide of fortune does seem to have changed even more quickly than usual," said Emily.

"Quickly enough. For on Friday evening, he had about 120 votes and [by] Saturday he had upwards of three hundred and forty. And then I had to make my appearance before Lord Sunderland, to thank him for his support, to regret that support had not been more efficacious, which of course I could not often attribute to his lordship's want of zeal or influence etc, etc. And his Lordship was kind enough to tell me that, with all my talents (his Lordship's expression), I knew nothing about elections, that my speech to the mob would have done capitally in a novel or among patriots on the stage, that he thought the character of William Tell would suit me quite as well as Macready.[1] But that a *real* mob was a different thing entirely and a patriot on the hustings, not of the same species with a poetical one. At last, he put me entirely out of patience by telling me I should have promised as fair as Dunstan did. In vain I argued that I had promised all my conscience would allow, and that I had understood my sentiments to agree exactly with his lordship's. His only answer was, –

'Pho, pho, my good friend. A drunken mob have no idea of conscience, and those who are sober enough to understand half what you say, give you credit for the quarter of it being sincere. You know there have been members for M____ before you were born. And how many do you think *did*, or were *able* to do – half that they promised? Dunstan promised them every thing. Therefore, if by the same comparative rule he performs one half, the borough of M____ will be better off than it has been for several scores of years. Goodbye, I am very sorry you have lost your election, for your own sake as well as for mine. But please Heaven, I will see to it yet. And remember another time my young friend, when you are addressing an English mob, to give them five words, not five *sentiments*. And to rail at Sheil and O'Connell[2] instead of giving your feelings upon governments in general and English government in particular.'

I took my leave, excessively disgusted with elections. Voters (more particularly those of M –) and old Earls, who fancy themselves able to bring young men into parliament by a nod of the head, or wave of the hand, to an obstinate coarse savage illiterate set of –"

"Hush hush, my dear Everard," said Emily, laughing and putting her small soft hand on his mouth. "I cannot let you rail any more against poor Lord Sunderland, who depend upon it, is just as disappointed and ten times as angry as you can be. I wonder tho' what he meant by saying he would see to it yet. Has he interest in another borough?"

"I am sure I do not know. And if he has no more than in the borough of M____, I do not particularly care. But let us leave off disagreeable subjects and think of pleasant ones. Where is the pretty, wild Baroness? And how is my little Alixe?"

"You should not put the pretty Baroness *first*, Everard, unless you prefer her," said Emily, with a gentle smile. Then, changing the expression of her countenance to one of anxious tenderness and laying her hand on his arm, she said, –

"Ah Everard, you do not know how unhappy it makes me, to see you growing so fond of a woman, who even were you free to choose and she to accept, is not half so worthy of your homage as the poor thing you have sworn affection to."

"My dear foolish Emily," said Everard, rather impatiently. "Here you have wandered from one disagreeable subject to another. What harm can it do, my admiring Madame de Valcone? And what man of your acquaintance is there who does not admire her? I cannot see why you should be at all unhappy about it."

"My own darling, it is only the fear that may make you unhappy at some future time, and poor little Alixe too. You are a man Everard, and men are unable to see beyond a woman's preference for them. The thousand little shades of feeling, the little anxieties of love, they cannot see. Satisfied with their conquest, they sit blindly down in contented forgetfulness; and many a man has accused a woman of fickleness, who perhaps after a long and bitter struggle, between her affection for him and the growing conviction that his disposition is too wavering to afford her any prospect of happiness, has turned with affected coldness and real anguish to the solitude of her own heart again. I have watched Alixe and seen her sad fixed gaze, when you have been laughing and flirting with Madame de Valcone. I have marked sighs that have been lost in the mutual laugh of yourself and a gay companion. And Everard, believe me, I am woman enough to see that it is not mere jealousy that actuates Alixe. She has too much *character*, I am convinced, to feel vexed only because you transfer your attentions from her to another woman. No, it is as a fault in you, that she deplores it. It is because she believes it equally against your happiness and renown. You think only of the present, a woman who loves instinctively links the present with the future. Would you spoil her bright dream of life? Would you teach her to distrust you before you are united till Death. Surely *les prémices*[3] of so innocent and warm a heart cannot be indifferent to you? Surely you would not wish to make her unhappy?"

"No, my dear grave Emily, nor you either, but I suppose even Alixe does not think me bound to be always at her side. I cannot be married to her just yet and I would not have her grow tired of me beforehand."

Emily shook her head with a mournful smile.

"Well good night," continued he, "for fear we should quarrel. And believe me that the Baroness with all her charms, natural and acquired, is in my eyes to Alixe, what the leaf is to the flower. Both are beautiful of their kind, but it is the flower that we prefer and that will do without a contrast to give it resplendency. Kiss me like a good girl, for my last sentence is very poetical and I will go to bed and not allow the Baroness to enter even into my dreams."

How far Everard performed his promise can never be known, as he gave no account of his visions at breakfast the next morning. But after he had heard Miss Herbert harangue for an hour on what she called "his Misfortune" he went to Lady St Clair's and from thence his truant steps wandered to Park Lane, where the beautiful Baroness resided. He was shown as usual into the boudoir, which was richly hung with pink and white muslin. The tables were loaded with pretty trifles. A guittar with a long blue ribband lay on a low ottoman by the window thro' which floated the heavy perfume of heliotrope and jasmin and others of her favourite flowers. As Everard made a momentary pause at the door, he saw the Baroness sitting at a low table. Her round arms were crossed and her head with all its velvet curls leant on them. For a moment, there flashed across Everard's mind his interview with Alixe at his mother's house. Alixe, his betrothed! But he chased away the comparison. As he entered, Madame de Valcone raised her head. The big bright tears were standing in her eyes. She rose with a languid smile and said, –

"Oh, is it you? I thought it was the Baron. I am rejoiced to see you." But the tone that lingered on the word did not agree with it. Everard was touched.

"You have been reading," said he gently. And he took up the book that was lying on the table. It was a small copy of Camoëns' Poems.[4] Her tears still wetted the page. Everard observed that several of the passages were marked. He was reading one of these when Madame de Valcone, rising, drew the volume from his hands.

"Do not," said she, without lifting her eyes. "I cannot bear to see that book in the hands of another, far less in yours. Ah si vous saviez combien il n'est chic."[5] And she sighed. Nothing is more infectious than the sigh of a pretty woman. Everard sighed too. The Baroness took the Camoëns and locked it in a worktable drawer. And she returned to the seat on the sofa, by her companion.

"I am jealous, Baroness," said Everard, half smiling.

"Jealous! Mon Dieu, of what?"

"Of the person who gave you that Camoëns."

"Ah mon pauvre petit Camoëns! You need not think of the person who gave it to me, for he is gone, gone from this world for ever!"

"But you love him still?"

"No, je le *regrette*. Il a emporté avec lui, ce beau songe de la vie qui ne vient qu'une seul fois: le songe d'un bonheur parfait sur la terre."[6]

"Is it possible," said Everard tenderly, "that one so bright and apparently so happy can weep in her solitary hours, hours *so* solitary, that you have not even a friend to weep with you."

At this mention of friendship by a handsome young man, the Baroness mournfully raised her eyes, –

"Where," said she, "do you think Honorine should find friends? In the world? No, I glitter there as a happy beauty at home and here –". Madame de Valcone shook her head with a melancholy smile. "No, at home, I cannot. I did once hope, but I have been disappointed, really disappointed," and she leant her pale cheek on her hand with the deepest despondency.

"How beautiful she is," thought Everard, "and how little they all think who admire and laugh with her how unhappy she is."

"Beautiful Honorine," exclaimed he. "I am not to you surely, the same as the vain multitude whose love of an hour is no more to be depended upon than their smiles. It is impossible to see and know you without admiring, without being interested about you. I love another. I have avowed that affection to you. But if you will permit me to be your friend? If you will allow me the satisfaction of thinking that I can prevent or at least alleviate your sadder moments, believe me, the privilege will be almost as dear as that one love of my heart."

The Baroness wept without speaking for some minutes and then extending her hand, she said, "Oui j'ai besoin de consolation, oui vous serez mon ami."[7] Everard could do no less than kiss the hand that proffered, tho' he had some pangs of remorse during the performance of this piece of gallantry.

"I will hide nothing from you," continued the Baroness. "I had once a friend dearer than anything ever can again be to me. Pauline D'Olbach, the companion of whom I was speaking the other day, had a brother who used frequently to come and see her. Le Comte D'Olbach was gay, young and handsome, and to me appeared perfect. Pauline raved of him. Every thing that was noble and generous she attributed to him, till I felt that I loved him more as the personification of some hero in a fable, than from what I myself knew of him. In the anxious simple kindness of her young heart, Pauline often expressed to me her ardent wish that I should be united to her brother and that a friend of his would obtain her hand. Le Comte D'Olbach frequently told me it was his determination to ask me in marriage of my father as soon as I was out of the convent. It was he who gave me that Camoëns. It was he who marked those passages, who used to read them in this low soft voice when we were alone. It was he who saw me married to another without one effort to save me, tho' he knew I depended on him! I saw him afterwards, once, and he addressed me with the same soft voice. The same gaiety was in his eye, his very laugh was so much the same that for one instant a dark dream seemed to dissipate, and I thought we were again lovers. It was but a moment. I never saw him more. We parted in coldness and long afterwards I saw his name in the paper amongst the list of killed at Waterloo. Il etait perfide – mais je l'ai perdu – et la mort qui grave si profondement sur le coeur, les charmes et les vertus de son victim[e], efface les erreurs."[8]

"And Pauline?" said Everard, after a pause.

"Pauline? She too, has woke from her dream. She was not allowed to accept Eugéne de Villemort. Her hand was disposed of, in that dreadful *foreign* way, to a Monsieur de Calzean, a man possessed of enormous riches and nothing besides. I have her picture, she was very beautiful and resembled her brother. So much that her portrait was once finished for him."

Everard looked at the picture which was presented to his notice. It was a half-length miniature of a tall, very dark and very lovely person, with a rich Italian skin and hair braided round her head in one long plait of the richest black.

"And now, adieu dear Baroness," said Everard, as he rose to take his leave.

"Adieu, remember I am always at home to you." And Everard vainly imagined that the invitation was given and received in the purest spirit of friendship.

He walked home and stopped mechanically at his own door, his head full of the blue lake of Geneva and the different buildings on its shores. It was natural he should think of it, for it is a most beautiful spot, one of those I am fondest of, of all I have visited. But it was a pity that his mind dwelt so exclusively on the beautiful villa where Madame de Valcone used to receive and entertain him. Alixe still shone forth as a star upon his path, whose pure quiet light was to guide him to happiness, and he would not then have relinquished his hope of her hand for all the beauty that blest Europe. But the Baroness bewildered, intoxicated, him. She pleased his eye and worked upon his feelings. He determined to marry Alixe, but he thought only of the Baroness. Nevertheless, we may not blame him since all this was done, not in Love, but in *Friendship*.

Chapter 16

"Here is a pretty affair, Emily," said Everard, after reading with bent brows those long pages of a letter closely and rather illegibly written, and he handed her the epistle in question. After spending some time and trouble in decyphering it, Emily collected that Lord Sunderland, the writer, had proved satisfactorily to himself and, as he hoped, equally satisfactorily to other people, that Dunstan's election had been carried entirely by bribery. And he had written to express his determination to Everard of petitioning his rival out of the house, as soon as he should take his seat.

"Well Emmy?" said Everard, who had been watching her countenance.

"Well love, I think if he has obtained his election by unfair means, he certainly ought not to sit. And I am glad Lord Sunderland has taken decided steps about it. For if Dunstan has wronged and injured you in so base a way, he is no longer worthy of the name of friend."

Everard sighed, but he answered: –

"Why Emmy, it is done at all elections almost, and I am afraid it was more my affection for Harry Dunstan than my horror of bribery, that made me so conscientious at the election of M____. I felt I could not bear to take an unfair advantage of him."

"And he has abused your generosity," said Emily warmly. "Everard, he is not fit for a friend. He is dangerous, even as a companion. For if, the moment his interest clashes with yours, he is willing to betray you, what dependence can you place on such a man? Oh, shame upon him! Who could pretend to feel injured, when he knew that he was winning the victory by the Devil's own weapon of Subtlety? But he will fall, he must fall, and I shall see you, dear Everard, where your talents ought to place you."

Emily's prophecy was realized. Lord Sunderland gained his point and Everard took his place in the House of Commons as member for M –. And did Harry Dunstan take his disappointment calmly? No, he vowed vengeance, deep unremitting, untried, unsatiated vengeance on the head of his rival friend. But the oath was inaudible, save to Heaven and Hell. And the smile with which he had greeted his victim was the same cold bright smile which he had worn for years before, the smile which had dazzled Prinny Dure, the smile which had deceived Colin Campbell. Perhaps, had the present object of his hatred been poor and helpless, the tiger heart would have disdained to wear a mask, and have trampled its victim at once into the dust. But Everard was still useful to Harry Dunstan. When the former, half reprovingly, half playfully, hinted that his friend's resources were chiefly the result of his success at cards, particularly at Hunsden, he was nearer the truth even than he guessed. Dunstan had so totally ruined himself that he actually had not a farthing he could count upon, from one year's end to another, of real income. The turf, the gaming table and dice box, which had been his favourite amusement, now became the resources to which he looked for his daily bread. That a man with such very uncertain means of living should endeavour to stamp certainty on one at least of these means, was at any rate natural. And Dunstan's success at cards was proverbial. So much so indeed, that several of his nominal friends were exceedingly shy of playing with him. Everard Price was a rich man, fond of cards, quickly excited, and an easy dupe as far as regarded suspicion of unfair dealing. For he would as soon have expected to have been stabbed in one of the clubs, as to be cheated by a gentleman and that gentleman his professed friend. Dunstan felt bitterly the loss of all the advantages he had struggled and plotted for. He had become so embarrassed that a seat in parliament held, in its power of securing his person against his creditors, a charm as powerful for *him*, as the ambition of distinguishing himself did for Everard. To win the hand of Emily Price the heiress, to make his friend the constant spring from whence he was to draw resources, till that desired marriage was obtained, and finally to wreak a little vengeance on Everard, yes, even on Emily and the innocent Alixe, these were the demon hopes that filled his mind. Alas! as he stood firm in his treachery, with a soft salutation to each, and an expression of regret from those perfidious lips for having availed himself of a custom he did not doubt Everard, too, had yielded to, why could no guardian angel whisper in their ear –

"He is a serpent! Throw him from your bosoms!" But no such voice was permitted as a warning. The frank way in which he half blamed, half defended himself, the cheerful sweet-tempered manner with which he bore his disappointment, softened the hearts of his young friends, who in the plenitude of their own happiness, were ready to share it with another, even tho' faulty in their eyes. There was but one in the whole party who could not look on Dunstan with an unprejudiced eye. From what Charles heard from Alixe, he was prepared to dislike his acquaintance before they met. And all that he heard of him since, joined to the false manner and cold eye which distinguished Captain Dunstan, only seemed to increase his aversion for his character. Two greater contrasts were certainly never thrown together. Charles St

Clair was so natural, so noble in his ways of thinking, so warm and cordial in his manner, so sincere and generous in the expression of every feeling of the heart. His soul glowed so at the thought of any mean and unjust action, that his contempt and dislike for Dunstan's character was only equalled by his wonder that such things should be on the earth, and all the inhabitants of it not rise up against them.

Joined to his dislike of Dunstan, Charles had another source of discomfort in the conduct of Everard Price towards the Baroness. For a moment, a little moment perhaps, when he first thought of the apparent inconstancy of the former, a gleam of hope for himself sprung and lighted on his path. But the selfishness of human nature fled when he caught his Fairy's eye dimmed by a half-seen tear or the sad expression of her countenance, as she watched the unconscious Everard and Madame de Valcone. If Charles expressed a fear or doubt on the subject, Alixe repelled it gently but firmly.

"He cannot marry me yet," she would say. "And I cannot expect that my society should be the only one pleasant to him. I must expect after I am married that he will have friends and companions besides myself, and I hope I shall always be able to love all he loves." Thus, would she reason. But Charles saw that she suffered and often he would heave a sigh, a heavy sigh to the memory of what might have been. Often did he yearn for his home and Alixe out of the tiresome bustle of the world, or for the employments and dangers of the ocean, where on his lonely watch, however painful his conjectures might be, they could not be more painful than the reality. It was one of those sighs, perhaps, that drew Emily Price's attention, as they were sitting side by side at some magnificent ball. She looked round. Charles's eyes were wandering after Alixe.

"How fond you are of Alixe!" said Emily, with a gentle smile. "But I do not wonder at it. Being always with her and constantly seeing all her perfections, must make one adore such a sister!"

"She is not my sister, Miss Price," said Charles, in a tone that ill corresponded with the gaiety of the scene around them. "But you say true, one cannot live in the house with her and see her constantly without adoring her." "I beg your pardon," added he, as he rose. "Let me lead you to the supper room, this is grown hot."

The pale cheek of his companion had flushed a deep rose, and her arm as she took his, but Charles St Clair saw nothing round him. He offered his arm mechanically and they followed others of the crowd to supper. Emily Price saw in a moment thro' all the concealed feelings of his companion. In a moment the real state of the case flashed across her mind. She felt that Charles was Everard's rival in his affection for Alixe, tho' it was evident that the beautiful orphan preferred the accomplished man of the world to her adopted brother. She knew not whether she was glad or sorry, as she gazed almost unconsciously on her partner, who was listlessly leaning over the supper table after his first offer of helping her to something. It certainly was a triumph for Everard and proved how deep the love must be, which could resist in his favour, the influence which Charles's mind[1] might be supposed to hold over his adopted sister's mind. But then it was surely a pity that one so interesting, so worthy to be loved, should be thus disappointed, and his dearest hopes blighted in the very springtime of life. And Emily sighed again. Charles might have been gratified had he known he was the subject of so much melancholy musing, but he did not even hear the sigh. He was busied carefully examining the structure of some vegetable flowers which decorated a dish before him.

"How pretty that is," said he at length, breaking silence and striking with a knife a white rose made of turnip.

"Very," said Emily, who did not even see what he was pointing at. At this moment, Alixe entered the room, leaning on Everard. She seemed in high spirits and, giving a glad smile to Emily, made her way to the end of the table where she stood.

"I certainly am the most patient of mortals," said she gaily. "Would you believe it, Emily, we have been stopped seven times in our passage from the dancing room to this, merely that your brother might receive the congratulations of soi-distant[2] friends on his seat in parliament. And I never even frowned or testified the least intention of letting go his arm and coming on alone!"

"Wonderful indeed," said Emily. "You will need refreshment after such a journey. Everard, why do you not think of offering your partner something?" Her brother turned round and did as he was bid, in spite of the vicinity of the beautiful Baroness, who was playing with a saucer of strawberry ice and looking pale and disconsolate. Alixe looked up with her arch laughing eyes.

"I really believe you are thinking of something or somebody else, you are grown so grave all of a sudden. It will be my turn to offer you something, what will you take?"

Everard was beginning some smiling answer, when a sigh, so deep and distinct that half the party turned their heads round, startled him. Alixe looked. It certainly was the Baroness. She looked ill and unhappy. Our heroine thought of moving towards her and trying to raise her spirits. But Everard was before her. He turned away and the instant afterwards was standing by his foreign friend, bending with an air of deep interest to hear one of her languid sentences. Charles and his adopted sister returned with Emily to the dancing room.

"Alixe," said the latter, "should you not like to see poor Pamela Ainslie? She is better now and expressed a wish for your visit this morning."

"Yes indeed, I have thought of it often, but I did not think she saw people."

"She saw very few, but Annette is come to town and she thinks it will do her good to see her friends and you know you were always a great favourite."

"I will go certainly, poor thing." And Alixe went accordingly. She was shown into the darkened room where her unhappy friend lay. They had shaved all her beautiful dark hair from an apprehension that the brain would be affected. She was grown thin and altered and was scarcely recognizable even by those who had known her best. She raised herself on her sofa and flinging her arms round her visitor's neck, she wept long and bitterly. Alixe wept with her. The door softly opened and Annette Darlies made her appearance. She kissed her sister on the forehead and begged she would not agitate herself and bring on a relapse of the fever. And then sitting down, she conversed fluently with Alixe on the topics of the day, ending by asking her if she was going to Lady Linton's that evening.

"I am asked," said she gravely, half wondering that Lady Darlies could talk of gaieties while Pamela was there.

"Asked! Oh then, of course you mean to go. It is to be the most beautiful thing, illuminated gardens and fireworks and all that is splendid. I would not miss it for the world."

"Are *you* going?" said our heroine, with unfeigned surprise.

"Certainly, why not?"

"Is it tonight, Annette?" said her sister languidly.

"Yes love, but I shall not go till long after you are in bed and asleep, I hope?"

"Oh, I would not have you stay away for me for the world. I was only thinking it was a pity it was not some other day, as Mamma has never been in bed these three nights. And I thought perhaps you would take her place. But I am getting a foolish habit, wanting someone to watch by me. And I would try to do without, but that when I wake and hear thro' the dreary stillness of the house the ticking of the clock and the heavy breathing of the nurse, I get such nervous horrible thoughts!"

"My dear love, there is no need of your trying to do without, for I am quite sure Mamma would watch there equally, whether I was there or not. And tomorrow, I shall try and persuade her to leave me alone with you, tho' I fear she will not."

So saying, Annette rose and, kissing Pamela with the information that she was going out to pay a few calls, she left the apartment. Soon after, Alixe also rose.

"Oh, do not go yet!" said the invalid eagerly. "I am so wretched, the moment I am alone, and Mamma is lying down just now. Do stay a quarter of an hour longer." And our heroine remained patiently while the bright day went down and the weary half-hour past, trying to amuse and interest the wretched nervous being who, even amid her thankfulness, showed so much sadness and listlessness that it was discouraging to those who were endeavouring to give back to her mind the little energy it once possessed. At length, the door opened.

"Oh, here is Darlies, kind Darlies," said Pamela with more animation that she had yet shown. "He will stay with me till Mamma comes." Alixe rose to depart.

"Annette," said Lord Darlies, "it is not. Lady Darlies, it is not. Alixe St Clair,[3] I beg your pardon," said he, in a tone of deep disappointment. "I thought to have found Annette with her sister." Then addressing himself affectionately to the beautiful sufferer, he sat down by her and our heroine returned home, wondering at the selfish coldness of that heart which could seek for pleasure at the expense of the comforts of those who have the strongest claims upon our tenderness and attention.

The scene at Lady Linton's was truly splendid. The green lamps hung among the trees like fairy lights and the winding walks were filled with the young and gay and beautiful. Alixe was perfectly happy, leaning on Everard's arm, who was in one of his kindest gayest moods, she walked up and down the shaded promenade, enjoying the warm still night and thinking, in the fulness of her joy, even the murmur of voices around her sweet and harmonious. The mingling of music and laughter, the beauty of the illuminated gardens, nothing escaped her. Love breathed the witchery of its spirit over all. And there existed not in the wide bright world, the being to whom she could have said "I envy you!" But all her happiness would not prevent her feeling tired and after having replied three times in the negative to her companion's anxious enquiries, she suffered herself to be led back to her mother. She sat down under the trellis doorway, among jasmin and roses. Everard stood by them for a little while, but his friend Henry Dunstan came up and after conversing gaily and fluently with Alixe for some minutes, he requested her companion to step aside as he wanted to speak to him. They walked away together and Alixe's attention was successfully occupied by her different beaux for about an hour afterwards. She was left alone for a short time and amused herself by watching the different parties as they moved on in the gleaming light beyond the steps of the house where she sat: mothers who were watching, as the spider watches its prey, self-entangled in the mesh spun for its destruction, some young unconscious heir, who saw nothing round or beside him but the blue eyes and long curls of the would-be wife, who from time to time took "sweet counsel" by the eyes from her parent as to her next step; girls who were endeavouring to delay the departure of their only beau, who walking with three females in a string, all waiting and watching for his least word and laughing loud and long at his least joke, was ungrateful enough to be keeping his eye fixed on some particular party before them, whom he meditated joining on the first opportunity; others, who paraded in pairs with the lovers, whose escape was now impossible, whose intentions had been torn from their heads or hearts when but half matured, who had proposed they hardly knew what, on account of the alarm inspired by the aunt or mother they hardly knew how, and who felt and looked discontented they knew not why. Other unfortunates again, being in the habit of flirting with younger brothers and *useless* men, or being under the care of some severe and uninterested chaperon, or worse, one who had still pretensions to please, walked sad and solitary by their sides with a forced smile at their brilliant jests, and pretended humility during the speech.

"How impossible it is to please you. You are never contented. I have walked up and down here all night for your satisfaction and you look as if you were in an iron collar, taking a lesson in drawing. If you are so tired, I am sure we had better return." And weary and disappointed, the passive victims get into the carriage, give one long sigh to the contrast between their expectations and the reality, and hope that the next time they will be more fortunate.

Alixe watched the different groups and amused herself by conjectures as to the feelings and destiny of those she did not know. She was just wondering who a very tall grave fair young man could be, who past alone and apparently unoccupied, when she was startled by hearing her own name pronounced in an ironical tone. She could catch but a few words of what Lady Darlies (for she it was) was saying, but those few were not pleasant. Annette was leaning on Everard's arm, as Alixe saw when they passed under the illuminated porch. She was talking eagerly and almost angrily.

"It is quite as well to deny it, for no one could believe you. Such a simpleton as to trust of marrying her. It was very well to flirt a little when she first came out. A new beauty is fair game; but to marry!" Alixe heard a few more words, but indistinctly. Lady Darlies seemed to accuse him of tameness about Madame de Valcone and to insinuate that Everard's fortune must be of greater consequence than his heart, since she bore his error so patiently. It was but a moment. They past on.

"What unprovoked wickedness," thought our heroine. "She is married to a man she sought eagerly and won easily. She has everything this world can give. Why does she wish to make me unhappy? And Everard too? And Madame de Valcone? A year ago I should have thought it impossible! And *now*, how will it end, and what can I do but be patient, as *I* am, as I have been blamed for appearing."

Charles interrupted her thoughts. He had just discovered an old schoolfellow in young Lord Linton, whom he presented and who was the identical pale melancholy-looking man Alixe had remarked. But she scarcely saw him and answered at random. Charles saw something was the matter and he asked if she was tired and wished to go home? She answered in the affirmative and the carriage was called. Lady St Clair and her young companion got into it and for some time all were silent. Charles broke the silence. His mother, wearied by the extreme lateness of the hour, had fallen asleep.

"Alixe," said he gently. "What has happened to fret you? The beginning of the evening you seemed so happy and I was telling your friend Emily I thought you were never more gay." It was too true. Alixe remembered how happy, how very happy, she had been the former part of the evening and how needlessly and cruelly that happiness had been crushed. She sobbed aloud.

"Alixe! my own Alixe!" exclaimed her agonized brother and the remembrance of that day at the cottage, the last day she had leant that beautiful head in the confidence of sisterly affection on his arm, rushed over his mind and for a moment empowered him. His first impulse was to fold her to his bosom to conjure her, with the energy of a devoted heart, to leave "the world," and Everard, whose inconstancy he doubted not, was the subject of her grief – and to trust to *him*, who loved her beyond all that earth contained, to console her, to make her happy. But he checked himself. He was to be only her friend, her brother. The tears shed in his arms flowed for another. The grief for which she silently bespoke his sympathy arose from a cause unconnected with him. He heard all she had to tell composedly and answered with what he could of comfort, tho' he inwardly despised and cursed Everard's wavering, unsettled disposition. He told her that, –

"What Lady Darlies had chosen to say could not affect her lover, unless indeed he was weak enough to let ridicule outbalance his affection for her." She had not heard Everard's answer. It might be silent contempt, it might be proud and indignant reproof. And Alixe felt comforted, and drying her tears slumbered on that kind and friendly arm till their carriage stopped and Charles withdrew his eyes from the blue sky, which was brightening into daylight, with a heavy sigh and assisted his no-sister into the house.

Chapter 17

As our reader may perhaps like to know the substance of Dunstan's conversation with his friend Everard, we subjoin a letter from the latter containing apparently the substance of what had been started the night before:

My dear Dunstan,
    I enclose the loan you requested, tho' I assure you I can but ill spare it. I am afraid I shall soon be like the feverish patients who are bled till they can bleed no more. But were it the last drop in my veins, you are still welcome to call upon me for it. As to the other points you touched upon, for which the scene of yesterday was much too public a place, I wish I could answer them as readily. I do not think Emmy, poor girl, is in love with young St Clair and I am quite certain he is not in love with her. At the same time, my dear fellow, I must confess I see no chance for *you* there, that you wrong me if you persist in thinking I serve you feebly or privately assassinate your character. On the contrary, I do not think I ever allowed you in her presence to possess a single demerit. Nor do I believe you possess one that time and a good wife would not cure, particularly as you say your Uncle George is in such bad health, as his death would take away half your temptations to evil. On the whole, I advise you not to part with Chlöe, as you are pleased to call Peggy Tell. You say you are certain Madame de Valcone is in love with me. I thank you for your very flattering opinion of my irresistible qualities, but I must doubt the fact and even if it were so, all-charming as she is, beautiful in her lonely sorrow as she rises now before me, do you think me at once so mad, so base, as to relinquish Alixe for the hopes of what? Of gaining the heart, in other words of ruining, a beautiful being who had confided in me, from whose husband I have received nothing but kindness. No, I confess at times I am bewildered, intoxicated. I confess it to you my friend, tho' till you spoke I would hardly have owned it to my own soul, I would fly till I was freed from the strange infatuation. But you know as well as I, that to go abroad, which would naturally be my wish, would destroy all my hopes of settling my affairs, which I hope to be able to do in a year. I, that used to dread marriage, now actually (independent of my

love for Alixe) long for the time when my rebel heart will be fettered beyond the possibility of changing – Lady Darlies too, but I defy the imputation. I will meet the danger (if there is any) of Madame de Valcone's eyes and words, and come off victorious.

Yrs ever
E.A.P.
To Captain Dunstan, Miller's Hotel

Captain Dunstan took out the enclosed loan, carefully deposited it in his pocket book and having read his friend's letter from beginning to end, he sank back in his chair and laughed, the low triumphant laugh of a successful demon.

"Yes, struggle, flutter in the net, but if you break the meshes, poor bird, you will be stronger than I believe you. And the poetical description of the feelings that exist for these two angelic woman, one a finished coquette in the midst of the tenth 'grande passion,' and the other a mere simpleton, who has become so enamoured of the ideal Everard, that his faults really have ceased to be faults in her eyes. And I verily believe, if he had a mistress and refused to part with her when he married, she would clothe the action with the glorious name of Constancy. Oh, my orator and patriot! My hero in public and private! Your hour is come. Look to it." And Harry Dunstan rose to book some Doncaster bets, which was one of his resources.

Meanwhile, our little heroine was sitting quietly in the drawing room at home, musing (but no longer painfully) on the events of the night before. Charles was attentively keeping her company at the late breakfast, in which fatigue had obliged her to indulge, half-wondering as he did, at the easy way in which his fairy's spirits rose again. He yet rejoiced at the reflection that if sorrow sat so light on that young heart now, it would easily recover any blow Providence might think fit in its wisdom to inflict hereafter. Alas! poor Charles had yet to learn that the almost unnatural buoyancy of the spirit in its first freshness, proceeds neither from levity in the affections, nor from that firmness which enables us to bear misfortune without sinking under it, but from the unquenched, the almost unquenchable, hope which burns within us, in those blessed days before sorrow had saddened us, or distrust and suspicion sown anxiety like a baleful weed among our brightest most cherished feelings.

The door opened and Lady Louisa Whittaker was announced. She was just come to town and Alixe, as she rose joyfully to receive her and her little girl, could not help contrasting her situation last spring with her present good fortune; and the scorn which the Aimwells felt or affected for her imprudent marriage, with the eagerness with which Lady Darlies now courted her society. Blest with all that this world could give, young, beautiful and beloved, Lady Louisa was too happy in herself to be harsh to others. Drest simply as she had been when the slightest extravagance would have ruined her husband, with the same fond confiding expression she returned Alixe's greeting, and was introduced to Charles. After much conversation on first and present subjects, Lady Lousia said, –

"And you are not the least tired of any of your gaieties?"

"No – that is perhaps I am a little tired of being at the same balls over and over again, but I am never tired of the people I meet there." And Alixe blushed slightly as she concluded. Her friend smiled, –

"What a pity you are not more discontented, to give greater brilliancy to my offer. For do you know, I actually come to propose a new pleasure? One at least, I think, must be new to you."

"Oh, what is it? Do tell me."

"It is a place in the ventilator in the House of Commons.[1] Were you ever there?"

"No, never. But I should like to go exceedingly."

"Well, I am happy to say I can gratify your wish and you can hear all the members of parliament, new and old, say all their wise and foolish sayings. It is to be a very interesting night and *somebody* is expected to make his maiden speech." Alixe raised her eager eyes and met those of her friend. She coloured deeply. "Farewell for the present. I will call for you a little after five."

The door closed and our heroine was left to her reflections. She should hear Everard speak, how her heart beat at the thought. He would stand unconsciously within her hearing, perhaps within sight, admired by all, beloved of one. Charles interrupted these high-flown reflections by reminding her that if she was going to the house it would be necessary to take some steps towards procuring an early dinner or at least some meal that would stand in its place.

Dinner! What did she care whether she ever ate dinners again? The very thought was an intrusion. Lady St Clair was informed of the place and readily acquiesced, though she feared Alixe would be fatigued. But her adopted daughter, on the contrary, was perfectly certain she should not be the least tired. She was impressed with the idea that to sit several hours in the ventilator must be of all things the most refreshing and invigorating. She only wondered people were not more eager to go. It must be much more amusing than any ball. In short, she was quite sure she should like it of all things. Punctually at 5 o'clock did the splendid equipage of Lady Louisa Whittaker drive up to the door. And Alixe, ready to the moment with shawls to keep her warm and fans to keep her cool, got into the carriage.

"And this is the ventilator!" said our heroine, as she entered the large, cold and dreary apartment, where the wives and sisters of young members may creep unseen, unheard, in breathless anxiety to the eight-inch square hole where they may hear these dear familiar tones which gladden their homes.

"Hush" said Lady Louisa, laughing and whispering. "This is the ventilator and you can sit here and put your head thro' that little hole when you are *very* anxious to hear what is going on!" Alixe did as she was bid and listened with mute attention. But for a long time, no one rose that was at all interesting to her and she withdrew her head and was beginning to think the subject of Currency exceedingly dull, when Lady Louisa touched her arm.

"Listen," said she, "Brougham is speaking."[2] Again, Alixe's whole soul was in her ear, while the orator's firm and impassioned eloquence held the house in silent attention, only broken by cheers from time to time, uttered like a low murmur. But Brougham's speech, tho' a long one, did not last the whole evening. His voice ceased and he sat down again. The long dry speeches and the short foolish ones provoked the impatient Alixe. She sat till nearly ten o'clock. Her head grew stupefied and she almost gave the point up in despair.

"Will you have some tea dearest," said Lady Louisa, pitying her suspense. The offer was accepted. Tea was ordered and during that refection, Charles St Clair and the honourable Augustus Barrymore, Lord Linton's friend, who was a member, came up. Mr Barrymore was very polite and not very entertaining. He stood talking to Lady Louisa on the debates past, present and future of that evening, while Charles woke Alixe from the weariness and abstraction into which she was plunged. They were still chatting and Mr Barrymore had just given the welcome intimation that "they expected the new member, Mr Price, to speak presently, heard he was clever, etc." When the voice so long expected and so fervently wished for, broke upon the ear of our heroine again, she took her station at the little square aperture. Again, her soul was rivetted more deeply than ever to the words of the speaker. As Everard proceeded and those clear musical tones rung thro' the house, Alixe leant her brow, in which the quick pulses were throbbing, against the wooden partition. The big tears stood in her eyes, her cheek glowed with all the triumphant energy of her lover's speech. And every murmur of applause thrilled thro' her heart. At length, he sat down amid loud and repeated cheering and Alixe smiled tho' her tears as Lady Louisa rose and warmly congratulated her on the success of her darling Everard, success won deservedly by his talents. Of course, Alixe thought that success unequalled, those talents unrivalled, and the speech she had just heard infinitely superior to any that Burke, Fox or Pitt even made in their most inspired moments.

She returned home and reported the entertainment of her evening to Lady St Clair; and retired to rest, to dream of glory, patriotism, Everard and the

Paper Currency. If there was anything which could add to an affection which scarcely admitted of increase in our heroine's heart, it was the thought that Everard should distinguish himself as he had done that night. She thought she had never loved him as well after this display of his eloquence. He would cease to employ his mind on trivial objects. He would think no longer of the flattery of the fair sex or the temptations he was led into, by comparison of his own. No, Everard the orator and patriot would be a different thing from Everard the man of the world, and Alixe fell asleep in the midst of a vision of herself making tea at home (*her* home and Everard's), his favourite books laid on the table and her guittar ready tuned to relieve his weary mind after a long evening spent in listening to dull debate. But dreams are not reality and this evening of evenings was spent by Everard Price neither in dreams of domestic happiness, nor public glory. It was spent (after the toils of the house were over) at Madame de Valcone's. The Baroness was ill, so she had told him. She was unhappy, so she had persuaded herself, and what could an attached friend do less, than spend at least one half-hour in soothing her mental malady, if he could not relieve her headache. When Everard entered, Honorine de Valcone was alone. Her husband was gone to one of the clubs with a friend. Ennuyée, in spite of all her gaiety, and piqued and jealous in spite of all the attention paid her, the disconsolate Baroness peevishly received every attempt to soothe her. Everard began to feel rather bored and cast several wishful glances at the door, half hoping someone might come in to break this very disagreeable tête a tête. But this was not at all what Madame de Valcone intended.

"You are wishing to go, mon ami. This scene is too melancholy for you. Go then, do not let a forced pity hold you here. Go, and leave the miserable Honorine to her own loneliness." And the Baroness wept.

"You wrong me, Honorine," said Everard. "I have no wish to leave you. I – I feared the presence of another was irksome to you just now."

"You mock me, where is the being beside yourself whose presence would be welcome to me? Did I not send for you? And when you come, you are unable to bear the listlessness and sadness of a wounded spirit. Go, you are no friend. I am only doomed to feel the bitterness of disappointment thro' my life."

"I *am* your friend, my lovely Honorine, your devoted friend. It is cruel to doubt me. Trust me dearest," and he took her passive hand. "There is nothing you could require of me I would not do. The success of this evening is nothing to me in comparison of one of your smiles." The only reply was a sigh and there was a deep silence. Suddenly, the Baroness raised her large flashing eyes with an expression of wildness and terror and fixed them on Everard.

"No, you must go, fly [from] me. I feel too deeply the deceit we would mutually practise, Everard! We are not friends, we cannot be friends. We must part, wide as seas can sever us, wide as the world will allow. If distance can bid us forget, we will forget that ever we met, that ever we parted."

The last words were nearly inaudible and his head sunk in its shame and emotion, till it nearly rested on the hand that held hers. Everard's first impulse was to obey her literally. Alarmed at the lightning flash of danger that burst on his mind, he had almost started from his seat and left her for ever. But the hand that trembled in his was not withdrawn. To spurn her? To leave her? He could not, he would not.

He spoke, he himself hardly knew what, murmured words of consolation and tenderness, sentences which he *meant* should mean nothing, but which by the consolation they afforded appeared to mean a great deal. Honorine drew her hand away and covered her face. The big bright tears trickled thro' her fingers. Everard rose and gently took her hand away.

"Honorine, listen to me, a word, a breath from your lips and I fly to the uttermost part of the earth, if such is your will. But why, Oh! why, should I leave you? Trust me, for you may trust me. I will never again revert, even in thought, to this evening. I will never by word, look, or sign, appear to drain any feeling in your heart which ought not to be mine. Honorine, beautiful, look at me, speak to me!" The Baroness looked up and holding his arm with startling energy, she exclaimed, –

"Swear then never to leave or forsake me, never to reproach me with my folly." And her eyes grew wilder and fiercer as if in wrath at the bare supposition of such a taunt. *And Everard swore.*

Chapter 18

Charles St Clair rose early the morning after Alixe's parliamentary entertainment, and after pacing the drawing room backwards and forwards for some minutes, he grew impatient at the laziness of his adopted sister, who was seldom absent from the breakfast table at her usual home. At length, he sent up a message and received for answer that Alixe had such a violent headache in consequence of the heat the night before, that she could not come down yet. He ate his solitary breakfast, read his newspaper and then wisely began to meditate on his sister's affairs. After revolving in his mind a thousand romantic plans for serving her, his brain became so confused and heated that he decided a cool ride in the park at this early hour would do him all the good in the world. He ordered his horse and employed himself, after galloping for about half an hour with unabated activity, in settling how he could effect his great end of making Everard sensible of the glowing impropriety of *appearing* at least to make love to one woman while solemnly engaged to another. Charles stifled his anger and contempt, which these reflections never failed to raise, and at length persuaded himself that it was his duty, however little it might be his inclination, to endeavour to win the confidence and friendship of the object of his meditations. Surely, if he was so fond of Dunstan and allowed *him* to exercise so great an influence over him, when he was after all a shallow friend and a bad man, he might easily be won to like and esteem one who never professed more than he felt, or allowed himself to feel unjustly or any occasion, as far as the light of reason allowed him to judge. Having settled these points in his own mind, he turned his horse's head to Grosvenor Place with the intention of congratulating Everard on his success the night before. He was admitted without delay, and tho' he thought he heard Everard reprimanding his servants for letting anyone up, yet he proceeded with tolerable good humour. The door was flung open and Everard, who appeared to be following his visitor's habit of perambulating the apartment, made a dead stop. They shook hands and sat down. And Charles, having turned his intended compliment as gravely as he could, – without producing any great visible effect on his auditor's countenance, paused. But his companion did not seem inclined to carry on the conversation, for after a cold curt acknowledgement of Mr St Clair's civility, he remained perfectly silent.

"You have not been exempt from fatigue," said Charles, looking at the table on which the breakfast things still stood. "But I do not wonder at it, for even Alixe, poor little thing, who was only a listener, is still in her room."

"Alixe?" said Everard, looking with insult and wonder at his companion.

"Yes, she was in the ventilator. I thought perhaps you might have known it. She never was there before, and was much delighted." Charles pronounced this last compliment with pain and it certainly appeared to afford anything but pleasure to the person he addressed. The latter leant back in his chair with the expression of acute mental anguish and he compressed his lip and muttered something his visitor did not hear. Charles was surprised, –

"You do not seem well this morning," said he kindly.

"Well, I am quite well. Will you have any breakfast?"

"I have breakfasted, I thank you."

"Then I will at least ring and have these things taken away." The servant came and proceeded to obey orders. At length, the man ventured after many cautious inquiring glances towards his master, to demand whether he could not have something hot brought up *now*.

"Ho, Fool," said Everard, angrily. "If I had wanted it, I could have ordered it. Take everything down stairs." His peremptory command was duly executed and once more Charles found a difficulty in conversation. It was laboriously carried on for some minutes longer. When he rose to depart, Everard seemed relieved, –

"Give my love to your sister," said the latter, "and say I hope to see her in the course of the day." Charles left the house, and the master of it, throwing himself into his chair and leaning his head in his hands, groaned aloud. A gentle tap at the door roused him. It was his sister, Emily.

"How late you are, dear love. Miss Herbert is fuming and fretting below stairs and vowing you must have made yourself ill. Now do not sit moping here, but come to us in the drawing room. You really grow quite ungallant."

"You should have come a little sooner, Emmy, and you would have found a more suitable beau in young St Clair, who is just gone." Emily coloured, but did not raise her eyes or make any answer. She dragged her brother from the library, and having placed him the large armchair, said playfully, –

"There now, if you will only think out loud, we will consider it as conversation, for I suppose you will seldom condescend to talk to ladies again after raising your voice for the public good."

"Humph," said Miss Herbert, in a discontented tone. "It had need be for the public good, for I'm sure his last night's employments have done little good in private."

"What do you mean?" said Everard sternly.

"There now, do look at his countenance! Mean? Why I mean that if speaking in parliament is only to teach you pride and misanthropy, to lock yourself up in your own room and never pay the slightest attention to the ladies of the house, you had much better tell Lord Sunderland that you will give it back."

"Give what back?"

"Your seat in the house, to be sure. And who but you, since we are on the subject, would have thought of going, young and hot-headed as you are, to stand up and speak oratory to a parcel of Torys, without first reading over your speech to older heads! I'm sure I was thunderstruck when I learnt you had actually spoken and never so much as told me of it beforehand."

Everard rang the bell and ordered his horses – and then walked out of the room. And Miss Herbert continued for a full hour longer to descant on his conduct, ending by declaring she never would have believed his head would be so easily turned.

Meanwhile the object of her animadversion was slowly riding, or rather suffering his horse to lead him, to Alixe's house. But the noble animal, being merely acquainted with his master's habits and not his thoughts, made a pause under the Baroness's balcony which was the nearest point in their journey. Everard, startled from his reverie, looked up, and the scene of the previous evening coming full over his mind, he angrily struck his spurs into his horse's side. The horse,[1] alarmed at this unexpected correction, plunged, reared and finally threw him, in spite of the efforts of his groom, who had instantly dismounted. Captain Harry Dunstan was at that moment coming out of the house, and he assisted the man to heave in his senseless master and lay him on a bed.

The first sight that greeted Everard's half-conscious eyes was the form of the beautiful Baroness, who stood with fear and sorrow in her countenance at the bedside. She clasped her hands when he looked at her and uttered some fervent expression of thankfulness, but the words were lost on the sufferer. The sight of Honorine de Valcone brought confusedly to his mind sensations of shame and pain. He dimly felt that he had been tempted and had been weak enough to give way to the temptation. And that in some manner or other, the Baroness was the cause of his being where he was. With a low groan he turned away, wishing, in the mixture of bodily and mental pain he was suffering, to relapse again into the eternal insensibility from which he fancied he had awoken. Honorine could only sigh and sit down to watch again till the surgeon came. He came, after a proper delay, to prove his consequence and extensive practise, and after talking Latin, and moreover doctor's Latin. For half-an-hour he condescended to say in plain English that his patient had dislocated his shoulder and received a violent blow on the head [and] "must be kept cool and quiet. All agitation to be avoided, must be bled, no sort of danger unless indeed fever should ensue."

The Baroness, greatly relieved, departed to inform her husband of the result. It was decided that for the present, Everard should not be moved and a room was accordingly prepared for him. And the good-natured little Baron declared, rubbing his hands and smiling, that if anything *could* console him from such a horrible accident, it was the thought that he should again have his friend Mr Price in his house, as at Geneva, where they were all so happy and pleasant together. After enduring this species of consolatory friendship for about a quarter of an hour, Everard faintly requested he might be left alone. Dunstan had gone to Grosvenor Place to break it to Emily and from thence with still greater pleasure to inform Alixe of the accident. The former received it with apparent composure, though her cheek flushed and her hand trembled, as she tied on her hat, with the resolution of instantly going and judging for herself how far her brother was injured while Miss Herbert strode up and down the room, wringing her hands and vociferating her sorrow, so as to deafen those who were unfortunate enough to be expected to sympathise. Alixe was working embroidery by her mother and quietly awaiting the performance of Everard's promise of calling. Harry Dunstan studiously threw into his countenance an air of tragic embarrassment, which for him, who never attempted to express his feelings otherwise than by the medium of speech, was more alarming than it would have been in other persons, whose countenances are *sometimes* consulted as a clue to their sentiments. Charles, who had just returned from his ride, sat gloomily down to await the departure of his obnoxious visitor.

But Dunstan had no intention of hurrying himself. He hemmed and hawed, talked of the weather and looked everything that was deplorable. At length, he said he was sorry that a great friend of his, and he believed a friend of Lady St Clair's, Mr Everard Price, had met with a serious accident. Alixe uttered an exclamation and dropt her needle on the tambour frame. Dunstan continued his story, carefully describing where and how the accident happened, the beautiful Baroness's fear, and her ecstatic joy when Everard first recovered his consciousness and spoke to her. There was one circumstance which Dunstan did not know, but he would equally have omitted it, had he known it, which was, that the cause of his friend's being thrown from his horse was his wish to pass that balcony filled with heliotrope and jasmin, where he was accustomed to pause and come on to his expectant Alixe. Our heroine could not guess this, or it would have given her comfort. As it was, there appeared no gleam across the waste to which she looked. With every shade of colour driven from her cheek and the blood beating in the heavy pulses of her heart, till the feeling almost amounted to suffocation, she had just sufficient command over herself to choke back the tears that rose to her eyes; till Harry Dunstan rose and left the apartment, satisfied that every word had dropped like molten lead on the souls of his hearers, and that he had nothing further to expect of gratification to his cruelty.

Alixe then rose and sunk with bitter tears into the extended arms of her kind parent. Charles rose too, and after many attempts at consolation, he finished by declaring he would go and see Everard and judge of his situation, as he doubted not (and in his emotion, he spoke it boldly) that Dunstan made the worst of it. Alixe was proportionately grateful, but it hung heavy on her mind, that her love whom she might not see would be watched over, and that tenderly, by a woman whom she had many reasons to fear and doubt, in spite of Madame de Valcone's kindness and fascination of manner, in spite of Alixe's indulgence and generosity, which prompted her to attribute the Baroness's influence over Everard more to her natural talents and beauty, than to the efforts the former was accused of making to obtain the heart of her lover.

Charles soon returned and gave a good account of the patient, tho' he confessed that he did not suppose he would leave his present home for some little time, but that in three weeks he hoped Everard would be in the drawing room and then they could see him. Three weeks! It was a long time to live in doubt and suspense, but they must be borne.

Chapter 19

Emily Price watched with the untiring affection of woman by her brother. Naturally impatient, and at this moment suffering mental as well as bodily pain, Everard required all that gentleness and fond attention which his sister showed, to make him support with tolerable patience the irksomeness of his situation. Charles came often and Emily could not help admiring the sweetness with which he bore her brother's peevish gloomy answers or cold manner; the cheerful good-humour with which he strove to amuse by anecdotes he thought might be interesting to his companion; the eager manner in which he entered into, and encouraged, Everard's taste for politics; and above all his accounts of Alixe, so free from selfishness, so entirely forgetting all but the wishes and happiness of his adopted sister.

And deep indeed must have been the love that could have blinded Charles to the kind interest and admiration of that dark soft watchful eye and the blush that wavered on the pale and weary cheek, whenever the anecdote he told aroused the best of her pure and affectionate heart. He saw in Emily, Everard's sister, Alixe's friend, but for himself nothing. The anxious tones of that one dear voice in his home, rung in his ear even while talking to others. And his eyes, while they seemed to be perusing mournfully some strange features, gave him back the bright, laughter-loving glance of his fairy.

Meantime, Everard grew better. He was able to come downstairs and tho' still forbidden to stir his arm, might at least see and converse with his friends and relieve the ennui that consumed him. Lady St Clair brought Alixe after his first few days of comparative liberty were announced. And the buoyant spirits of her adopted child rose in proportion as her fears had been great. Overjoyed to be once more with him who was her chief object in life, she saw no cloud in the brightness of her future, but laughed, talked, and looked gaily up at her lover, as she sat on a low ottoman by his sofa. But Everard was not in the mood for gaiety and in the midst of the low silver laugh of his companion, he turned his head away with a murmur that almost amounted to a groan. If the sudden change of countenance Alixe exhibited could have satisfied him with its expression of tenderness, grief and alarm, or could her soft tones – "You are in pain," and when that was denied – "I have wearied you" – have fallen on a less preoccupied ear, the feelings that were gnawing Everard's heart would have been at least soothed and lessened. But the look and the words were lost in the torture of memory which was busy with other looks and other words. Alixe departed and tho' she saw her lover frequently, now that he was getting well, yet there was one who was with him from the hour of his rising, to his retiring for the night. Honorine de Valcone saw that her influence over Everard hung on a balance difficult to keep, even as it stood, and which might be destroyed by a moment's imprudence. She saw that his admiration for her was struggling with his shame and deep affection for the pure-minded Alixe. Had she been the wife of his bosom or even stood in the place of the gentle Emily, she could not have watched his eye in order to guess his feeling with more meek, more unremitting as assiduity.

Often when Everard had half resolved to gaze with stern reproof on her efforts to please, the timid mournful expression of fondness which she threw into her large black eyes unmanned his resolution, and he smiled when he had meant to frown. Often when he was meditating on a plan he had formed of going to Hunsden as soon as the session of Parliament was over, and then remaining alone and wrapt up in his affairs, the notes of her guittar and the rich languid swell of her voice, as it died away in some melancholy Italian air, thrilled thro' his soul and drove everything from his mind, except the sensation of her presence. Still, when the witchery of the hour was over, he returned to his plan. From Hunsden he was to come to Lord Felix Brandon's uncle and former guardian to Lady Louisa Whittaker. *There*, at least, he would be safe from the power of the enchantress. *There*, the magic circle would no longer be drawn around him. Alixe and the Whittakers, he was sure to see there, he knew they were asked. Perhaps Annette Darlies, but the beautiful Baroness was not even acquainted with any member of the family. She had told him so. And he wondered that he sighed when he thought of the impossibility of their meeting.

Harry Dunstan watched, with the eye of unsatiated revenge, each step to destruction that he fancied his victim took. Every struggle in Everard's soul was to him a feast. He wound himself by serpent approaches into Madame de Valcone's confidence. Possessing the coldest and purest regard and duty, and hinting the fullest acquaintance with his friend's feelings (which of course he persuaded her were entirely filled with a passion for her, which his endeavours to stifle only rendered more valuable by proving its intensity), Dunstan gradually made himself an object of importance to Honorine and wielded an unseen, but not the less certain, power over her actions. Slowly, sorrowfully, did Emily admit the truth that broke on her mind: that her brother, that brother so admired, so troubled, so beloved, was laying up shame and grief for himself and ruining a future that promised to be as bright as any that a mortal could look forward to. But she had strong hope that if he would listen to the voice of reason and affection in time, if he would consent merely to part in reality from the object that had fascinated him, all would be well. In doubt and fear, she broke the subject to him. She conjured him by all that was precious in life and honour, by all that used to bind him, by the fear of heaven and the memory of his idolizing mother, to cast away the shackles that bound his spirit. She wept as she held his hand in both of hers and spoke of Alixe and his inviolable engagement. And in the visionary picture of domestic happiness which she drew, made Everard himself feel how worthless the object for which he might be obliged to renounce so much good.

He parted from the beautiful Baroness and thanked her for all the kind attention which she had shown him during his illness. And though his voice faltered, as he pronounced the adieu that was to be all but eternal, he went without one lingering wish to meet those bright large tearful eyes again, till time and distance should have taught him more government over his own mind. Madame de Valcone's last words were "remember we are still, we are ever, to be friends." Till Parliament was over, Everard could not leave town, and he again eagerly mingled in politics: many a bright dream of fame and glory, such as young minds do feel when first a wider scope for their powers opens to them than in the narrow circle of home, many a plan of distinction and vision of liberty stole over his soul in the excitement caused by the pursuit of his favourite study. He was envied by the young, complimented by the old, and many were the prophecies kindly whispered in his ear which he did not think the least improbable, tending to fill him with the natural hopes of being one day at the head of the administration. While his mind was thus diverted and the excitement lasted, all was well, and his sacrifice appeared nothing in his own eyes. But when the hurry and turmoil was over and he was quietly settled at Hunsden, the long evenings of Autumn brought back his ennui. And often when his sister fondly flattered herself he was reading or slumbering, his thoughts were with Honorine de Valcone; her voice rang in his ear, her form floated before his eyes and he half wondered where the soft step had vanished that used to creep round his sofa when he was in pain, where the bright glance had sunk that used to light up his soul with its wild gaiety.

Lady St Clair, her son and Alixe had returned to the cottage. Charles was much happier now that the London season was over. If he had nothing more to hope, at least he had no more trials to undergo. All the quiet rational unemployment which to him were a part of home might be enjoyed without interruption. Once more he was alone with Alixe. Once more their feelings mingled, their pleasures and sorrows were the same. His adopted sister was happy also. Everard was well, and her confidence in his love and his honour were unbroken. Alas, neither that love, nor confidence, were shared by him. The words of Lady Darlies at Lady Linton's assembly, though he would fain have persuaded himself he scorned them, returned ever and anon to his mind. And yet could Alixe be capable of interested motives? And in the peevishness of his own conscious heart, he persuaded himself that at least she could not love him deeply, warmly, as he ought to be loved. No, she cared little for a rival. She was neither angry, nor out of spirits. What could it be? Was she cold and indifferent? Was she blind enough not to see his partiality for Madame de Valcone, or did she think herself so secure of her prize, that he could not escape her? And the last supposition deeply offended her captious lover. An invitation to Lord Linton's woke him from the lethargy and ennui which began to oppress him. Yes, he would go there, it would just fill up the time he must have spent at Hunsden, where he had no party. To Lord Linton's they accordingly proceeded, and after a long and moody journey they arrived one evening just in time for dinner. Lady Linton received them very graciously, assured them they had been anxiously expected, and that her son would be overjoyed to see them. Then, advising them to commence their toilettes, she swept her ample drapery through the long corridor and disappeared.

After the necessary preparations were over, Everard and his sister descended into the drawing room. It was full of people, some of them friends, or more properly acquaintances, some of them utter strangers to Emily and her brother. Lord Linton was standing with his back to the marble chimney piece; he advanced three steps to testify his rapture at seeing them and then fell back into his former position. The Honourable Augustus Barrymore seized upon the reluctant Miss Price, having been obliged for the last quarter of an hour to entertain several old, dull, dry dowagers, the beauties of Lady Linton's day, who with a quantity of rouge and a sort of fever light in their eyes, still seemed to claim all the homage that could be spared to them. Everard remained, standing opposite Lord Linton. There was a pause in the conversation and Everard turned to glance carelessly over the "galaxy of eyes" that were round him. He recognized Lady Darlies and bowed to her. The half-smile which accompanied that bow still lingered on his lips, when his eyes wandered back again round the circle; they were rivetted with perplexed earnestness on the form of a lady who sate near the place where he and Lord Linton were standing. He could only see her throat, shoulder and the back of one of the most beautiful heads ever sculptured. He watched for some moments. She turned her head and caught his glance, exhibiting a face of the most statue-like beauty; a high fair forehead, round which turned in a single braid the whole of her rich black hair; large dark eyes and pale melancholy features, pale even to her small full lips; all these seemed familiar to Everard; yet she did not appear to know him. She slowly withdrew her eyes without allowing the slightest change of expression to steal over her countenance and again turned her long swan-like throat to her companion. Everard still gazed till his arm was touched by someone. He started. It was Harry Dunstan.

"I see who you are looking at so earnestly," said his friend, smiling. "Is she not beautiful? It is Madame de Calzean!" The name thrilled thro' Everard's frame. It was that of the baroness's friend and schoolfellow.

"Yes, indeed," said Dunstan, as if in reply to Everard's thoughts. "And they say she is as good as she is beautiful. Mountain snow could not be purer. Linton was very much in love with her when he was at Rome. But she was marble to the poor youth, yea, cold as the statue of the Venus de' Medici."

"It is a happy thing," said Mr Price, who felt he was called upon to say something and hardly knew what the words were.

Dunstan continued, "And yet she does not seem happy, poor thing, but no wonder. Look at her husband." Everard did at last detach his eyes from Madame de Calzean and fixed them on a fat *walrus*-looking individual, who with a newspaper in one hand and the fingers of the other holding tight by the collar of his coat (displaying on the fourth finger an immense diamond), was watching with cat-like avidity the opening of the door which was to introduce the welcome announcement of dinner. Many times the portal swung back. And as often did Monsieur de Calzean turn with a look of blank disappointment from the pretty woman or perfumed dandy who came gliding in, and sink back in his chair with a sigh like that of a dying porpoise. At length the welcome tidings struck on his famine-sharpened ear. He rose with speed that would have done honour to Mr Albert and stood puffing with impatience, while the different couples were marshalling to go down the marble staircase. At length that was over.

Madame de Calzean had, as Everard thought, fallen almost by magic to his share and mechanically they walked down stairs. On sitting down, Mr Price found himself next to Lady Darlies. He thought she looked at him with a meaning smile, provoked and embarrassed. He directed his conversation entirely to his new acquaintance. Madame de Calzean, however, was impenetrably silent. Nay, had she not been so very beautiful it might have been called stupidity. Her lips certainly moved when she uttered her short, soft replies to the string of questions her companion flattered himself were to produce conversation. But her eyes, those large deep southern eyes were never raised, and the short quick smile that convulsed, rather than played over, her features, left a painful impression. There was a long pause. It was broken by Madame de Calzean, who for the first time asked a question in her turn.

"You are acquainted with my friend the Baroness de Valcone are you not?" As Everard turned to answer the inquiry, he encountered her eyes. Raised, and fixed full upon his own for an instant, they were expressive, or he fancied so. Whether it was this, or the proximity of Lady Darlies, or the consciousness of the great confidences made by female friends to each other, Everard felt uncomfortable. He answered, however, in a cool careless manner that he had had the pleasure of knowing the Baroness, both at Geneva and in London. No more was said. And Everard felt relieved when the statue-like beauty rose and glided away.

   The next day was the first of the Doncaster Meeting and Lord Linton's seat being near that far famed place, many of the party had determined to go. Everard was in no humour for races or any other amusement. Listless and dispirited, hardly knowing himself what he wished, he sullenly turned from the attempted rallying of Harry Dunstan and the petition of his other civil friends and watched carriages and horses as they departed with something like satisfaction. When the parties returned, fatigued and worn-out with over-excitement, they maintained a stupid silence, sometimes broken by praises of a favourite horse which they expected would win and which was the more interesting as it had not been anticipated previous to the Meeting. Dunstan and a few others appeared in spirits, the former particularly. He laughed, talked and drank to the success of particular horses, adding in a significant tone that an hour might change the favourite into the last horse people would bet upon. Towards the end of the evening, Everard could not help thinking his friend rather tipsy and (why he knew not) the circumstance added to his ill-humour. He heard a confused murmur of bets, sums staked that would ruin the loser and which in some instances he was quite sure they had it not in their power to risk. Wearied and disgusted, he walked off to bed. He was still ruminating, or rather indulging in a waking dream on the interesting subjects of Alixe, Madame de Valcone and her friend, when he was roused by a tap at the door. And Dunstan answered the summons of "who's there?" by walking in. After some desultory conversation, in which the latter certainly did not shine, he said, –

   "Ah Everard, my dear fellow, if all goes well tomorrow, I'm a made-man."

   "I thought that it was very unlikely you could succeed. I understood your interests to be directly opposite to those of Pegasus, the present favourite."

   "That, my dear fellow, is nothing. I shall be a rich man tomorrow, or –" added he suddenly, pausing, "I shall be ruined." And a frightful expression mingled itself with the vacancy of intoxication. He left the room and Everard, who thought his conduct very strange, returned to his slumbers.

Chapter 20

The morrow rose, as bright, as beautiful, as it was possible for day to be, and the eager followers of the sports of the turf looked out with gladness. Lady Darlies declared it was the most gratifying spectacle, the most enchanting sight. And having provided herself with one female companion and two males, set off in her new open carriage, perfectly contented with herself, her equipage and the admiring crowd. Many, tempted by the day, the assurances of their companions, as to its being the best worth seeing of any race that had ever been run in any part of the United Kingdom, and their dislike to be left to comparative loneliness in a large country house, followed her example. And except a few fat men, old dowagers and one old maid who had, after being half promised a place in somebody's carriage, been obliged to give it up to a Colonel Worthington and who sighed in a corner, Everard and Madame de Calzean found themselves almost alone. Why, he knew not, but Mr Price certainly stood in awe of his new acquaintance. She seemed so different from what he really believed her to be. She was not stupid, for she conversed well and fluently on most subjects, but all she said or did was said or done like a beautiful automaton.

"Surely," thought her companion, as he looked at her, as she bent over a small picture she was finishing, "she must be acting. Where is the gaiety, the enthusiasm, the playful talent, Honorine used to describe to me? Where is even the expression which Madame de Valcone's picture of her throws into those dark passionless eyes?" He had just finished his reflection, when Madame de Calzean looked up from her drawing.

"You are meditating?" said she, in her slow calm voice.

"Yes."

"And may one ask the subject of your reverie?"

"I was thinking," said Everard smiling, "what could be the subject of that happy picture over which you have spent so many hours?"

"It is just finished. Would you like to look at it? It is a present I intend for Honorine de Valcone." Everard eagerly availed himself of the invitation and placed himself opposite the picture. It was beautifully finished. Perhaps prejudice made him think the design French and complicated. A beautiful female figure, which at once struck Everard as being intended for the Baroness, was placed on the left side, shading her eyes with her hand from the bright light, which burst on the scene. And gazing on a statue of Friendship, by the side of which a young man stood with his back to the spectator, apparently watching the effect of the scene on the female, a *something* with wings, hovered over her and appeared to be vainly endeavouring to call her attention in the direction to which it pointed: viz. to a little fat French cupid, who peeping from behind the statue, was taking aim at the lady's heart. Everard wished very much to say something. He struggled and dug for a compliment but every time his lips opened, his eyes again fixed on the figure on the right side of the picture. The more he looked at it, the more convinced he felt that Madame de Calzean had made it from a sketch of his person. It was his very air, his attitude, the way in which he threw back his haughty head when triumph or scorn swelled in his heart. He stared at the picture, as if he expected the figure would at length turn round and reveal its features.

"Well?" at length said his companion. He turned and met her glance. It rivetted him for a moment in speechless surprise. Her deep Italian eyes gleamed with the expression of a sorceress. There was something wild, almost savage in them, as they met those of Everard Price. His first momentary impression was a confused idea of supernatural power in the form before him; his second, hatred and anger against the woman who thus meddled unmasked in his plans and feelings. And then a thousand confused thoughts rushed over his soul, and turning away he heaved a deep miserable sigh.

"Are you going?" said Madame de Calzean. There was a slight, very slight tremulousness, in her voice that altered the intended harshness of Everard's answer.

"I am going to walk in the park," said he after a pause.

"Bon, we will walk together, shall we not?" added she, as she looked up into her companion's face. It was one of Honorine's looks. Everard started and assented.

It was a bright soft evening and the welcome breeze came thro' the thick branches of beech trees which swept the ground with a mixture of perfume and freshness that was delicious. Whoever, after deep and painful emotion, has wandered out from the works and the wiles of man to the glorious works of God; whoever has felt the soft winds of heaven fanning a brow whose temple veins are throbbing and starting with human passion, and looked round with heavy and angry eyes on the calm majesty of Nature, which appear to wear, in the sunset, the melancholy smile of love which accompanies a mother's reproof to her child, till the tears start and the heart swells, has felt with Everard that evening. They walked silently, side by side, for some time.

Everard was the first who spoke. He talked of indifferent subjects, but his companion had relapsed into monosyllables. At length, they paused to contemplate a superb view, which was one of the lions of the park. They stood on one side of a deep ravine, planted with Scotch firs. The other side was covered with beautiful trees intermixed with some ever-greens. Below them at a fearful distance rushed a foaming torrent, boiling and raging over the opposing roots and stones it met with. The dizzy height on which they stood, which sent a thrill into the stoutest heart that looked down and instinctively thought of the chance of death, a mangled death, to any one who made a false step or advanced to near the edge. The beauty of the opposite bank, where the dark green of the unfading fir and laurel mingled with the autumnal tints of the fading trees, whose waving branches caught the sunshine as if in sport and bent again to the waters beneath: all sunk with that sense of beauty which is overpowering even to sadness on the gazers' hearts.

"Beautiful! Beautiful!" said Everard, in a low tone, as if fearful of dispelling the magic scene by a word.

"Beautiful indeed," said his companion, whose dark eyes were fast filling with tears in the effort to speak. "The true majestic beauty of nature. Art could give no mimicry of it. Description to those who had never seen it would be vain. No picture could give us the dancing of the waters, the gloom of this side of the torrent or the showers of light which play on the opposite bank." After a pause she added quickly, –

"Apropos of pictures, you did not seem to like mine this evening."

Everard started. At length, he said somewhat coldly, –

"I do not know what I have done to inspire Madame de Calzean with so much interest for a stranger, or by what right she sketches an allegory of my action and interrogates me as to the success of her lesson."

"I have the right of friendship," said his companion calmly. "Not for yourself but for another. I will not deny that you inspire interest, for I came here prepared to hate you from the bottom of my heart. I thought to find you a scheming artful man of the world, without one interest except in the success of his selfish plans; without one feeling for the miseries of others, even when caused by himself. I find you different, with much of passion and folly. You have also the elements of what is good and noble. If you do not mar it, your future may be a bright one, very bright. But if you obstinately refuse all warning, believe me the storm is brooding above that will crush you. Listen to me patiently and I promise never again to *look* as if I had thought of you beyond the other human creatures who glide through Lord Linton's drawing-room. I might even plead the right of age," added she, half-smiling, "to lecture you since I am full five years your senior." Everard looked incredulous and Madame de Calzean continued, –

"You have professed to feel regard for Honorine de Valcone, to love her, to be her friend. Alas, how would you deceive yourself and her. *I* love her, dearly and well. She was the most joyous, the most innocent, the most lovely of God's creatures when first we met. She is to me a creature of the past, connected with all I loved, with every scene of my happy, – I would say of my *happiest* days. I repeat, I love her and therefore I know and feel that you do not, for you would make her miserable."

"God forbid," muttered Everard hastily. "And at least you cannot accuse me of her present unhappiness. She is unhappy because she is united to a man she does not, she cannot love."

"You are mistaken," returned his companion. "There is nothing to prevent her loving Baron de Valcone sincerely. You men, whose love is the impulse of the moment, know not, and never can know, how much a woman's affection is the force of habit. Her habitual feelings are stronger than almost any others. Take any two people who love one another passionately and are just united in holy and eternal bonds. The man in the ardour of his passionate adoration would fly with the object before him to the world's end, nor leave one regret behind. But with his bride the case is different. Weeping and hesitating on the threshold of the house from which she is a voluntary exile, she clings to the arms of her mother, her sister, her brothers, watches the last look of those familiar faces which smiled in the dreams of her childhood, and sinks with a gush of tears by the side of him whom she professes to love better than all the world. Again, be her life ever so bright, her new home ever so happy, tell her she shall revisit the scenes of childhood, that she shall return, if it be but for a time, to her old house, her old prayers, and the rapture that sparkles in her glad eyes would make you believe that she tasted no happiness elsewhere. And she will greet even the old watch-dog with kisses and tears. And thus, even if a woman be united to a man with whom she is not passionately in love, provided that man be kind and estimable, no more is required. She will love him from the mere force of habit warmly, sincerely, and lastingly. His interests are hers, his hopes and fears are confided to her, his children are her chief object of love in the universe."

"You do not believe me," added she, as she looked at Everard, "and yet I speak from a knowledge of my own heart. At your first entrance into life, you formed to yourself many thousand plans of fame, glory, ambition and power. So, at my entrance into a more narrow sphere, I looked to woman's single dream of happiness: the romance of love. I woke from that dream," continued Madame de Calzean, in a low and tremulous voice, "and thought life with its enjoyments was at an end. And yet, I do swear to you on the faith of woman that I have tasted much tranquil happiness. I had two children. It pleased God to take them to himself but I was happier in the hour of my sorrow, mingling my tears with him to whom I had been a faithful wife, to whose children a fond mother, than if a guilty passion had stood in place of the love I bore those little ones. Honorine de Valcone might be happy with her husband and child. I have seen her perfectly contented, fondly smiling on the man whom you say she cannot love, but it was where no tempter came, where the beautiful feelings of nature were left to themselves. Why should you act the part of Satan to bring guilt and misery into a peaceful home? Oh pause, while it is yet time for her sake, for your own, for one who should be ever dearer than self. *Pause*! And mark me, I know Honorine and can judge of her feelings far, far better than you can. If ever you bewilder her reason and inspire her with the unholy passion which ends in misery, she, Honorine, will hate you! Surrounded by the glare of vanity, admiration and flattery, with a romantic imagination and a heart that wanders from home, you may captivate, intoxicate, for an hour. She may appear to love you with devoted tenderness. But when the bubble bursts, when the guilty magic has ceased to brighten the scene; then, when she finds herself degraded and despised, Honorine de Valcone the beautiful, the loved, will hate you with all the deep, deadly and eternal hate of an injured woman!" And as she spoke, she lifted up her prophet eyes to the countenance of her companion. Beautiful, very beautiful, was Pauline de Calzean at that moment. The look of inspiration lighted her brow and her pale cheek flushed with emotion. But Everard saw her not. He was murmuring a faint prayer to that God to whom he so seldom bent the knee or raised the appealing and petitioning hands, –

"Pray! Pray to thy God, sinner, that he may save them!"

"And now," said Pauline de Calzean, gently relinquishing the hand she had taken in that moment of irrepressible emotion. "I have but few words to add, and on a different subject or rather a different person. I would speak of your friend Captain Dunstan. Whatever I know of you and my unhappy friend has been communicated by him. He had been in the confidence of each. Oh, Mr Price, beware the man who could thus play the traitor to both, that you might be the sooner irrevocably ruined. Thank Heaven he mistook the character of Honorine de Valcone's early friend. Hark! Surely, I heard voices. But it is so dark here, I cannot distinguish anything. List! There again. Do you not hear it? Let us go from under the shadow of these fir trees."

"We had better cross the little bridge," said Everard. A few moments placed them on the opposite side and they distinctly heard voices, one in a smothered tone of determination mingled with curses, and the other in the feeble moans of supplication with earnest assurances of eternal secrecy. Both our pedestrians felt alarmed. For a moment, the latter voice was slightly raised and Pauline de Calzean, every fibre in her body instinct with emotion, said in a voice scarcely audible, –

"It is Lord Linton, they are murdering him!" At one and the same time, Everard and his companion sprang forward into a little open glade that shelved down towards the water. It was indeed from here the voices had proceeded. Dunstan, his features deadly pale and convulsed with passion, the gleam of murderous intention under his knit brow, his white teeth clenched and the beautiful serpent lips compressed, so as to be almost as pale as the rest of his countenance, slowly raised himself from above his victim, whom he had apparently been dragging to the edge of the precipice. As he started up and stood firm before them Everard uttered his name. With the speed of lightning, Dunstan drew a pistol from his bosom and fired it. Then rushing from the spot, he disappeared and they heard the furious galloping of a horse in the distance. It was indeed Lord Linton who had been so nearly the victim of Dunstan's demoniacal plan. The young man had fainted from exhaustion. And as Everard bent, regardless of the pain in his arm (which had been wounded by his treacherous friend), to gaze on what he feared was the corpse of their young host, the beautiful, fair and almost boyish features, torn and bloody with his struggle, seemed to prove a double barbarity in the ruffian who thus abused his strength. After a few drops of water had been flung on his face, he partially recovered, his eyes opened and the fair curls which had left a stain of blood where they lay, were raised from Madame de Calzean's shoulder, who had supported him during the short period since Dunstan's departure. He looked wildly round and meeting her large dark anxious eyes, his features heightened.

"Pauline, my beautiful! Is it possible?" Madame de Calzean rose and delivered him over to Everard and then, overcome by the scene and perhaps by some touch of tenderness for him, whose love for her had thus saddened his young life, sank down by a tree and sobbed bitterly. Everard remained for some minute irresolute. Then, as Lord Linton leant his head against his arm, he said, –

"Something must be done. One of us must go to the Castle and procure help." Madame de Calzean started up, –

"I will go this instant."

"No, you had better stay with him, I think. Your dress will betray you and someone ought to break it to Lady Linton, who will be exceedingly alarmed."

"Pray, pray, do not leave me," said the unhappy young man. "I assure you I can walk, I *will* walk. We shall meet some of the carriages coming home, but I could not bear to remain here alone." And a convulsive shudder passed over his slight frame as he pronounced the words.

"And pray, when you see my mother, say only that I have had a fall from my horse, if you think it necessary to say anything. But indeed, I dare say I shall be quite well before dinner."

After continuing for a little while silently sitting in the evening shade, Lord Linton declared that he felt quite able to proceed and he accordingly proceeded, supported by his kind friends, for some little distance, when he became again quite faint. Luckily a carriage, the last almost from the races, drove past and Everard shouted to it to stop. Lady Darlies, the fair occupant, immediately turned out her companions, male and female, and Everard, Lord Linton and Madame de Calzean were invited to take their vacated places. Everard declined, saying he preferred taking the short cut home by the little bridge and that he would warn Lady Linton of her son's accident. He accordingly joined the party of pedestrians, all eager to know what had happened to Lord Linton, what Everard had done to his own arm. And to reward him in return, gave him a confused account of something that had happened at the races. They were not, indeed, particularly well qualified to tell the story, having been in Lady Darlies' carriage nearly the whole time of the grande scène and only catching the account by hearsay from the different agitated spectators. But this much they were sure of: that the favourite had suddenly died from the effects of poison as was firmly believed; and indeed confessed, by a man who (and this was the part of the story on which they most greedily fed) declared Captain Dunstan was the instigator of this most ungentlemanlike and criminal expedient for turning the fortunes of the day. Lord Linton, who was one of the stewards, had rode round to see the dying animal, which he had had some thoughts of purchasing and which was truly beautiful. There were words between him and Captain Dunstan, but nobody could repeat what the words were, except that Lord Linton had said in conclusion, –

"I fight none but gentlemen."

They reached the House in time to break to the agonized mother the tidings of her son's misfortune, which was supposed to be a fall from his horse, who had dragged him in the stirrup for some yards. Lady Linton rushed forward. Her grandeur, her stateliness, were forgotten in the rush of human feeling to her bosom; and had the whole world stood with opera-glasses inspecting her conduct, she could not have restrained either her exclamation, – "My boy, my dear boy!" or the tears which gushed forth, as she pressed his pale and wounded forehead to her bosom.

Chapter 21

For many days Lord Linton was considered in danger of a brain fever. His mother watched over him with unremitting assiduity and many of the strangers who formed the party at Linton Castle departed, finding it exceedingly dull to spend their time in asking after their host's health. Everard, however, remained. Emily was far too kind-hearted to care for amusement, when others were in pain either of body or mind. Besides which, she had formed a strong friendship for the strange and beautiful Madame de Calzean. To Emily, Pauline was neither cold and abstracted, nor passionless. She entered into all her feelings, smiled with her in her gladness and soothed and sympathized [her] in less happy moments. As long then as her friend remained, Emily was content to stay. And there was not a chance of their departing an hour sooner than they at first intended, as Madame de Calzean resolved to eat the excellent dinners of Linton Castle till another engagement which she had in view, should afford a promise of edible enjoyment elsewhere. It was true that Lord Linton had loved Madame de Calzean. Nay more, that he did love her with an intensity of devotion less common to his age that to his melancholy and romantic disposition. He was but nineteen when he first became acquainted with her. Two years had passed away, and his love remained as fresh in his heart as ever. That Madame de Calzean should refuse the homage of a boy ten years her junior, was perhaps only to be expected, but her refusal proceeded neither from caprice nor coldness. She had loved once, the passionate and devoted love of a pure-minded woman. And many had since sighed for the smiles of the majestic Pauline, but she pursued her own course in calm, undeviating rectitude and frequently declared her disbelief of the possibility of a woman loving truly more than once. How could she form to herself two idols or persuade her heart, after a first disappointment, to turn again to the visionary happiness it once built upon? Such were her feelings and as I never was in love except with my uncle's dairy maid (who jilted me), I leave it to others to decide whether she was right or wrong.

Certain it is, that Lady Linton esteemed and loved the person who, instead of luring her only son from the paths of peace and virtue, had, with a mother's cautious tenderness, spoken words of advice and warning which had sunk deep in the heart of him to whom they had been addressed, even if they had not the power to eradicate his unfortunate passion. Every day, Lady Linton communicated with a kind smile the progressive improvement in the health of her precious boy to his true friend. And when at length his recovery was completed and the mother's feelings gradually gave way to her habitual ones, her plans for an evening dance in the illuminated garden adjoining the house were submitted to Madame de Calzean, and she was requested to make use of her taste in the necessary engagements. Madame de Calzean accordingly good-humouredly acquiesced in taking all the trouble on herself and leaving the lighter part of this "labour of love" to Lady Linton. Meanwhile, the object of their attention had returned to his usual amusements and employments and it was within a few days after his leaving his room that he gave Everard Price an account of the transaction in which he so nearly lost his life.

When it was first discovered that the favourite was unable to run, a scene of confusion ensued which has no parallel. Execrations the most gross and violent, accusations and remonstrances the most insulting, mingled their hoarse sounds with shrill exclamation of curiosity and surprise, while the voice of the man who had the care of Beauty (the dying horse) rose in vehement appeals, first to Heaven, then to his honour and finally to *Jim*, a groom companion on whose friendship he appeared to place the strongest reliance. And the low muttered oaths of disappointment and rage in the owner were heard in the momentary pauses for want of breath of the several clamorous throats. At length, threats, promises, persuasion and compulsion induced the appealer to Jim, to let fall something which, though mysterious, caught the owner's ear as he stood watching the struggles of the poor animal. He turned sharply round and after swearing that "if Beauty dies" he would, "not only hunt out her murderer, should he be concealed in the wilds of Kamchatka, but would proceed against him with all the rigour the English law would allow." He declared he would "take no further notice of the crime in any one who would give a true account of the occurrence." Jim, who had been standing quietly, gazing in the speaker's face, gave a loud "hem" and thrust his hands deeper into his pockets, as he glanced from his friend to the ground.

At length, the silence was broken and the sullen and hitherto mute offender confessed that something certainly *had* been given to Beauty, that he took his "*davy*"[1] – he did not know exactly what – that a "gentleman" had bribed him to do it and had told him it would severely prevent her running, and that as to any intention of poisoning such a fine animal, he was as innocent as the babe unborn. On being further pressed, he pointed out Dunstan as the instigator of the action. All eyes immediately turned to the accused, who sate sideways on his horse with his arms arched, looking on. He was too far off to hear what was said, but the instant and deadly paleness that overspread his face, when he observed the earnest gaze of the crowd, left no doubt in the minds of Lord Linton's and the gentleman who owned Beauty as to the truth of the man's statement. They went up to Dunstan and expressed surprise, couched in no very gentle terms at such ungentlemanlike conduct. At first, Dunstan attempted to express suspicion, but even his well-tutored features refused to obey the wily workings of his mind on this momentous occasion. His lips quivered and turned the colour of ashes. His very teeth chattered with mingled rage, disappointment and fear. He saw that a moment more might ruin him and resolved to make one desperate effort to save himself. Gnashing his teeth together, as if in hope to acquire firmness by the action, he muttered something like a compromise. He offered to give whatever Linton would have given for Beauty previous to her accident. But the suppressive fury of her owner only blazed the more fiercely.

"Sell her to you! You barbarous brute! If you had the will and power together to indemnify me for the loss of her for this one day, I would not sell you her corpse the end of it for twenty thousand pounds."

Lord Linton, provoked and irritated by his own disappointment and Captain Dunstan's unequalled assurance, spoke in no very conciliating terms and finished by regretting that he had even invited to his house a man whose conduct had been so unnatural and blackguard, giving a hint at the same time that his company at Linton Castle would be dispensed with for the future. Dunstan bent forward, as if he would have stabbed the speaker to the heart. And then muttered that he would bring him to a reckoning, which speech gave rise to the angry affirmation of the young nobleman that he fought none but gentlemen. The owner of Beauty had turned away for a moment to speak to someone. Dunstan looked round him and suddenly, striking the spurs into his horse, the animal reared, plunged and kicked – and finally, as the alarmed crowd widened to escape from being trampled upon, set off with the speed of a winged arrow from the course. Anyone but Dunstan would have been thrown, but his firm tho' graceful figure bent not, save with the motions of his horse. And tho' his hat fell and the winds waved thro' his dark wild hair, till he looked like a fiend in man's shape, he paused not even to look round, till he was at some distance. Then, checking his horse so suddenly that the spirited animal nearly fell on its haunches, he turned and shook his clenched hand at Lord Linton and disappeared. It would seem he left the animal he rode bridled and saddled, as it was on the open road, which induced many to believe he had been thrown and killed. This was just what Dunstan wished for. He wisely calculated that, if he succeeded in his plan of vengeance, he could take his host's steed. And if he failed, there would be no need of any.

When Lord Linton passed thro' the park gate on his return home, the first intimation he had of the presence of another human being was given by observing a shadow darken across his steed's path. As he had, for the sake of arriving some minutes sooner at home, taken the short cut, he felt something like alarm at this proof that he was dodged, and checking his horse, called peremptorily on the person, whoever it was, to come forth. The summons was instantly obeyed and before Linton had time to recover his surprise, he was flung to the ground with all the supernatural strength with which rage and despair had invested his opponent. Relying on the utter loneliness of the place and the apparent impossibility of escape, Dunstan had with a diabolical refinement of cruelty depicted to his victim in glaring colours that awful scene in his early life when *he* had so nearly been cut off in the midst of unrepented sin: his struggles, his agonized entreaties for mercy, his wild gaze for aid which none could give; the cold clammy drops that crept over his brow as the conviction burst upon him that entreaty and resistance were alike unavailing. And the last, almost mechanical effort of pulling the trigger of his gun. *All* was told to the helpless and shuddering boy, and but for this delay Linton would never [have] seen the sun rise after that day. With the last sentence Dunstan had dragged him to the edge of the precipice and was lifting him over it, when the arrival of Everard and Madame de Calzean saved him from the most horrible of deaths. The whole of this strange and horrible scene was detailed to Everard under a promise of inviolable secrecy, which he gave the more willingly from being unable yet utterly to cast from his kindly feelings the friend and companion of his boyhood, tho' he shuddered at the sound of his name.

The night for the projected entertainment in the grounds approached. It was the last Everard and Emily were to spend at Lord Linton's. The constant attendance of the former by the sickbed of his friend had prevented his seeing much more of the interesting Madame de Calzean and now she appeared to have almost relapsed into her automaton manner. The fete went off with unrivalled brilliancy and the youthful object of this singular mark of maternal affection appeared in spirits and restored health. Towards the end of the evening, as Everard was musing alone in one of the illuminated walks, Madame de Calzean suddenly joined him.

"You are going tomorrow to Lord Felix Brandon's," said she. Her companion started and assented and then hardly knowing why, he sighed.

"You will meet *her* there," continued Madame de Calzean. "Perhaps I may also be enabled to come. I have warned you – beware!" And as she spoke, she laid her fingers for a moment on Everard's arm. Bewildered and astonished, he murmured some few words of thanks, surprise and of farewell. And before he had recovered his composure, his strange and beautiful companion had disappeared.

Everard slept but little that night and when he rose he could scarcely decide whether it was, or was not, a dream, in which he had been informed of the certainty of Honorine's presence at a house where he had thought it impossible he should meet her, where she was hardly known by name when he left town. Some feeling of its being his fate to be constantly thrown into this temptation struck his mind, as with gloomy discontent he followed Emily to the carriage which was to convey them to Lord Felix Brandon's.

Chapter 22

It was in the dreamy twilight of an autumn evening, about a fortnight after the arrival [of] Everard and his sister at Lord Felix's seat, that Alixe, accompanied by her friend Emily, stepped lightly and hurriedly along a superb gallery which joined the library.

"Oh wait, Emily, wait one moment. I never, *never* shall have firmness enough to go through the scene I am preparing for myself." And so saying, Alixe sunk on a low cushioned seat in the embrasure of an old fashioned gothic window and burst into tears.

"My dear Alixe, you agitate yourself needlessly," said her friend, soothingly. "Have we not both agreed that it *must* be done, and the sooner the better. A little courage now and you will spare yourself and one whom, I am persuaded, is dearer than self, much future misery. Go dearest, and may the God of the fatherless be with you."

Alixe accordingly rose and advanced to the library door. What would she have given to have doubted his presence in that dreaded apartment? But no, she knew he was there, she knew he was alone. She stole thro' the end of the dim gallery and, trembling like a guilty thing, paused before the door. She listened. All was so still that she fancied the beating of her heart might be heard in the distance. At length, summoning all her strength and calling rapidly to mind the different arguments for the step she was taking, which but last night appeared so incontrovertible, she turned the lock and entered the room. Everard was at the other end of it. He turned, on hearing the door open, and Alixe felt there was no longer any chance of retreat.

"Ha, my pretty Alixe, I almost took you for a spirit. You came in so softly I had thought you, with all the rest of your gay companions, were at the archery meeting. However, it is a lucky accident that brings you, for I was growing quite melancholy."

"Everard," said Alixe, while the big tears stood in her eyes. "I knew *you* were not going to the archery meeting and I came here to – to speak with you. It is not accident that has brought me and I would beg of you to hear me patiently for a little, a very little while." Her lover dropped the hand he had taken, and retreating a few steps, leant against the window.

"I know, Everard," said his companion, "that few would do as I am now doing, that the world, *your* world, would blame and ridicule me for voluntarily seeking an interview with one who has appeared to – to neglect me. But I also know that I am following the dictates of my own heart, of my own reason. I know what it has cost me to make up my mind to say what I am about to say. I am come, not to trouble you with an angry woman's accusations, nor a fond and foolish girl's reproaches, but to perform a duty, a solemn duty. Since we have been together in this house, I appeal to yourself whether your conduct has been that of a man who held himself bound by indissoluble ties to one worthy of his affection? Do not look angry at me Everard, I will not weary you. Your love is gone from me. Perhaps it was vain of me to expect it would last. I feel that I am different from those around you and that this difference was perhaps all the charm I had in your eyes. I feel too that this chance is gone, that we never can be, that –." But the voice of the speaker utterly failed in the attempt to choke back her tears.

"Alixe, my own Alixe!" said Everard, as he passionately took her hand. But she withdrew it.

"No, let me finish, while I *can*. I have thought it all over and I believe it will be better I should release you from your voluntary engagement. I do not ask you to think no more of me. I will not commit the feminine affectation of saying that I shall not regret you. I am no hypocrite or I might have won you back perhaps at last. And now, Everard, that you are *free*, that you cannot think I speak from a jealous fear of losing your affections, hear me, this only once, before we are strangers for ever! Your heart is full of a sinful love for one whose sworn vows are another's. Oh! Everard, *my* Everard, if I ever was dear to you, if you ever looked forward to pure happiness with me the day your mother blessed us, if the world has not deadened every noble feeling, every religious principle, spare me the agony of knowing that in relinquishing you I destroy the last tie that yet holds you back from crime! My love is not a worldly love, Everard, nor a vain and selfish one. I could bear to see you happy with another. I could love her for your sake. But I could not bear to see *that*; it would break my heart! I have not said all I meant and hoped to say. Nor, I fear, as I should have said it, but what I have spoken has been for you Everard, for *you* and not for myself. And you will think of it when I am not by you, when I can no longer warn you, when I can only pray to God for your welfare?"

It was some minutes before Everard Price raised his eyes, and when he did, Alixe was gone.

A thousand wild bitter feelings rose in his heart. He cursed his fickleness, his imprudence. He thought of the fascination, the passion of the Baroness and felt a desperate rage against her, against himself. He thought of the pure simple love of her he had lost, who thought him unworthy, and it maddened him. He repeated in the depth of his heart her low melancholy warning till, as every tone and word echoed in his ear, he lifted up his voice and wept.

"And have you really said all to him, Alixe?" said Emily, as pale and breathless, the unhappy girl entered her room.

"All, all I could remember in that moment of agony, all I could say, all I dared say, all I could have uttered without throwing myself upon his heart and conjuring him not to forsake me. Yes, it is over now. And *now* let me weep!" And she flung her arms round her friend's neck and sobbed convulsively.

"Nay dearest, this is wrong," said Emily gently. "You promised me there should be none of this."

"Yes, but when I promised, I knew not how it would end. I did not know he would have given me up without a struggle. I thought at the bottom of my heart that he would speak kindly and comfort me. And perhaps, yes, I thought he would have renounced the Baroness and begged of me to love him as, as I *do*. Oh, Emily if I lose him for ever, remember you advised me to this."

"But do you mean that my brother heard all unmoved?"

"All? No, when I spoke of his past love of his mother, he seemed touched. But, but – oh he must have thought me very cold!"

"Dear Alixe, your sorrow has bewildered you. You have done what was right. He cannot think the worse of you. If he is the brother I have known from infancy, he will be reclaimed by this, if anything can reclaim him. Believe me, he will, Alixe."

"Ah! Emily, you know how gladly I would believe you. But I am so miserable! Surely if Madame de Valcone knew it. Emily, I will go to the Baroness. I cannot suffer more than I have already done. I will appeal to her generosity, to her feelings. I will tell her all – how happy we were – and beg *her*."

"My poor little Alixe, your appeal would be vain. You would even have a better chance if the Baroness loved Everard as you do. But Madame de Valcone, whatever she may have been, is *now* a woman 'of the world': that comprehensive expression which signifies that all your best and most maternal feelings are swallowed up, all your holiest ties and duties hidden by the false glare and excitement of an all-engrossing vanity. Happy are they whose hearts have been saddened early into reflection, whose love and friendship are not of 'the world.'"

"But surely, dear Emily, she would feel shame – what could she say?"

"Dear Alixe, be advised by me the step you wish to take would be worse than useless. The Baroness would feel no shame, for she can have no principle and these things are done often in 'the world.' And I will tell you what she would say. She would say 'Mais c'est ironi!'[1] and her feeling on the subject would be one of simple wonder."

NOTES

Preface

1. *The Selected Letters of Caroline Norton*, ed. Ross Nelson and Marie Mulvey-Roberts, 3 vols (London: Pickering and Chatto/Routledge, 2020), 1: 174.

Introduction

1. The setting of the novel is most likely to be 1825–1826, since the description in Chapter 17 of an actual contribution to the paper currency debate in the House of Commons by Henry Brougham corresponds to a speech he delivered on 20 February 1826, during the Promissory Notes Bill (https://api.parliament.uk/historic-hansard/commons/1826/feb/20/promissory-notes-bill, accessed on 18 February 2023). The following day it was reported verbatim in the *Morning Post*, 21 February 1826, where Norton may have read it. Brougham's other two interventions in the Promissory Notes debate were relatively brief (https://www.historyofparliamentonline.org/volume/1820-1832/member/brougham-henry-1778-1868, accessed on 7 February 2023).
2. Norton appears to have also drawn on Helen's experiences in writing the descriptions of the voyage to Egypt and of Alexandria that appear in her later novel, *Lost and Saved* (London: Hurst & Blackett, 1863), 1: 165–179. Whereas Caroline never visited Egypt, in 1858–1859 Helen and her son, Frederick Dufferin, sailed to Egypt in his yacht, visited Alexandria and Cairo and "set sail up the Nile for Aswan" (Andrew Gailey, *The Lost Imperialist* (London: John Murray, 2015), 74–77), events which preceded the writing of *Lost and Saved*. The youthful collaboration of the sisters, as well as their later independent literary careers, to some extent echoes that of the Porter sisters (see Devoney Looser, *Sister Novelists* (New York: Bloomsbury Publishing, 2022)) and anticipates that of the Brontës (see Claire Harmon, *Charlotte Brontë, A Life* (London: Viking, 2015)).
3. Helen Blackwood to Caroline H. Sheridan, 11 September 1825, Public Record Office of Northern Ireland, D1071/F/A/3/1.
4. Helen Blackwood to Caroline E. Sheridan, 4 March 1826, Public Record Office of Northern Ireland, D1071/F/A/3/5.
5. I. A. Taylor, "The Hon. Mrs Norton and her Writings," *Longman's Magazine* (Jan. 1897), 29: 234.
6. Norton, *Lost and Saved*, 1: 66.
7. Benjamin Haydon to Elizabeth Barrett, 3 March 1843, ed. Philip Kelley and Ronald Hudson, *The Brownings' Correspondence* (Winfield KS: Wedgestone Press, 1988), 6: 347.

8. *Love in "the World"*, 12.
9. *Love in "the World"*, 12.
10. *Love in "the World"*, 35.
11. Jennifer Phegley, *Courtship and Marriage in Victorian England* (Santa Barbara, Denver and Oxford: Praeger, 2012), 5-12.
12. George Norton, The History of Parliament: British Social, Political and Local History (http://www.historyofparliamentonline.org/volume/1820-1832/member/norton-hon-george-1800–1875, accessed on 30 June 2022); Lord Grantley, *Silver Spoon* (London: Hutchinson, 1954), 13.
13. *Love in "the World"*, 13–14.
14. Antonia Fraser, *The Case of the Married Woman* (London: Weidenfeld & Nicolson, 2021), 45.
15. *Love in "the World"*, 22.
16. The editors of the present volume performed the song for Lady Antonia Fraser, when she was starting work on her biography of Caroline Norton, at the Atheneum Club in Pall Mall, London in February 2019. Caroline Norton was acknowledged to be "among the beauties in the balcony" at the Athenaeum in the *Champion and Weekly Herald*, 1 July 1838, 6. "Juanita" was written for her son Brinsley's guitar when one of her children was ill. See Patricia Hammond, *She Wrote the Songs: Unsung Women of Sheet Music* (Scarborough: Valley Press, 2020), p. 89.
17. *Love in "the World"*, 48.
18. *Love in "the World"*, 132, Chapter 8, n8.
19. William Hazlitt, "The Dandy School," *Examiner* (18 November 1827), rpt in ed. P.P. Howe, *The Complete Words of William Hazlitt in Twenty-One Volumes* (London: J.M. Dent and Sons, 1934), 20: 146. Hazlitt particularly had the work of Theodore Hook in mind, among other authors, whose *Sayings and Doings* (1824) is regarded as having started the Silver Fork genre.
20. See Louisa Devey, *Life of Rosina, Lady Lytton* (London: Swan Sonnenschein, Lowrey & Co, 1887), 50.
21. It is unclear whether or not this was co-written. According to Jane Gray Perkins, it was a collaborative venture (*The Life of Mrs Norton* (London: John Murray, 1909), 8). However, the 1831 "Living Literary Characters" article (see note 23) attributes sole authorship to Norton, although an unpublished volume of poems that came next was apparently collaborative.
22. Thomas Lister's novel *Granby* (1826) established the genre.
23. See Diane Atkinson, *The Criminal Conversation of Mrs Norton* (London: Preface, 2012), 39. The source of this information is an article of 1831, most likely to have been written by Mary Shelley, "Living Literary Characters, No II, The Honourable Mrs. Norton," *The New Monthly Magazine & Literary Journal*, vol 31 no 1 (January–June, 1831): 181 (https://books.google.co.uk/books?id=NmlEAQAAMAAJ&pg=PA180&lpg=PA180&dq=%22Living+Literary+Characters,+No.+II.+The+Honourable+Mrs.+Norton%22.&source=bl&ots=vQEQf93Rvb&sig=ACfU3U1-x9YU2-OmvsE_EdsvI8fAQIqPg&hl=en&sa=X&ved=2ahUKEwi9_YL6lNb4AhXKfMAKHXaPA6EQ6AF6BAgSEAM#v=onepage&q=%22Living%20Literary%20Characters%2C%20No.%20II.%20The%20Honourable%20Mrs%20Norton%22.&f=false, accessed on 10 June 2022). Mary Shelley was Caroline Norton's friend and correspondent. For a list of Norton's letters to Mary Shelley, see the index in *The Selected Letters of Caroline Norton*, ed. Nelson and Mulvey-Roberts, 3: 328.

24. https://digitalarchive.tpl.ca/objects/198178/the-dandies-ball-or-high-life-in-the-city#, accessed on 27 June 2022.
25. Thomas Carlyle, *Sartor Resartus: The Life and Opinions of Herr Teufelsdröckh* (Boston: Dana Estes, 1892), 206.
26. https://digitalarchive.tpl.ca/objects/198178/the-dandies-ball-or-high-life-in-the-city#, accessed on 27 June 2022.
27. *Love in "the World"*, 15.
28. *Love in "the World"*, 46.
29. *Love in "the World"*, 104.
30. Randall Craig, *The Narratives of Caroline Norton* (New York: Palgrave Macmillan, 2009), 26.
31. Women writers of the Silver Fork genre are included in a six-volume series, whose general editor is Harriet Devine Jump, *Silver Fork Novels, 1826–1841* (London: Pickering and Chatto, 2005). See also Tamara S. Wagner, "From Satirized Silver Cutlery to the Allure of the Anti-Domestic in Nineteenth-Century Women's Writing: Silver-Fork Fiction and its Literary Legacies," *Women's Writing*, 16 (2009): 181–190.
32. See Craig, *The Narratives of Caroline Norton*, 31.
33. Antonia Fraser, *The Case of the Married Woman* (London: Weidenfeld & Nicolson, 2021), 45.
34. Caroline Norton, *The Wife and Woman's Reward*, 3 vols (London: Sauders and Otley, 1835), 3: 293.
35. Norton also adopts a masculine guise as a character in *Love in "the World"*: "I never was in love except with my uncle's maid, who jilted me", 137.
36. Norton, *The Wife*, 3: 296.
37. Ibid, 3: 26.
38. Ibid, 3: 42.
39. Ibid, 3: 42-3.
40. Introduction to *The Wife*, in ed. Oliver Lovesey, *Victorian Social Activists' Novels*, 4 vols (London: Routledge, 2011), 1: 5, citing Craig, *Narratives of Caroline Norton*, 210.
41. Lovesey, *Victorian Social Activists' Novels*, 1: 8.
42. Norton, *Lost and Saved*, 1: 63.
43. Ibid, 1: 68.
44. Ibid, 1. 252.
45. Ibid, 1: 91.
46. Ibid, 1.70
47. Ibid, 1: 69-70.
48. *Love in "the World"*, 145.
49. *Love in "the World"*, 108.
50. *Love in "the World"*, 42.
51. *Love in "the World"*, 42.
52. *Love in "the World"*, 34.
53. Norton, *The Wife*, 3: 254.
54. Caroline Norton, *The Coquette, and Other Tales and Sketches* (London: Edward Churchton, 1833), 1: 6-7.
55. *Love in "the World"*, 37.
56. Maria Edgeworth to Mrs Ruxton, 9 March 1822 in Augustus J. C. Hare, *The Life and Letters of Maria Edgeworth*, 2 vols (London: Edwards Arnold, 1894), 2: 66–67. Quoted by Amy Galvin, "Out of Site, Out of Mind – Women of the

Ventilator" blog for Women's History Network, 4 June 2017 (https://womenshistorynetwork.org/out-of-sight-out-of-mind-the-women-of-the-ventilator/, accessed on 30 June 2022).
57. http://historyhoydens.blogspot.com/2006/11/maid-marian-she-wasnt.html, accessed on 30 June 2022.
58. The painting was restored in 1935 to reveal that under the layers of oil there was a portrait of Mrs Musters wearing a red riding habit with black fur hat.
59. See Fraser, *The Case of the Married Woman*, 79-91; Atkinson, *The Criminal Conversation of Mrs Norton*, 147-205 and Alan Chedzoy, *A Scandalous Woman: The Story of Caroline Norton* (London: Allison & Busby, 1992), 9–23 and 122–127.
60. The poor sound-quality is demonstrated through the AHRC Project, "Listening to the Commons," run jointly by York University and the UK Parliament which attempts to reproduce the soundscape experience of women listening through the ventilator shaft in the old House of Commons (https://www.york.ac.uk/history/listening-to-the-commons, accessed on 30 June 2022).
61. *Love in "the World"*, 114.
62. Daniel Maclise, *The Spirit of Justice* (1850).
63. Lovesey, *Victorian Social Activists' Novels*, 1: 7.
64. Helen Blackwood to [Richard] Brinsley Sheridan, 24 February 1829, Public Record Office of Northern Ireland, D/1071F/A/3/3.
65. [Jane] Georgiana Sheridan to [Richard] Brinsley Sheridan, 24 January–8 February 1830, W. H. Mallock and Lady Gwendolen Ramsden, eds *Letters, Remains and Memoirs of Edward, Twelfth Duke of Somerset* (London: Richard Bentley and Son, 1893), 22. Manuscript held at Devon Heritage Centre, Exeter, Seymour M/L/1392/30/6.
66. Troy J. Bassett, *The Rise and Fall of the Victorian Three-Volume Novel* (London: Palgrave Macmillan, 2020), 2–3 (https://rhollick.wordpress.com/2015/10/26/circulating-libraries, accessed on 22 February 2023).
67. Caroline Norton, introd. S. Bailey Shurbutt, *Lost and Saved* (Delmar: Scholar's facsimiles & Reprints, 1988). Caroline Norton, *Old Sir Douglas* (London: Macmillan, 1877).

Editorial Note

1. Caroline Sheridan Norton Collection. General Collection, Beinecke Rare Book and Manuscript Library (https://archives.yale.edu/repositories/11/resources/641, accessed on 20 April 2023).

Foreword

1. Perkins, *Mrs Norton*, 8.

Chapter 2

1. "Our Hero" written above in pencil as a possible replacement for "He."
2. "Poor little harp" annotated with pencilled underlining and speech marks to indicate Alixe's use of the same phrase in the previous chapter.
3. "fairy" underlined and annotated in pencil: "too often repeated."

4. Possibly a musical adaptation of a poem by Gabriel de Querlon, voicing Mary Stuart's feelings on her departure from France, first published in the *Anthologie Francoise* (1765):

> Adieu, plaisant pays de France,
> O ma patrie,
> La plus chérie,
> Qui a nourri ma jeune enfance!
> Adieu, France, adieu mes beaux jours.
> La nef qui déjoint nos amours,
> N'a ci de moi que la moitié;
> Une part te reste, elle est tienne,
> Je la fie à ton amitié,
> Pour que de l'autre il te souvienne (*The Collected Poems of Amelia Alderson Opie*, eds. Shelley King and John B. Pierce (Oxford: Oxford University Press, 2009), 547).

Chapter 3

1. Between 1805 and 1864, this was the second highest rank in the Royal Navy (below Admiral of the Fleet).
2. "a mere nobody" underlined in pencil and annotated "that's not fair to N [or M]."
3. "Bored" (French).
4. French name for a species of daisy, known in England as "Herb Margaret." So called because it appears at about the time of the Feast of St Margaret, formerly celebrated by the Catholic Church on 10 June (as for her charity, ecclesiastical reforms and religious faith, Queen Margaret of Scotland was canonized by Pope Innocent IV on 19 June 1250).
5. Either (1) a misspelling of "caisse" which could refer to the French for box, *La caisse* might be an allusion to a dress with box pleats; or (2) an Archaic form of "chasse," i.e. "hunt" (French). The reference might be to Van Dyke's *La Roi à la Ciasse* (1635) portrait of Charles 1, who like Alixe was of diminutive height.
6. Military man (French).
7. "Be he" corrected on both occasions to "Is he" in the MS transcript, but "be he" seems to work better here.
8. Bay St Louis, near New Orleans.
9. Annotated "(This is an excellent chapter.)"

Chapter 4

1. "Simpering" (French).
2. "A string by which the occupant of a carriage may signal to the driver to stop" (*OED*).
3. Mob cap.
4. In the sense of blowing a kiss goodbye.
5. "Big party": the correct French is "grande partie."
6. "x Good Chapters" written in pencil at the foot of the folio page.

Chapter 5

1. "Until death" (Italian).

Chapter 6

1. An early medieval castle in Rhineland-Palatinate, destroyed in 1523 and subsequently a ruin. "Drachenfels" translates from German as "Dragon's Rock." An anonymous poem entitled "The Drachenfels" was published in the 1828 edition of *The Keepsake* (105–106), later edited by Caroline Norton.
2. "Recently" (French).
3. This quotation has not been identified, but clearly refers to an episode in Lord Byron's poem, *The Bride of Abydos* (London: T. Davison, 1813), where Zuleika visits a cave to read the Koran and play her lute (2. 101–102).
4. "Fickle heart" (French).
5. "Dazzling" (French: correct spelling is "éblouissante").
6. "Let's change the subject" (French).
7. "Natural behaviour" (French: "comportment" may equally have been omitted here).
8. "Beautiful Alixe, I will come back when you call me back" (French).

Chapter 7

1. "Awakening" (French).
2. Preoccupied (French: correct form is "preoccupée").
3. "A bit flighty" (French).
4. "Absence and time destroy love" (French: correct form is "détruisent").
5. Caroline-Stéphanie-Félicité, Madame de Genlis (1746–1830), a French writer of the late eighteenth and early nineteenth century, then known for her many novels and her theories of children's education. There are numerous portraits of her.

Chapter 8

1. "Unbeknownst to him" (French).
2. "Beloved mother" (Italian).
3. For ever (French).
4. "Really my dear, you make me impatient" (French).
5. Thomas Campbell, *The Soldier's Dream*, l. 4.
6. In the late 1820s and early 1830s, Caroline Norton and her sisters, Helen and Georgiana, were known as "The Three Graces." Caroline Norton's sister, Helen Blackwell, the author of this note, was married to a captain in the Royal Navy, Price Blackwell (1794–1841).
7. The wedding reception is intended here.
8. An asterisk in the text is linked to a note at the foot of the page by Norton: "This is for the benefit of young ladies and in humble imitation of some pages in 'Pelham' devoted to the costume of the other sex." Edward Bulwer Lytton's *Pelham* was published in 1828, indicating that the above section of the novel must have been written after this date.
9. This passage asterisked with an explanatory comment: "You're a delightful woman!"

Chapter 9

1. The *HMS Britannia*, a "great vessel of 120 guns and measuring 205 ft x 55 ft" (*Sea Breezes*, Vol. 51 (1977), 437), was launched in 1820 and remained in service until 1869 (Brian Lavery, *The Ship of the Line – Volume 1* (London: Conway Maritime Press, 2003), 187.
2. A naval punishment in which the sailor was tied to the top of the ship's mast.
3. The transcriber (Helen Blackwood) pencilled "committed to" as a replacement for "flung into."
4. "She was a bountiful and a doting mother and they all loved her very much" deleted.
5. Eight-word deleted sentence.
6. Byron, *The Corsair* (London: John Murray, 1814), I. l. 281–82: "None are all evil, – quickening round his heart, One softer feeling would not yet depart[.]"

Chapter 10

1. Originally "they also left town" but this is clearly incorrect as they had already left town in the previous paragraph. It seems likely this oversight would have been rectified in CN's final draft (possibly as it has been done here).
2. Archaic word for "accustomed".
3. The handwriting here changes from that of Helen Blackwood to that of Caroline Norton.
4. A shed often used for storing agricultural products.
5. Based on the first stanza of "You Meaner Beauties of the Night" (1624) by Sir Henry Wotton. The final line in the original is: "What are you when the sun shall rise?" (https://rpo.library.utoronto.ca/content/you-meaner-beauties-night, accessed on 1 July 2021).

Chapter 11

1. "Considerate" (French).
2. A Scots dialect ballad by Lady Anne Lindsay (1750–1825), written in 1772 about a young woman abandoned by her lover, who to rescue her destitute parents is forced into an arranged marriage with the financially secure Robin Gray. CN may have seen the poem in Mary Wollstonecraft's *Maria: or the Wrongs of Woman* (1798), which CN referenced – together with Wollstonecraft's *A Vindication of the Rights of Woman* (1792) – in 1851, when subpoenaed to a trial concerning an unpaid carriage bill and interrogated by her barrister husband, in her declaration: "I do not ask for my rights. I have no rights. I have only wrongs." In Wollstonecraft's novel, the ballad is sung to the protagonist, placed in an insane asylum by her husband, by another abandoned inmate, who during her own arranged marriage had been driven mad by a jealous older husband (Mary Wollstonecraft, *Mary* and *Maria: Or, The Wrongs of Woman*, ed. Gary Kelly (Oxford: Oxford University Press, 1976), 88).

Chapter 12

1. Felicia Hemans, "Evening Prayer at a Girl's School," ll. 29–30.
2. Shakespeare, *Macbeth*, Act 5, Scene 5, ll. 28–30:

   "Life's but a walking shadow, a poor player
   That struts and frets his hour upon the stage
   And then is heard no more[.]"
3. In the sense of a marriage proposal.

Chapter 13

1. Specifically, execute a chassé dance movement; in a more general sense, dance.
2. "Convolvulus" is meant here.
3. "That's enough!" (French).
4. Depending on the outcome, duelling was still tolerated during this period. On 23 March 1829, during the writing of this novel, the Duke of Wellington, who was then Prime Minister, had fought a duel with the Earl of Winchilsea. After Wellington fired first and missed, Winchilsea discharged his weapon into the ground. It is unclear whether Wellington intended to hit Winchilsea, but he was aware of the consequences if he had killed him, allegedly remarking to the Earl of Ellenborough that "he considered all the morning whether he should fire at him or no. He thought if he killed him he should be tried, and confined until he was tried, which he did not like, so he determined to fire at his legs." However, as Wellington's biographer notes, "he may simply have been looking for an excuse for missing!" (Rory Muir, *Wellington, Waterloo and the Fortunes of Peace, 1814–1852* (New Haven: Yale University Press, 2018), 344–345). As Captain Aimwell had mortally wounded Lord Ainslie, he would be subject to arrest if he remained in the country.
5. From 1817 to 1840, the Earldom of Sunderland was held by George Spencer-Churchill, 5th Duke of Marlborough (1766–1780), though he was very differently situated to the influential political magnate depicted in the novel, who is certainly not based on him. The Duke had been involved in politics in his twenties and thirties but by the era of the novel lived in retirement at Blenheim, where he attempted to recoup his debts by selling fishing and shooting rights, but seemed unable to prevent the continued mismanagement of his estate. Mary Russel Mitford observed that "the mansion [Blenheim] is worse even than the common run of bad great houses – they kill two oxen and twenty sheep a week, and the waste, riot, and drunkenness that go forward from morning to night are sufficient to demoralize any neighbourhood in the world" (Mary Soames, *The Profligate Duke: George Spencer-Churchill, Fifth Duke of Marlborough, and His Duchess* (London: William Collins Sons & Co. Ltd, 1987), 169).

Chapter 14

1. "But if you knew how much this 'think of me' weighs in my heart" (French).
2. "But what is the use of suffering?" (French: correct translation is "souffirs").
3. On the final page and inside the back cover are written a list of the novel's characters and a poem by Norton:

   How vain the love I bore thee
   In youth's first happy hours

When sunny skies shone o'er me
And life seemed strewed with flowers

Oh love me – love me still
Though thou are doomed to leave me
While thou are blest no ill
Of frowning fate can grieve me

Oh love me love me still
What though the cold world smile
Tho its scorn can never move thee
Turn then a little while
To her who cannot cease to love thee

Oh love me love me
And as the crushed flower sends
Its last faint perfumed breathing
To him whose footsteps bends
The blossoms neath him wreathing
And dying haunts him still
Love's last faint forms sinking

Volume II

1. Annotated "2nd Volume Novel when I was yet 'in my teens.'"

Chapter 15

1. William Charles Macready (1793–1873) was one of the leading English actors of his generation.
2. Daniel O'Connell (1775–1847) was then the political leader of Roman Catholic majority in Ireland and the Irish leader in the House of Commons, to which he was elected in 1828. Richard Sheil (1791–1851) was an Irish politician and orator and one of O'Connell leading supporters.
3. "The beginnings" (French).
4. Luís Vaz de Camões (1524-80).
5. "If only you knew how chic it is" (French).
6. "I regret it, he took with him this beautiful dream of life that comes only once: the dream of perfect happiness on earth" (French).
7. "Yes, I need consolation, yes you will be my friend" (French).
8. "He was treacherous – but I lost him – and the death which engraves so deeply on the heart, the charms and the virtues of his victim erases the errors" (French).

Chapter 16

1. "(for candidly he must [be] allowed to possess many)" deleted.
2. Probably in the sense of "so-called," although "self-identified" could also be intended.
3. "said the former" deleted.

Chapter 17

1. The Ladies Gallery Attic in St Stephens, from where women could listen to debates by gathering in the space above the ceiling of the Commons Chamber, was then the upper part of the original Chapel of St Stephen. Floorboards and chairs were placed round the ventilation lantern, providing a restricted view down into the Chamber below.
2. Henry Brougham, 1st Baron Brougham and Vaux (1778–1868), had campaigned for the abolition of the slave trade and been elected to Parliament in 1810, moving to the Lords in November 1830, when he was appointed Lord Chancellor in Earl Grey's Whig administration. A champion of the poor and an advocate of legal reform, he was a regular parliamentary speaker and holds the record (six hours) for the longest House of Commons speech.

Chapter 18

1. Annotator has replaced "spirited animal" with "horse."

Chapter 21

1. i.e. "he took his oath" or "swore."

Chapter 22

1. "But that's irony" (French).

PUBLICATIONS, WEBSITES AND ARCHIVES CITED

Publications

Atkinson, Diane, *The Criminal Conversation of Mrs Norton* (London: Preface, 2012)
Bassett, Troy J., *The Rise and Fall of the Victorian Three-Volume Novel* (London: Palgrave Macmillan, 2020)
The Brownings' Correspondence, Volume 6, eds Philip Kelley, and Ronald Hudson (Winfield, KS: Wedgestone Press, 1988)
Byron, Lord, *Bride of Abydos* (London: T. Davison, 1813)
———, *The Corsair* (London: John Murray, 1814)
Campbell, Thomas, *The Complete Poetical Works of Thomas Campbell* (London: Phillips, Sampson and Company, 1853)
Carlyle, Thomas, *Sartor Resartus: The Life and Opinions of Herr Teufelsdröckh* (Boston: Dana Estes, 1892)
Chedzoy, Alan, *A Scandalous Woman: The Story of Caroline Norton* (London: Allison & Busby, 1992)
Craig, Randall, *The Narratives of Caroline Norton* (New York: Palgrave Macmillan, 2009)
Devey, Louisa, *Life of Rosina, Lady Lytton* (London: Swan Sonnenschein, Lowrey & Co, 1887)
Fraser, Antonia, *The Case of the Married Woman* (London: Weidenfeld & Nicolson, 2021)
Gailey, Andrew, *The Lost Imperialist* (London: John Murray, 2015)
Galvin, Amy, 'Out of Site, Out of Mind – Women of the Ventilator', blog for *Women's History Network* (4 June 2017)
Grantley, Lord, *Silver Spoon* (London: Hutchinson, 1954)
Hare, Augustus J. C., *The Life and Letters of Maria Edgeworth*, 2 vols (London: Edwards Arnold, 1894)
Hammond, Patricia, *She Wrote the Songs: Unsung Women of Sheet Music* (Scarborough: Valley Press, 2020)
Harmon, Claire, *Charlotte Brontë, A Life* (London: Viking, 2015)
Hazlitt, William, 'The Dandy School', *Examiner* (18 November 1827)
———, ed. Howe, P.P., *The Complete Words of William Hazlitt in Twenty-One Volumes* (London: J.M. Dent and Sons, 1934)
Hemans, Felicia, *Poetical Works* (London: Phillips, Sampson & Company, 1849)
Hook, Theodore, *Sayings and Doings*, 3 vols (London: Henry Colburn, 1824)

Jump, Harriet Devine, *Silver Fork Novels, 1826–1841* (London: Pickering and Chatto, 2005)
The Keepsake (1828)
Lavery, Brian, *The Ship of the Line – Volume 1* (London: Conway Maritime Press, 2003)
Lister, Thomas, *Granby*, 3 vols (London: Henry Colburn, 1826)
Looser, Devoney, *Sister Novelists* (New York: Bloomsbury Publishing, 2022)
Lovesey, Oliver, ed., *Victorian Social Activists' Novels*, 4 vols (London: Routledge, 2011)
Mallock, W. H., and Lady Gwendolen, Ramsden, *Letters, Remains and Memoirs of Edward, Twelfth Duke of Somerset* (London: Richard Bentley and Son, 1893)
Morning Post, 21 February 1826.
Muir, Rory, *Wellington, Waterloo and the Fortunes of Peace, 1814–1852* (New Haven: Yale University Press, 2018)
Norton, Caroline, *The Coquette, and Other Tales and Sketches* (London: Edward Churchton, 1833)
———, *The Wife and Woman's Reward*, 3 vols (London: Saunders and Otley, 1835)
———, *Lost and Saved*, 3 vols (London: Hurst & Blackett, 1863)
———, *Old Sir Douglas* (London: Macmillan, 1877)
———, *Lost and Saved*, introd. S. Bailey Shurbutt (Delmar: Scholar's facsimiles & Reprints, 1988)
———, *The Selected Letters of Caroline Norton*, eds Ross Nelson and Marie Mulvey-Roberts, 3 vols (London: Pickering and Chatto/Routledge, 2020)
Opie, Amelia, *The Collected Poems of Amelia Alderson Opie*, eds Shelley King and John B. Pierce (Oxford: Oxford University Press, 2009)
Perkins, Jane Gray, *The Life of Mrs Norton* (London: John Murray, 1909)
Phegley, Jennifer, *Courtship and Marriage in Victorian England* (Santa Barbara, Denver and Oxford: Praeger, 2012)
Sea Breezes: The Magazine of Ships and the Sea, vol. 51 (1977)
Shelley, Mary, 'Living Literary Characters, No II, The Honourable Mrs. Norton', *The New Monthly Magazine & Literary Journal*, 31, no. 1 (January–June 1831): 180–83
Soames, Mary, *The Profligate Duke: George Spencer-Churchill, Fifth Duke of Marlborough, and His Duchess* (London: William Collins Sons & Co. Ltd, 1987)
Taylor, A., 'The Hon. Mrs Norton and her Writings', *Longman's Magazine*, 29 (1897): 231–41
Wagner, Tamara S., 'From Satirized Silver Cutlery to the Allure of the Anti-Domestic in Nineteenth-Century Women's Writing: Silver-Fork Fiction and its Literary Legacies', *Women's Writing*, 16 (2009): 181–90
Wollstonecraft, Mary, *Mary and Maria: Or, The Wrongs of Woman*, ed. Kelly, Gary (Oxford: OUP, 1976)
Wotton, Sir Henry, and Sir Walter Raleigh, *Poems* (London: W. Pickering, 1845)

Websites

https://digitalarchive.tpl.ca/objects/198178/the-dandies-ball-or-high-life-in-the-city#
http://historyhoydens.blogspot.com/2006/11/maid-marian-she-wasnt.html
https://rhollick.wordpress.com/2015/10/26/circulating-libraries
https://womenshistorynetwork.org/out-of-sight-out-of-mind-the-women-of-the-ventilator/

https://www.historyofparliamentonline.org
https://www.york.ac.uk/history/listening-to-the-commons

Archives

Public Record Office of Northern Ireland, Belfast
Beinecke Library, New Haven
Devon Heritage Centre, Exeter

Printed in the USA
CPSIA information can be obtained
at www.ICGtesting.com
JSHW020010130923
48245JS00001B/3